PONTI

Sharlene Teo

PONTI

PICADOR

First published 2018 by Picador
an imprint of Pan Macmillan
20 New Wharf Road, London N1 9RR
Associated companies throughout the world
www.panmacmillan.com

ISBN 978-1-5098-5531-5

1 3 5 7 9 8 6 4 2

A CIP catalogue record for this book is available from the British Library.

Printed and bound by CPI Group (UK) Ltd, Croydon, CR0 4YY

PONTI

1
SZU

2003

Today marks my sixteenth year on this hot, horrible earth. I am stuck in school, standing with my palms pressed against a green wall. I am pressing so hard that my fingers ache. I am tethered to this wall by my own shame.

I am in trouble again. I keep finding myself in trouble. It takes me weeks to wade out of it. There is something dishonest about my face, even when I'm telling the truth. What can you do when you're born with a bad face? I think that's why most people don't take to me. Yes, take to me, the way that ducks take to water or kids take to certain talents. The way the other girls in school seem to be best friends in seconds, in-jokes and easy laughter.

When I was eleven I used to hope that puberty would morph me, that one day I'd uncurl from my chrysalis, bloom out beautiful. No luck! Acne instead. Disgusting hair. Blood. I take after my father's side, apparently, the homely, ashen Ngs, a family of grifters and gamblers, smugglers and runaways. People are superficial, whether they admit it or not. I wouldn't be stuck here if I looked even a tiny bit more like my mother, who is a monster but so stunning that she can get away with anything. Even when she's not around, I can feel my mother's eyes on my back; the pinprick glare of her disapproval.

True horror fans know her as Amisa Tan. Screen name: Amisa Tan Xiaofang. Day to day, she is the kind of woman who never sweats, who wouldn't be caught dead talking with a mouth full of food. She eats like a bird, smokes like a chimney. Back when she left the house more often she used to get fruit and flowers offered to her (like some sort of pagan goddess) at the wet market, by stuttering men of all ages, who also competed to help her with her bags. She accepted the free gifts but declined the manpower, made me carry all the shopping instead. All the way home, cars slowed in stately reverence as my mother sauntered down the roadside, me trailing behind her. Strained plastic handles cut into my palms, the weight of future dinners ached my shoulders and forearms.

Right now I keep staring at the wall because if I shut my eyes I might fall asleep for a second, standing up, like a horse. This wall is the shade of carsickness and cheap mint ice cream. Behind me is the staffroom. I hear the teachers going in and out of the swinging wooden doors. If I strain my ears I tell myself I can make out the scratching of ballpoint pens. Scritch-scratch, wrong answer, incorrect. Right now Mdm. Goh and Mrs Fok and Mr Singh are marking our test scripts: Mother Tongue and Elementary Mathematics and Chemistry. I already know it, I have that familiar sinking feeling in my stomach, that I am not going to do well. *You are not doing well, Szu. You need to buck up,* Mrs Fok tells me, and that is part of why I am in public detention. The other reason is because I am 'disruptive',

2

and also too old, Mrs Fok continues, to be upsetting my classmates with the things that I am saying.

Elizabeth Kwee is the new girl who transferred over from St Magdalen's Secondary School two weeks ago. She is half a head shorter than me and as sweet and manufactured as Japanese candy. She has a cluster of ripening pimples spread across her right cheek, inflicted, perhaps, by a dirty pillow and firm preference of sleeping angle. I thought maybe we could be friends. But she is the one who told Mrs Fok that I am a compulsive liar and that I spend all day whispering 'weird, creepy things' to her.

The part about talking to her all day is true, especially during the draggy afternoon periods. The weirdness I disagree with. I am the most normal person that I know.

Singapore lies just one degree north of the equator and it feels like the bullseye where the sun is aiming a shot at the earth with the intention of killing it. In the afternoons this building heats up like a copper coil stove. The classroom is so sweltering that all thirty-three of us sweat out half our body weight, a form of suffering which the girls most committed to their eating disorders view as beneficial and beautifying. The cooked classroom smells like Impulse deodorant and soiled sanitary pads. The perspiration makes our starched buttoned blouses turn translucent as onion peel and stick to the skin. Lurid bra straps and push-up cup lines emerge like litmus blooming through filter paper: neon pink, acid green, boudoir red; unorthodox colours for our prim and proper all-girls' school. My own bra is always beige.

3

Mrs Chan, who is in charge of Pastoral Care, has already swapped my sitting partner five times this year. I've exhausted everyone. My classmates call me Sadako after the *Ringu* drowned girl and prefer to leave me alone. That is, until they get intolerably bored and decide to make my life miserable. For now, even the cruellest and most perfect girls prefer to pretend that I don't exist.

Clara Chua, Lee Meixi and Trissy Kwok are a three-headed vision of stem-glass necks and crystal-clear skin, branded satchels and understated sexual experience. They are as idle and cunning as crocodiles. They are unknowable and invincible. Their limpid eyes judge and glint. Every morning, in unison, they twist their shampoo-advert hair gently in their hands and draw it over their shoulders like a rifle sling.

Ours is a convent school, the Whampoa Convent of the Eternally Blessed, but there is nothing pious about the things that teenage girls inflict upon each other. In this place it is not the weird girls, the too freakish to engage with, who are minced meat, but the less well-off, the ones who can't afford good school bags or sports shoes, or else the weaklings, the watery-eyed and too quick to please. I've seen girls torn to pieces for agreeing with the wrong thing, I've seen girls strung up like joints of char siu or roast duck in the dirtiest toilets, panties exposed, gulping back tears for offending one of the crocodiles or associates of the crocodiles. Always in some minute, impossible way – blinking for too long so as to appear contemptuous, coughing too comically, saying some misjudged, stupid thing.

4

I don't believe in holy ghosts, but right at the start of my time here (three forever years ago, at that inauspicious age of thirteen) I used to say this prayer every morning, in time to my footsteps before I entered the gates:

I pray to birdshit,
I pray to the trees,
I pray to the walkway,
I pray to the construction cranes.
Nobody be bad to me,
Let me be okay.
Amen, amen, amen.

The wrought-iron school gates are painted the same shade as banana foam gums, to mimic the pliability of marshmallows when there is no easy escape. A nauseating candy palette forms the colour scheme of our school, to soften the blow of the horrors within; mint-green walls by the staffroom, senile lilac by the concourse, blush pink and cloud blue on the tall, tacky spires that make up the east and west wings. I spend more time in this compound than I do anywhere else. I wish it would burn down in my sleep.

*

Yesterday I saw a mirage on the whiteboard. If I believed in God I would call it a holy vision. Mrs Fok's marker-pen squiggles began to jump around on the surface, flow and skip like the volume lines on a monitor; I felt like I was either going to faint or leap up from my chair and start dancing. My blood swelled. My bones brimmed with an overwhelming sense of expectancy, as if the thing I had waited for all my life, without being able to name it, was finally happening. Just then I had the greatest urge to talk to Elizabeth Kwee. Her small pink ear was a receptor of infinite wisdom; invited it. My palms and feet were cold even though the rest of me was boiling.

'Oi, Elizabeth, do you want to hear something?' I whispered.

She kept her eyes resolutely on the whiteboard.

'Oi, want to hear something cool?'

'No,' Elizabeth hissed. She drummed her right hand on the grey plastic table. The fleshy underside of her palm was stained with blue ink. I leaned over to her ear.

'My mother is a monster,' I whispered. I was so close to her. I knew how hot and stinky my breath would be, in this endless 2.30 glare, this humidity. Someone behind us shifted in her chair. Elizabeth moved away from me gently. She didn't want to risk detention.

'Stop talking,' she said under her breath.

'No one can hear,' I replied. 'You won't get in any trouble. So you know about my mother?'

'*Yeah*. So what?'

'You can still get video copies of her movie, in Malaysia, pirated—'

'The one about the Pontianaks. Yeah yeah, I was sick that day. But I heard you did a presentation.'

Last Friday for National Education I did a PowerPoint presentation on my mother's film career. My voice shook the whole way through my introduction. The girls in the back row sniggered. *Ponti!* (not to be confused with *Pontianak 1957*, *The Pontianak*, *Curse of Pontianak* or *Return*

6

of the Pontianak) was the best and most underappreciated film to come out of Singapore in 1978.

Ponti! is a cult movie. It is the first and undeniably finest of a trilogy, even though hardly anyone knows about them and it's difficult to obtain copies. But film fanatics find a way. My mother has received four letters from America, three from Indonesia, two from Japan, one from Holland, from these superfans telling her how much they love her. Once in a while she takes the letters out from their manila folder, smoothing the creases, and rereads them silently. I told her if we got a computer she might get even more fan mail, but she doesn't trust the Internet and neither does my aunt. My aunt says that too many wires will piss off the local spirits, and when I tell her it doesn't work like that she gives me a small smile and waves me quiet.

In the best (and only) role of her working life, my mother, in cheap prosthetics, plays a hunchbacked, congenitally deformed girl named Ponti who makes a deal with a bomoh to become beautiful. She will do anything, pay any price. A lifetime of ugliness is unbearable. My mother was nineteen when she filmed it, close to my age. *Please, Datuk, I beg you*, she says to the camera – and the voice that comes out is a total stranger's: an American dub, sweet and small and foreign.

The witch doctor grants her wish. Emerging from a dust cloud she looks as radiant as a pearl, even in the grainy footage.

With Ponti's beauty, however, comes a thirst for male blood. She is the *Pontianak* now, a cannibalistic monster. She must find and feed on victims in order to maintain her looks. She wears an off-white dress that hugs her hips, and seduces men who are travelling alone along the lampless dirt roads of Pantai Dalam. It's all in keeping with the Pontianak myth, told by worried wives to make their husbands wary of young, beautiful girls walking alone at night. Of course, the men don't listen. And she looks so alluring. She brings her victims right up close and gives them a long, wet kiss that sucks the soul and youth out of them. The sight of my mother kissing an actor makes me squirm in my seat. Blood splatters. And then the camera pans to the tops of palm trees. You can see the leaves shaking. The sound of hungry slurping off screen. They didn't have the budget for more gore, so we are spared the actual defilement.

In the next shot she's standing alone in the artificially lit glade. This is the clip I showed in class, rather than the seduction and murder before. It's a wordless scene, and my favourite. My mother is breathing heavily and looks clammy and defeated. Her shoulders are uncharacteristically slouched. The front of her dress is drenched in diluted corn syrup, more pink than red. She peers up slowly, and when she's facing the camera straight on she blinks like she's coming out of a trance. And then her expression crumples; she's too tired even to cry. I always want to hug her here. At this point the projection flickered, as if in agreement with me. I glanced around the darkened classroom, trying to make sure everyone was paying attention. Trissy grinned at her phone. Meixi had her eyes closed. Vanya and Lin, however, were staring impassively at the screen.

My mother raises her hand to brush some dirt off her left forearm. She's trembling; it's not just the jolty camera. Her long dark hair is flared in that style so popular in the seventies. Backlit in milky light, she looks like she's on the moon. Up close, her face is soft and unguarded. I've never seen this expression in real life. She seems like someone I might get along with, a girl full of worries and affection who will one day solidify into my mother, but not just yet.

Ponti! ends with a chase scene. My monster is pale and frantic, but still proud. She keeps her chin up as she tears through the lalang field. The long green stalks shudder around her. The hero is in close pursuit. I used to watch this through my fingers. I never wanted him to catch her. But he's the one cut out for victory. He knows how to defeat the Pontianak: a sacred, rusty nail, driven into the hole in the back of her head, the one the bomoh drilled to curse her beautiful. The legend dictates he must also stuff a bit of her own hair into her hole. The actor finally does this with the bored purposefulness of someone pushing pizza flyers through a letter box. I have memorized the final frames: the rustle of rain-soaked leaves; my mother's bare, dainty feet pattering through the mud, followed by heavy boots. There is a clap of lightning as our hero overcomes her. He raises the hammer, drives the nail in, along with some of her hair. And then an awful crunching sound as my mother's eyes widen.

'Watermelons. That's the trick,' my mother said. 'If you chop the centre of a watermelon quickly, with a long knife, it sounds like stabbing a tummy. If you drop a watermelon from three metres it's just like a skull being cracked open. If you rattle coffee beans in a tin drum it sounds like a rainstorm. But everyone knows that last one.'

This was many years ago, when I was still a cute kid. We used to sit together and watch the trilogy over and over until I knew each film down to the minute, and she would tell me stories about the making of them, back in that free, wonderful life she enjoyed before me.

'Wah lau, they made such a mess on set,' I whispered to Elizabeth. 'Watermelon pulp everywhere, hacked-up brinjal and white carrots and tomatoes and radishes all over the floor, so sticky. They filmed in a sound stage in Johor, in June, when the weather was damn hot. The whole place stank of rotting vegetables.'

'*Don't care*,' Elizabeth said. She looked ahead, eyes glazed, and had stopped drumming her hand on the table; instead she pushed her chair closer to her desk, as if to tuck her whole body away. The metal legs made a screeching sound on the floor.

'Anyway, even though my mother dies in *Ponti!*, she gets resurrected for *Ponti 2*. And even though she gets beheaded at the end of *Ponti 3* it's left a little open-ended. You know how it is in horror movies? Always leaving the potential for sequels.'

Elizabeth swerved her head toward me with a pinched, decisive expression.

'Can you please just shut up?' she hissed.

'Fine, fine,' I said. We both turned to the whiteboard. Nothing written on there made any sense. Maths and other people were a foreign language. I heard the low, laboured hum of the ceiling fan whirring above us. A mosquito hovered near my left ear and moved along. Even the mosquito couldn't be bothered with me. I felt a skittering in my ribs, rising up into my windpipe. I didn't know if I was angry or sad or glad or all of the above. I tried Elizabeth one more time.

'I can lend you the VCD you know, Mrs Chong helped me convert the footage . . .'

Elizabeth clamped her hand over her left ear, the one closest to me. Her other hand smacked the table. The classroom fell silent.

'Elizabeth and Szu. Is everything okay?' Mrs Fok asked, pointing the uncapped marker pen at my face.

I felt the entire herd of classmates turning towards us. Now it was their stares that were like heat rays on the back of my neck, on my reddening cheeks, across my clammy shoulders.

I nodded and gulped, mute again.

'Madam, she keeps talking when I'm trying to pay attention,' Elizabeth said, in a wronged, snivelling voice.

'Szu Min, remember last week?' Mrs Fok said, waving her pen. 'I gave you two warnings already. What did I tell you, girl?'

I looked up at her from under my eyelashes. I tried to embody a sheep. Why do teachers ask these dreadful, rhetorical questions? I could see Meixi in the corner of my vision, flicking her shiny, ever-obedient hair. She looked disgusted but mostly bored by me.

'Public detention,' Mrs Fok continued, answering her own question. 'Tuesday, Green Post B, by the staffroom.

Be there at two. Stay still and quiet. You girls need to learn stillness and quiet. Don't try anything funny. I'll come check on you.'

*

'Oh, Szu, you're still here,' Mrs Fok says. Her shadow crosses the green wall. 'You can put your arms down.'

I turn around and look at her. My arms ache and I hate her for it. She's shorter than me; most people are. Her hair is greasy black with strands of grey, and lies flat against her skull. Her skin is sallow crêpe paper. She looks like a houseplant that has been neglected over the holidays.

'Your continuous assessment is in five weeks,' she says. 'Not long to brush up.'

'Yes, Madam, I know,' I reply, and leave it at that.

'Five weeks,' she repeats.

She fixes me with a glare and her eyes are two black beads. Because she teaches maths all day I think of the counters of an abacus. I think about the Elementary Mathematics scripts lying on her desk, right this moment, unattended. I think about how my own script is sitting there, marked and graded, and I wonder how low that number could be. She knows, and I don't. My failure dangles like a dripping laundry line between us.

'Szu, you've got to apply yourself,' Mrs Fok says. 'I know you have it in you.'

I blink slowly at her. 'It', I think. What is this 'it' she is referring to? A parasite? She doesn't know 'it' any more than I do, but right now I am practising how to lower my heart rate. I quieten my breath. I imagine that I am a spread of butter, applying myself to my examination paper, smearing it in oily yellow. I picture the scrawny number on my script bending and warping into something magnificent. An impressive 88, a stately 92, perfect 100 for all the right equations, or even beyond that – if she gave me 120 per cent, because I was exceptional and also because she adored my personality. I could then carry the extra 20 per cent over into another one of my weak, wheezing grades, boost it stronger. Everyone would be happy.

'How are you coping?' Mrs Fok asks.

'Huh? Sorry?'

She sighs.

'How are you coping with revision?'

'Um. Revision is okay.'

This is a lie, because in order for revision to happen one must have gone through everything at least once over. My workbooks and file folders remain untouched under my desk in the classroom. I can see the crisp, clean papers gathering dust and bacteria.

The guilt makes my tongue fatten in my mouth. Saliva pools underneath it. Perhaps I will drool. I glance away from her, I am a hangdog; Mrs Fok knows it. She sighs and crosses her arms and I stare at her scuffed black shoes. Her tired feet and angry arms have made the right assessment: I am Miss Frankenstein, I am the bottom of the bell curve, I can't even string long words together. *What does this girl know about anything?* she must wonder. *I hope my daughter doesn't turn out as useless as her.*

She dismisses me. We draw our faces into small, straight smiles. We say goodbye and walk in different directions –

me towards my school bag, she towards her mountain of scripts.

The eyes in the back of my head narrow at Mrs Fok. The mouth in my brain hisses at her: *I hate you and your stupid subject. I hope you get cancer. I hope you don't survive it.*

As I walk out of the yellow gates my palms ache and my legs are heavy with the weight of my birthday. How is it possible that anyone could celebrate this, throw a party where people look at them, giving a thumbs-up as they crookedly cut a cake? How could anyone actually enjoy being one year closer to a bad back, to sleeplessness, to gums drawing away from yellowed canines? Even with the bait of wisdom, old age still depresses me. I dread the day when my mouth is frozen into a life-formed snarl and I can no longer keep up with shitty pop music.

My bus arrives with a hiss. As I get on I think: how about this for a change – if every year, instead of wearing out and scarring the same awkward skin I could wake up with a fresh one. Shed my tall self like a snake. It would be the best present. I wish I could go away and become some-one else, again and again. But I have at least two more years of necessary education, and it is only Tuesday.

2

SZU

2003

We have always lived in this cul-de-sac. It is located at the leafy, surprising end of the road, and sometimes people wander down here and are disappointed that there is nowhere else to go. They shake their heads and retrace their steps.

I push open the rusty orange gates and drag my feet down the path. I don't want to go home, but I don't want to be outside either. Everywhere stinks. When I alighted from the number 67 at the overhead bridge and began my walk back I almost retched. The air reeks of rotten eggs, or burnt barbecue. If the other people at the bus stop had not been coughing and gagging as well I would be worried that I have a brain tumour.

No matter how many times my mother and aunt make me rake up the soggy leaves, the driveway never looks any better. The garden is overrun with weeds. All day long the crickets and cicadas won't shut up. We adopted a dog when I was ten, a scruffy white terrier, ostensibly to replace my dad. First I called him Egg, and then Kueh-Kueh. I finally settled on Biscuit. Biscuit used to yap and yap when I returned from school. He made a real racket for such a small guy: a four-legged home security system. Always so happy to see me. Silly twinkling eyes and a stuck-out pink tongue. Four years ago I was crossing the road opposite the cul-de-sac. Someone had left the gate slightly ajar: a crying client, perhaps. Biscuit charged towards me, paws pounding down the asphalt, just as a 20-ton lorry trundled down the road. For once, he didn't make a sound. Now he is a bare spot at the end of the garden, by the banana trees.

We keep an old frangipani tree and two shedding bougainvillea bushes in the garden. I say 'keep' but what I really mean is that these things exist, refusing to die even though we do not tend to them. The bougainvilleas are perpetually out of bloom, white and pink petals curled by heat, sodden with rain, and the frangipani tree sheds all year.

Our house itself is very old. My dad won the Toto lottery the year before I was born and they bought this place in the eighties, which is why we could afford a landed property. The building is flat and ugly, almost like a military barrack. I wouldn't be surprised if the Japanese used to torture people here during the war. Sometimes the wind makes the walls howl and during monsoon storms the roof rattles, as if to shake off a bad dream. The water-stained outer walls look like they have been slapped with long strokes of weak grey paint. It stinks of cigarettes, incense and my aunt's slow-boiled fungus soup. Everything is yellowing: every wall, every tile, every window.

When I get in I see the copper bell placed on the brass dish on the table. This means that we have a guest. The reception room is small and narrow with peeling wallpaper, cream flecked with jade. The altar is lit with two peanut-oil lamps in their lotus-shaped holders, flanked by four melted candles, red wax pooled on the dusty wrapping paper. Today it is set up with an offering of dried sponge cake, five oranges and a shallow dish of perfume. At the centre of the altar a rotation of deities and immortals stare from the eyes of idols or picture frames. If a client is around we light incense, bow our heads respectfully, invite him or her to join us in worship. My aunt mutters something under her breath. We kneel and touch our foreheads to the ground, all three of us. We wait until our guest begins to shift his or her body weight, squirming in polite discomfort. This can take anything between five and fifteen minutes. And then my aunt moves to ring the bell. We get up and she collects the 'door departure fee', which is additional to payment, and presented in a brown envelope. We see the person out of the door, our three female voices plaintive and gentle, our three different but related faces hovering by the grilled metal gate. Dialect, Mandarin, English, we've got it covered. *Goodbye, goodbye, see you another day.*

The amber bulb above the door frame is switched on, which means that the session is still in progress and I have to keep very quiet. I untie my canvas shoes and arrange them on the rack. I strain my ears to listen out for voices, but all I can hear is the unsteady surge and babble of the filter from the fish tank in the kitchen. I walk down the hallway and stop in front of the dark-brown door. I put my ear against it.

Aunt Yunxi is mumbling in a low monotone. She is speaking in dialect. It sounds like Hakka.

The client is making sounds of assent. Today it is a very old woman with a dry throat.

Aunt Yunxi does not allow any water in that room.

'But why?' I once asked.

'You've got to keep people thirsty,' she replied, and smiled. Thin, pursed lips. No teeth.

At the end of the hallway is my mother's bedroom door. It is shut, as usual, with no light coming from the gap underneath. I wonder if she is asleep, or if she is in the session room with my aunt and the client. My mother takes part in the sessions if the client has a lot of money or possesses desperate and excessive spending potential. She is an expert at discerning whom to target. It is not always the clients who are the best dressed or well coiffed, nor the ones who drive an Audi or Lexus, parked all shiny and out of place on our soggy driveway. Someone could turn up naked, or wearing rags, and smelling like shit, and my mother would still know if it was the right person.

'It's all in the face,' she says. 'A sad face is an open wallet.'

One day I will learn to be as expertly cruel as she is. She finds the weakness she wants behind the eyes, tucked within crow's feet and worry lines, all that fear and blind hope transmitted in the smallest tics and gestures. People are unaware of how much they want their weakness to be exploited; how much they want to be punished for being themselves. My mother locates the finest pinpoint of pain and presses on it. She promises these people everything, and she is so wonderful to look at, so dazzling and persuasive, that a few of them have even agreed to bring over their life savings. Both men and women fall a little bit in love with her. They present their love in fifty- and hundred- and thousand-dollar denominations, bundles of blue and red and brown, stuffed into plastic bags.

Aunt Yunxi stands off to one side during these transactions, eyes clouded over, in the throes of a trance. She is the medium after all, the giving conduit. *Thank you*, the clients say, after their loved one has once again departed, with a whimper and a howl, and my aunt's trembling body has gone still. She flops down towards the lace tablecloth like a rag doll.

Tears stream down the clients' cheeks. *Thank you, thank you, thank you* they say in Mandarin, Hakka, Teochew, Hokkien, English. After the session is over their leftover grief, for there is always too much, billows out over the room like a used parachute. My aunt lights a stick of star anise incense and opens the window.

'Did you see that? How happy that old man was?' she asks me. 'That went so well.' Her face is gleeful. 'Were you paying attention?'

Depending on the time of day and the angle, Aunt Yunxi looks anything between fifty and a hundred years old. She is as fit as a fiddle. In all the time that I have known her I have never heard her sneeze even once. She appeared on our doorstep nine years ago: 1994, the year my father walked out. My mother is the last person to ask for help or admit that she is struggling. She is too proud. But Yunxi simply *knew*. Call it sibling intuition. She swept into our lives after having travelled half the world. A tiny

19

Singaporean woman in her fifties, all on her own on the Trans-Siberian Railway. All she brought with her was one beat-up rattan suitcase and a spindly purple umbrella.

The truth is that my Aunt Yunxi is half woman, half violin. She screeches, she is narrow and stiff. She holds her arms out at odd angles, as if they don't belong to her. This is partly due to rheumatism but also an affectation. She is shrewd and shrill. Yet from time to time she is capable of emitting clear, startling notes of sweetness. She is the only person who buys me presents. When I was very young, and a long time before I would finally meet her, my father told me the story.

'Your mother will be too embarrassed to tell you this,' he said. 'Or she will think you are too young to know. But I don't.'

He said that Yunxi was a made-up name. She wasn't even a person but actually a rare violin, a Lipinski Stradivarius, the only non-touring Stradivarius in South East Asia. There were so few of these left in the world that you could count them on your fingers, and each model was signed and numbered. My mother had stolen it from a music college (how? I asked, and my father replied that 'how' was irrelevant) and disguised the priceless instrument as a woman, an older sister because my mother always wanted a sibling. And so the violin became this woman with frizzy white hair and liver spots across her cheeks, and fingers so thin and brittle that they look like they will fall off at any moment.

'All this is true,' he said, and tapped his nose.

My father loved old furniture. For years, he worked in an antiques dealer's shop as a repairman and apprentice restorer. After he won the lottery, he didn't have to work any more, but his love of antiques remained, the passionate hobby. He used to lull me to sleep with his long-winded, rhapsodic explanations about how a corner chair was made, its foresty provenance. Everything smooth was hewn from raw matter. Heartwood was hard and heavy. Mahogany bled a mess. Bean trees stretched into some abstract Thai sky. Dad spent so long in the workshop that he always smelt of wood shavings and the heady tang of what I came to recognize as paint thinner. He had a distinct smell, of that much I'm sure. Wax and wood and sweaty collars, beer. And then one day, when I was eight, he drove away and didn't come back. He disappeared so decisively it must have been after much contemplation, brewing in his head like slow-cooked stock, this wanting to leave. Or was it easy for him?

In my dreams my father is as real as I can remember. I always wake up both maddened and warmed by the sight of him. He has slopey shoulders, and he is neither tall nor short, with a broad, pockmarked face and a frown print between his eyebrows. He was always asking my mother in hushed Mandarin what was wrong. Something was always wrong. With her, with them, with me. His voice is vague. What I have is a paternal approximation, borrowed from daytime soaps. No recordings exist of him. Voices are the first things to go. Next, speech patterns. The turn of a phrase. What was meant as a joke and what was wisdom? You don't get to choose what sticks and what fades. Over time even silly untruths gain weight and sprout meanings, like mould on fruit.

*

If anyone asks exactly what my mother and Aunt Yunxi do, I've been instructed to say: they operate a small private business from home without employing any additional workers. They provide holistic wellness services. This includes transformative coaching and mind–body practices. My aunt learnt a lot of these practices from her travels all over China, Mongolia, India and Nepal. I can't go into much detail because services tend to vary due to the needs of each client.

My mother and aunt trade in hope. The fact that people come to them already guarantees half their success; these people want to believe in what they've paid for. To seek us out, to take down our address and be confused by the cul-de-sac, to wander tentatively down the driveway, that takes inordinate amounts of hopefulness. Some would call it desperation. The final-spurt effort of the last resort. Most of our clients are waiting to be consoled by the achingly familiar voices of the dead. They feel left behind and they want to be told what to do next. These people assume that the afterlife guarantees wisdom and foresight.

Only twice have we encountered incidents of clients complaining, calling Aunt Yunxi's bluff. Storming out of the bungalow after throwing a fistful of fifty-dollar notes on the antique table. I felt a kind of vindication both times it happened, a swelling in my chest, the spectator's fascination with trouble. Aunt Yunxi is a pro. She always keeps her low voice calm. She sounds like she is always in the right.

'I am sorry you feel this way.'

Reply: 'You're a scam artist, a joke.'

'We can't work with this kind of energy.'

Reply: 'You are full of shit.'

The clients reserve their swear words, their foul language, for Yunxi. It is easier for them to raise their voices at this small, sallow woman with sticks for arms and a pinched, beady-eyed face. Their anger is never directed at my mother, who takes the slightest cue – a narrowing of the eyes, a choked voice – to retreat with the measured, backward steps of a dancer. She trained in a youth dance troupe as a teenager. When I was little she told me I should do the same, but by the time I was nine I kept knocking into things, and every year my height sprang up, until puberty happened, this rambling gait.

*

The screech of a chair jolts me away from the door and into the darkened kitchen. I have taken off my socks and my toes are cold on the tiles. I stare at the large, dirty fish tank. The big-eye croaker and the two saddle grunts open and close their mouths, silver fins shimmering in the murky water. The milkfish is dying; its eyes are a curious shade of red and it swims too slowly, with unease, as if it will tip over at any moment.

I open the fridge door as my aunt and the client pass by in the hallway.

'But will things change?' the client asks in Mandarin.

'Will I feel better?' Her voice is shaky. I cannot bear to look at her.

'Things always change,' my aunt replies in her sage, show-womanly voice. 'It is the way of the moon, the light and flow. Change is the only constant.'

I roll my eyes at the fridge, which is so full that it looks like it will spill over. My aunt loves to cook. Leafy greens wrapped in newspaper, shrink-wrapped Chinese sausages, bolster pillows of tofu. From the wet market: red dates in a sickly pink juice, belachan in little jars. I am just looking. I call this the eyeball diet. Ocular callisthenics. No harm, no guilt just to look. Sometimes I squeeze the food; knead the tofu, poke the pig meat, tap the princely jar of Khong Guan biscuits. That's it. I am glaring so hard that my vision blurs.

'Ah girl. How was your day?' my mother asks.

I shut the door and turn towards her. She is wearing a blue pyjama set. Frayed silk blouse and long trousers. Her face is sharp and bright. She has never needed to diet.

'Not bad,' I reply. I do not hold her gaze.

'I haven't forgotten,' my mother says. 'Just in case you thought I forgot your birthday.'

She comes over and presses her head against my neck. I flinch. Her cheek reaches my shoulder. She puts her arms around me and squeezes my fat. Her sharp red nails dig into my school uniform. If not for the pain this proximity would seem unreal. How tiny her wrists are: fix-a-watch strap small, custom-made bracelet. How could this woman ever have contained me? Every day she is shrinking, not just getting thinner but losing density. Growing slighter, pellucid. Soon she will dissolve completely and I won't be able to remember the shape she leaves in a door frame.

'Aunt Yunxi has a surprise for you,' my mother says into my shoulder. I don't want to move; I feel like I might tip her over. I can't breathe.

'What is it?'

'You'll see,' my mother says.

She shepherds me into my room. Sunlight is streaming a cone of dust motes onto my bed. There is a rectangular white box in the middle of it. Long and straight like a doll's coffin. I try to undo the blue ribbon, which is tied tightly around it, but there is a dead knot so I have to use scissors. I slide off the cover and push aside the layers of tissue wrapping. Something that takes this much effort to uncover must be expensive.

I hear my Aunt Yunxi walking down the corridor. She pokes her head around the door frame and smiles, eyes crinkling at her crow's feet.

'Go on,' she says, and this makes my hands clumsier. The dress is folded neat and flat. I hold it up against the light; it is surprisingly heavy. Light pink and cinched at the waist, bodice studded with small white beads that are meant to look like tiny pearls. Aunt Yunxi comes over and presses the length of the dress lightly against me. It reaches down to my knees. The shiny fabric is stiff and scratchy against my skin. It looks like a dress you would find on a cake-topping ornament; those plastic princesses with no legs and fine nests of golden hair. Or like a dress that a woman in her sixties thinks that teenagers would wear.

My mother and Aunt Yunxi train their eyes on me as I

25

turn away and slip out of my uniform. My arms get stuck in my blouse and for a few seconds I wonder if I'll be trapped in here forever, in too-tight polyester with my sticky skin and body odour emanating from my pores, a potato stench.

'A young lady should have a nice dress,' Aunt Yunxi says, fastening the clasp of the zip. I cannot breathe. I am sweating and my face is red. One minute from crying. My mother stands to my left, watching me watching myself in the mirror. The dress doesn't fit. It makes my body look both too long and too wide. It is the colour of stale candyfloss and hugs my stomach, flaring out at the hips. The bright fabric of the skirt draws attention to the scabs on my knees.

I look at myself in the mirror but avoid my own eyes.

'What's wrong?' my mother asks. What she really means when she asks this is: what is wrong with you?

'You like or not?' Aunt Yunxi asks. 'It's the modern kind. Bought it for you from Golden Mile.'

'I love it,' I lie. 'It's really cute.'

'Good,' my mother says. 'Now thank your ah yi.'

'Thanks, Aunt Yunxi.'

I bow my head, cheeks straining.

For my birthday dinner we have century eggs with sliced ginger and sesame oil. It is six o'clock. Usually we eat at seven thirty, eight. Sunlight glints through the rusty curlicues of the window grille. I stare at the drooping bougainvillea bushes in our garden as I chew. The century egg tastes both bland and piquant. I can't stomach it. I think of swallowing an egg whole, how it would feel, gelid and aged, like a dinosaur's eyeball lodged in my gullet. I almost gag. Outside the window, a soft mist has settled over the grass, muting the colours. I swallow and feel chalky yolk clog my throat.

'Can you smell that? The air really stinks,' I say.

'I don't smell anything,' my mother replies.

'Me neither,' says Aunt Yunxi.

'Are you sure? It's everywhere,' I say.

'Don't be stupid. Shut up and eat your eggs,' my mother says.

I know better than to tell her I have no appetite.

Everyone knows that in order to transform an ordinary yolk into a century egg you must douse the uncracked shell in a salty brine of calcium hydroxide and sodium carbonate, then leave it in a plastic wrap for ten days. Zinc oxide helps to speed up the process; what would have taken months, and wood, and clay, in the slow old time before computers and digital clocks. I watch a shadow stripe the marble table: a car passing by. My mother taps her talons. After 240 hours of curing the egg is ready. It looks like an alien embryo preserved in rotten jelly. The egg white now translucent and yellowish, the yolk a dark, marbled grey. I slip another slice into my mouth, disgusting and familiar.

Aunt Yunxi raises her cup of tea and my mother raises a glass of wine.

'Sixteen,' they say at the same time, with the same solemn voice.

I stop chewing and stare at my dirty plate.

3

AMISA

1968

She was ten and things were changing. The war was long over; she'd been lucky to miss it. Malaya was done. The year before, there had been a two-month-long violent hartal that halted business on the island, and dust and dissatisfaction lingered over the shuttered windows and trashy streets of the main towns. The zinc-roofed village where she grew up was still holding on, shrinking, shirking factories and military bases and the tourists who would flood in eventually and litter potato crisp packets and soft drinks all around. Everything would soon be different and all the worse for it. But for now Amisa was a quiet child who wanted nothing more than her own turtle or monkey, this girl who often dawdled, so lovely and seemingly slow.

She was born and had lived her whole life here in Kampong Mimpi Sedih. The houses opened into the slate-green sea that some days slopped and slurred like a drunk, but mostly it was calm, kept to itself. A mangrove swamp slurped every other corner of her neighbourhood. There was no way to escape it, and it was beautiful in its own way, that wild farting water. When the wind blew sometimes her whole house stank of rotting eggs and Amisa wondered if

28

the smell upset the chickens, reminding them of failure. How awful life must be for a chicken, she thought, to have to sit in the scorching yards all day in a downy coat you couldn't take off, fucking and clucking to a point of focus. Imagine all your life's work being to crap out food for other people, until you got fat and old and beheaded.

The roots of the mangroves poked out of the water like turnip stalks or witchy fingers. She didn't play there. Not in the reeds full of stinging insects. Not amidst the secrecy of water snakes. The root palms propped up drooping trees older than anyone. Occasionally she heard big splashes at night, the sound of something flipping. It was crocodiles, or even older creatures, long-snouted or humpbacked or sharp-finned, her father said. She acted afraid, widening her eyes because it amused him when she seemed babyish. But she knew it was just mudskippers, or the corpulent ikan keli that thronged the waters.

She liked to hear ghost stories from her young, handsome uncle even if she didn't believe a word of what he said. Sometimes he talked too quickly and she didn't fully understand, just watched his eyebrows wriggling with animation instead.

'Watch out for the orang minyak,' her uncle said. 'Do you know what he does to pretty little girls like you?'

Amisa shook her head.

'He's covered in black oil, so he can slip away if anybody tries to catch him. And late at night, he sneaks into girls' bedrooms, and creeps under the covers with them. He has shocking white eyes, and greasy hands that go . . .'

He reached out and tickled her. Amisa shook him off,

giggling feebly. His hands felt quick and damp. Close by her father stubbed out a cigarette and looked the other way.

On the other side of the island there was a grand, creaking funicular that went all the way up the hill. The lily-livered British forces had used it, and then the brutal Japanese during the war. The carriages had wooden walls and rickety doors you had to use every ounce of strength to pull open. When it wasn't in use it was haunted, naturally. Part-time paranormal. The tracks were rusted and chipped, the colour of old blood. The wind rattled the holes in the metal. The hill was full of unmarked graves. Ditto the island. Such an old place, prone to disrespect. The teenagers dared sacrilege on each other, breaking into mosques and temples, discarding cigarette butts on tombstones, kissing on sacred ground.

That year, her mother was pregnant again. Amisa's mother was a dour former teen bride who always acted like her life was nearly over. Surely she had known how to be happy once. Was happiness something that couldn't be unlearnt, like swimming or riding a bicycle? Amisa suspected she was at least partly instrumental in her mother's misery. Every sibling was, but especially her. Her mother was the type of person it was impossible to imagine as having once been a child, and she imposed a laboriousness on even the smallest of things. Laughter, laundry, both duties. But who could blame her if she felt both clammy and corpse-like all the time and her sparking nerves signalled *hurt hurt hurt*? This trimester she sprawled on the divan near the stove breathing heavily as pain bloomed and seized inside her. Because there was a small wooden step-ladder to get in and out of the house she could barely leave.

Amisa's older sister, Jiejie, was also expecting. Jiejie was seventeen and had recently married the piggish lout who manned the cones at the charcoal factory. Seemingly overnight Jiejie had switched from a fun, cussing prankster to a grave woman with one hand always balanced on her growing stomach. Pregnancy scared Amisa; this swell of fear that entered through the navel and ballooned painfully outward, finally erupting in the guise of a small human.

Amisa had six brothers and they never stopped moving. They clambered around and shouted the house up to its rafters and were always getting into tussles. She liked her second youngest brother, Didi, best of all. He was a wry little shit with a capuchin countenance and a knowing way about him. Until recently, Didi had followed Amisa everywhere. From the moment he could walk he sucked his thumb with one hand and held onto her T-shirt with the other. Initially annoyed, she soon warmed to his eyes like brown marbles, and the gap-toothed ineluctability of his smile. Hand in small hand they had roved the nearby marshlands, but Amisa always made sure not to take him anywhere unsafe. No deep waters, or mud holes.

Xiao Gui, she called him, Little Ghost, until her mother told her to stop because it was inauspicious. But even though now at aged eight Didi considered himself too old to be trailing her everywhere, he was still her best friend, her toddling shadow. They had a similar temperament; both were mischievous, and liked to steal secrets. Somebody's shiny metal earring, taken from a windowsill, became a promise half kept. A crumpled ledger book left on a neighbour's wooden stool was a business secret. Buttons and bottle caps pilfered from countertops were secrets that would spoil a blouse, sour fresh milk. Secretly everywhere they found these scraps of other people's lives, the things they didn't mean to relinquish. Didi and Amisa liked to take and share the items, turning them over in their palms, cackling at the free thrill of theft.

Nowadays, Didi made less of a show of worshipping her every move and stealing secrets with her, and he often vanished down the trail of the fleet-footed games of the other boys in the kampong. Every night before bed, however, her Little Ghost still came over and hugged her until she thought she'd run out of air, and she never got tired of his small, skinny arms around her.

Some early mornings the two of them went on bird-watching expeditions with Khim Fatt, the kindly, patient old uncle who explained to them that every flutter overhead could signal the arrival of something remarkable. Maybe a bank swallow, or a blue-eared kingfisher, or a bay owl with its serial-killer stare and tawny sheath of feathers. She liked the stillness of their pursuit, the way she and Didi would move as a unit, crouching down, taking nimble steps back when instructed, both relishing the slow, orotund voice of the uncle as he named birds, reciting when which had migrated from where.

*

Amisa was becoming beautiful, even at ten, but she had something cold about her – everybody could feel it. This coldness was incongruous in the syrupy heat. It was plain to sense, even though she was so pleasing to look at with her dark hair that curved into a doll face, and that neatly stitched smile. She had the consciousness and poise of a cute child aware of her own cuteness, which unsettled both adults and peers. There is the same unforgeable alchemy to being dislikeable as to being universally loved.

Even without her accomplice, she still crept into other people's houses and stole small tokens. Nothing of consequence: balls of hair, onion peels. She kept these on a little shelf in her room. Working alone, she was less infallible. After she was caught a few times, the family became unpopular. They were like the irresponsible owners of a cat that thieved. Even her own mother didn't trust her. She preferred her panoply of brothers and trustworthy older sister. Amisa more closely resembled her grandmother, a haughty Peranakan beauty who had never hugged her children because she didn't want her kebayas crumpled.

'That one has the face of a princess but the heart of an ugly sister,' Amisa's mother whispered to her father after yet another thieving incident, and he just shook his head.

The other kids in the village shied away from her. She stared too much, took too long to respond. She looked pretty, but was she a bit stupid, they wondered? The girls called her Doll behind her back, *Xiao Wa Wa*, meant it meanly.

One day, Didi and her younger brothers were in the yard kicking chickens and deepening their male dialect; sniggers and innuendo they were too young to understand but absorbed from the older boys. The neighbouring kids did not invite Amisa to come and play marbles. She watched them hatch their plans and when one of the girls glanced towards her window, Amisa backed away and went to help her mother peel shallots. Who needs all that? she thought.

Still, when she left the house an hour later there was a sullen sinking in her chest, and she kept away from the beach where she might find them and went to the forest instead. Here the green hum filled her ears and did not rebuke her. She liked the stilt-rooted trees and the bird's nest ferns with their splendidly obscene undersides of brown spores, and the deep, spongy smell of vegetation. Amisa breathed out slowly until her stomach domed a small curve, and she tried to keep walking this way with her tummy stuck out, imitating her pregnant mother and sister. After a few minutes it felt uncomfortable and she stopped. She heard rustles. Monkeys were as unavoidable as air with their pelts of faded grey and their harried expressions. She didn't flinch when the leaves stirred, not until something clamped her shoulder.

When she turned around her heart jolted. There was a glistening pitch-black figure standing behind her. Amisa gulped. Her mouth went dry. Oily man. Slicked to his eyeballs. He was sinewy and loomed up like a pillar. He took his hand off her small shoulder. The whites of his eyes stood out, but the rest of his body glistened like fresh black ink. She remembered the orang minyak, the naked man who slipped through trees and fields covered in oil so he could elude the authorities. Her mother had warned her that the orang minyak could only be seen by young girls.

She wasn't sure what he did to them, only that it was bad, and that one way of fending the oily man off was for a girl to leave a pile of unwashed men's clothing around the bed, or even to wear a man's shirt. But it was too late for that.

'What time is it?' the man asked her in a hoarse voice. He spoke in Malay and then switched to Penang Hokkien. He had a creased face under the oil; he was older than her father. He stank like cars and sweaty feet.

'Four,' Amisa replied.

The man's eyes darted from her head to her toes. Her hands were empty except for a marsh stalk she had been twirling idly, which she now dropped. Amisa wore a dirty white T-shirt and frayed khaki shorts with pockets, but they contained only a garlic husk and a bobby pin. She clenched and unclenched her hands. Something rustled on the other side of her. She felt like an animal alert: hairs standing, her hands and feet cold despite the heavy heat.

A woman emerged from the foliage. She too was covered in oil, her flattened hair trailing past her shoulders. She looked like she was wearing similar clothes to the man under the mess. Now Amisa was truly scared; with that hair the woman could have been a langsuir, or a hantu pontianak. But when she smiled, she displayed a mouth of straight, shiny teeth and her eyes twinkled. She said to the man in Hokkien:

'She's just a little girl, she's got nothing.'

The man glanced from the woman to Amisa with a look that wasn't hostile, just tired. It was not only oil that covered them; they were caked in mud, swamp detritus, possibly shit, judging from how they smelt. She stared at their bare feet. The man's toenails were all smashed up.

The woman put her hands on her knees and leaned in to Amisa.

'Listen, what's your name?' she asked in a light, calm voice. 'We don't mean to scare you.'

'Xiaofang,' Amisa replied. Her face reddened; she should have lied.

'You're such a pretty girl, Xiaofang. Can you do us a favour? We really need your help. Do you live far from here?'

Amisa hesitated, and then shook her head.

'Can you bring us something to eat? It doesn't have to be much. And a rag if you can find it, just a long piece of cloth. If you're a good girl, I'll give you a reward.'

The man turned to the woman abruptly and shot her a glare. He threw up his hands, noticed Amisa watching and put them down. The woman nodded, as if to shush him.

'Do you think you can do that for me? Can you keep a secret?'

Amisa nodded seriously. She could keep secrets very well.

'Good,' the woman said, and beamed again. She jutted her chin out as if to indicate permission to leave.

Amisa backed away one step at a time, snapping tiny twigs as she retreated. The oily man and woman watched her, eyes ablaze, still as statues. When she was eight paces away she turned and broke into a run, helter-skelter non-stop, no chance if she could help it for four oily hands to grab her. She went so fast her breath heaped ragged. The undergrowth was uneven and unkind, scratching her shins.

By the time she got back to the kampong her T-shirt was drenched in sweat and her legs were covered in cuts.

'What's wrong with you?' her mother called out without looking at her.

Amisa shook her head and shivered. Her mother had shuttered the windows. Outside the sun still exclaimed from the middle of the sky, winking through the slats from time to time.

She winced. One of the cuts on her right leg was deep and it smarted. She sat on the wooden floor with its slanted boards and sole-prints, one filthy leg curled towards her and the injured one extended. She examined the cut on the inside of her leg, just by her knee, pressing it together with her thumb and index finger: blood oozed. She kept pressing until it stopped, the pain sharp and hypnotic.

'Ah!' Amisa cried out.

Her mother shifted and clicked her tongue. 'Be quiet. Stop disturbing me,' she muttered in Hakka. 'Just leave me alone.'

After a few minutes Amisa heard her mother's breathing even out and deepen. One of her brothers – it sounded like Didi – cackled from the alleyway. She heard the hyper-happy thwack of slippers hitting the floor as the boys chased each other outside. She reached for the rag lying by the stove and used it to wipe her leg. And then she stood up and moved as lightly as a whim, even though a serious impulse had overcome her. She took the rag outside and descended the small ladder carefully, landing lightly on the dirt. The giant hen, Goreng Pisang, bobbed her head out and stared with beady eyes rimmed in red. Amisa stared at Goreng Pisang's sagging comb and parted beak and felt tenderness for this poor, jurassically stupid bird stuck in the coop.

Her father would be out until late tonight, drinking beers with his fishermen, and the boys would come and go as they pleased. Right now her sister was likely preparing a meal for her husband, in her own home, so close yet so private.

Just around the corner from their house lived an ancient shoemaker named Ah Huat, whose family had gradually moved away or died. When Amisa was tiny she remembered him as sprightly and cantankerous, prone to drunken rows in the common yard. Now he lived alone, too old to work or bother anyone. Amisa peered into the house with its rusty grinding wheel in the corner and bare, tidy shelves. She saw him asleep as she expected, head thrown back over the wooden chair with its faded batik cushions, white hair as fine and fluffy as a chick's feathers, his bony chest rising and falling.

She stepped nimbly over the threshold. In here, she was an old hand: she often studied her neighbour as he slept, on late afternoons such as this when a stupor overcame Kampong Mimpi Sedih and even the animals napped. Ah Huat had one of those faces for which being at rest was transformative, conferring a quiet dignity, elegance in sleep. She stared at his smoke-stained mouth set in wrinkles. Times like this she imagined him as one of her grandfathers whom she had never met, both murdered in wartime. When she left she usually took a handful of peanut shells or a tab from a beer can as a souvenir for her own shelf: nothing he would miss, but today she boldly eyed the plate on the counter. Four slabs of watermelon, one half eaten, piled up in imperfect slices. She tiptoed towards the counter and eased the pieces into the plastic bag beside them one by one. Ah Huat stirred and she paused, but his mouth just opened and closed like a fish trying for air.

It was finally getting dark. The switch in the sky always happened like that: ridiculous sunlight all day, no segue, and then thin watery blues and browns as night-time settled and the flying insects emerged from their hiding places. She walked through the forest with slow, deliberate steps. Monkeys stared and chattered from the branches above but kept their distance. She carried the plastic bag in one hand and the rag cloth in the other. Her blood had dried and the smaller cuts didn't ache either. Perspiration cooled on her back. She remembered the path, straight through the trail and bearing left on the rickety wooden bridge, past the mossy old gravestones and through the thicket.

Amisa found them in the same spot, sitting opposite each other. They might have been easy to miss amidst the fronds if not for the seal-like shape of the woman's skull and the glint in her eyes as she turned to face her. The man started at the sound of her footsteps and the corrupt jiggle of her plastic bag. In the dimming light she saw that the oil on his skin had faded and rubbed off in places: a shoulder, a spot on the chin. Both their features were coming through with the insistence of injury, like pus through gauze. The orang minyak seemed altogether more human, as familiar as two factory workers she might have passed some time in town.

The woman got up first, followed slowly by the man. When she got closer he snatched the plastic bag from her with canine impropriety, opening it so forcefully he ripped the handles. She flinched. He held up the slice of watermelon with Ah Huat's bite mark parallel to his own mouth and set on it like he hadn't eaten in years. The juice dribbled down his chin and on to his sunken belly as the oily woman fixed Amisa with a look of pure gratitude.

4

SZU

2003

The next morning I wake up with a start. My alarm goes off two seconds later, a shrill and invasive beeping. I struggle to turn it off, eyes bleary. Sixteen years and one day old. My mouth tastes like smoke. Half awake, I picture my mother watching me as I sleep, blowing smoke rings into my mouth as I snore. My lungs feel dirty. I rub my eyes and reach over to the curtain, pulling it open.

A haze has settled over the garden. It blurs the outlines of the trees and terracotta pots. From my bedroom window the world looks like a low-budget film set. The neighbouring roofs resemble ridges folded from dark-orange paper. At any moment, a construction crane could reach down and scrunch all these houses up, dump them in the parking lot of some crumbling studio. That burnt-barbecue stench from yesterday is everywhere, and it's gotten thicker. Even though the window is latched shut the bad smell creeps all the way up my nose.

I stumble out of bed. I choke as I put on my uniform, my hands moving stiffly. I button up my blouse and zip up my skirt. It nips my waist. The skin of my finger snags on the zip.

'Fuck,' I mutter. I feel bitten. There is a bead of blood on my ring finger.

On the bus the radio is blaring from the speakers and I try to avoid looking at the television screen, which beams back the footage of commuters shot from three different angles. Nothing to make an early morning worse like being reminded of one's hideousness. None of the angles flatters me. The camera is low-grade and casts the interior of the bus in an ominous grey-blue glow, as if a spectre will appear at any moment. The macik behind me keeps blowing her nose. When she puts her hands on either side of her stubby nose and pinches she sounds just like the fuse from the kettle clicking at night. The uncle beside me jiggles his leg and keeps hitting my knee. I wish there was a bubble protecting me from every other human. I huddle closer to the window.

The radio announcer is a young woman with a smug, honeyed voice. 'Today's PSI is registered as 164. The public is advised to stay indoors as this is an unhealthy reading. If you must go outside, please wear a medical mask. Government-issued hospital masks will be available from the following public distribution points between 9.30 and 6.00 p.m. today . . .'

She lists the places, but I can't bear any more of her stupid, phoney, quasi-American accent. I put in my earphones. So I've heard the rumbles. The newspaper reports on forest fires in Sumatra, slash and burn, which sounds like the name of a bad rock band. I don't like rock music. I prefer the fuzzy distortions of shoegaze. I found out about shoegaze from a music magazine someone left on the number 67.

This shoegazey kind of music is made for me. It cancels everything out: the tedious hours ahead, the pollution all around me. Most of these bands are from northern England. I picture castles and cold air, drunk white boys with backcombed hair and bad teeth stumbling over the cobblestones. Canned air suspended on a bass line. The bus shudders and jolts. I hold my breath and squeeze my eyes shut.

*

By the time I reach the school concourse the haze has thickened into a grey shroud and I wave my hands in front of my face as I move forward. It's almost time for assembly. Through the haze I see two flags hanging on their poles. On a typical morning two prefects raise the flags solemnly to the piped, scratchy track of our national anthem. Even when the flags reach the top there is rarely enough wind to make the fabric fly photogenically. Instead, they just hang there – limp, rain-stained. The prefects go away. The anthem carries on for two verses and just when the sound cuts out we cross our right hands over our chests and mumble the pledge. *We, the citizens of Singapore* . . . I have mouthed all the words every weekday morning for the past decade. They have no meaning to me. Like meat that has been chewed flavourless.

This air tastes and smells stale. It's not like in *Heidi*, with all that clean, high-altitude Swiss air. This is second-hand smoke, a mess that hasn't been cleaned up and has drifted over to us. I don't know if we'll have normal assembly today. I shift my weight from one foot to the other. I can't see any teachers around. Through my daze I notice a group of girls gathered in the left-hand corner of the concourse. All I can make out is their clump of bent black-haired heads, rustling uniforms and mosquito-bitten legs shuffling around.

I nudge forward. There is a girl sprawled on the concrete. She makes a slight movement. She looks maybe two years younger than me. I have never seen her before. Her face is the sort you forget in a second. Not pretty, not ugly. She is looking at her own palm. Her mouth makes soft gulping shapes, like a goldfish out of a bowl. Her legs are splayed at obtuse angles, and I notice that her right foot has a smudged red circle around the ankle, no sock, and no shoe.

'One of the wild dogs bit her shoe off,' someone whispers. 'Ate her sock. Would have chewed up the rest of her if Faizah and Sarah hadn't passed by.'

'Serves her right,' someone adds.

At the back of our school is a secondary forest that the government grew to keep the air clean. It didn't work. The fir trees sprang to full height at double speed, unsettled by the heat. The conifers are dark green, with tall tips like the bristles of mascara wands. There is a blue wire fence around the forest because of the pack of wild dogs that roams the tall grass. From time to time a hole appears in the fence, whether made by clippers or bitten open by the pack of mongrel dogs, scraggly brown and grey; there's wolf in there somewhere. They run quickly, on sinewy legs. They never bark or howl. The authorities have brought in pest control and animal enforcement officers but these dogs are wily. They know how to hide.

I encountered one of them in my first year here. It came right up behind me when I was crying at the back of the canteen. As I watched my tears drip into my palms, so absorbed was I with feeling sorry for myself that I only sensed I had company when I heard loud, avid panting. My first thought was of Biscuit, back from the dead. I turned around and there was a huge, messy dog no more than two feet away from me. He – for it was a he, I could see his balls dangling – sniffed the grass in circles. I stared at his wet nose and yellow teeth, his long tongue discoloured like a piece of old steak, not pink like Biscuit's. There was, I thought, a certain grisly glamour to death by mauling. Yet the dog-wolf looked at me indifferently. After a few moments he padded away, haunches rising and falling. My heart shifted down from my throat and sank back into my ribs.

'Circe,' someone says. *Sir-see*.

The girl on the ground does not respond. A teacher comes up and makes us move aside.

'Circe,' the teacher repeats. 'Can you hear me?'

The girl's eyes roll round to where the teacher is standing. She moves her head and sits up, propped unsteady on her palms.

'What happened? Are you okay?'

'I'm fine,' Circe replies. Her voice is small and scratchy. She sounds like she has a sore throat. It must be from the haze.

45

'Girl, can you stand up? Are you sure you're okay?' the teacher continues. 'Later on you need to come and find me and countersign the accident report.'

'Okay. I'll action that. Just give me a few minutes.'

I lean in to get a closer look. What kind of person talks like this? Does she think she's in the army?

The teacher seems familiar with her. She nods, and walks away.

'Circe Low is such a drama queen,' someone behind me whispers.

'Thinks she's the shit. When she's not all that.'

'My dad knows her dad. Says they are nouveau riche, no class.'

Within a few minutes the crowd has dispersed, girls pairing off and mumbling small boredoms to each other. A flock of pigeons flies overhead. Circe and I look up at the same time.

'What's going on with assembly?' I ask.

She glowers at me. 'No idea.'

'Maybe they'll let us go home. Because of this haze. I can hardly see anything. My eyes are so dry.' I'm mumbling, and soon she will try to get away from me. 'Are you okay?'

'Yeah, I'm fine,' she says. She clutches her ankle and scratches her jaw with her other hand. 'A grey dog got my shoe. It looked like a mix between a wolf and a pony. Not cute. Came out of nowhere and it held on to my ankle and wouldn't let go. There's blood but it doesn't hurt. My Converse, though. Brand new. Converse 77s, special edition. What am I supposed to do with just one side? That fucking dog. Next time, I'll kick it.'

'Maybe you have rabies now. Or AIDS.'

'You can't get AIDS from a dog. Don't be stupid.'

'Of course you can,' I reply, even though I am not so sure. 'You should get a blood test. In case you're dying.'

I help her up and she brushes the dirt from the ground off her skirt. She looks at me out of the corner of her eye.

'Are you Ng Szu Min?'

'How do you know?'

'No big deal. I saw you outside the staffroom. You must have done something really dumb to end up in public detention.'

'I was talking in class. That's all.'

'Hm. Well, I heard you bite and lick people and make shit up.'

'Says who? That's not true,' I reply. 'People in your year are dumb and gossipy.' I eye her tiny frame up and down. 'And stunted.'

'What year are you in?'

'Sec Four.'

'I'm in the same year, stupid.'

'How come I've never seen you?'

'I transferred over last term. I'm not always in school,' Circe says. 'I have trouble sleeping. It's legit. I get some days off. I've got a medical cert. to prove it.'

'Wow. Lucky you.'

She shoots me an arch, shrewd look.

'I heard you're like the girl from *The Ring*. You never

47

wash your hair and you're fucking creepy. You climb out of TVs.'

Before I can react Circe shrugs, and then flashes a smile at me. She looks both twelve and like a cavalier twenty-something when she does this. I see that she is one of the 7 per cent of people in the world blessed with what is popularly termed a Truly Winning Smile. The sincerity of the smile makes my stomach lurch, like sitting in the back seat of a car as it goes over a speed bump. She hops on her bare foot. As we make our way into the school building and down the darkened corridor, she leans into my arm.

5

CIRCE

2020

Ever since my divorce I sleep better. Seven solid hours every night, right until my alarm goes off. I remember my dreams better, too. Lately I've had dreams about auditions and choir practice, sincerely hoping to be a professional singer, unaware of how discordantly my life would unfold. And even further back in time, dreams of being close with my brother – back when it was the two of us in collusion against adulthood.

Leslie and I would have done anything never to grow up. Even as kids, we knew what a cliché we were; we rewatched our copies of *Hook* and *Peter Pan* until the tape stripes wore out. Can't believe that my brother is now thirty-five, and has a goat-like wisp of facial hair, a bitchy banker wife and two smart, sulky children. Back when we were children ourselves, we hid behind the living-room curtains pale and tense as Daddy sat stony-faced at the dining table, sorting bills. Leslie and I hated seriousness. Adulthood seemed to us like an endless stream of paperwork and sighing. Frowning and always saying sorry, even when you didn't mean it.

'Yuck. Not the Borings again,' Leslie would proclaim at

the sound of guests' voices in the hallway. He would groan like the green monster from *Are You Afraid of the Dark?* because it was going to be a long, staid evening when our parents threw a dinner party.

When we watched TV Leslie and I made retching noises at any kissing scenes. When we got a fax machine connected to an extra phone line, we used to call each other from opposite rooms, inventing long jokes devoid of punchlines, telling elaborate ghost stories to each other until our ears grew hot from the receiver and Mummy wailed for us to do our homework. The year we had the Internet installed we listened in on the rainstorm jangle of data on the phone line, interrupting each other's connectivity. That was 1997: the dawn of the Asian financial crisis, a period of rapid currency decline and market upheaval – yet whilst other businesses crumbled, my father's hitherto limping luxury trading company unexpectedly thrived. It turned out that even in times of fiscal ruin people still harboured a bullish, avaricious appetite for certain kinds of jewellery, watches and double-breasted suits.

Our family moved out of the flat where I'd spent my whole life, straight into a two-storey detached villa on Margouliouth Road with floors so shiny I could see my gleeful face in them. We went from budget to five-star hotels, cushioned in my father's new money. Funny how long it takes to adjust to the removal of privileges, but how little time is needed to get accustomed to comfort. Hotel is a hotel is a hotel. Mummy used to berate Leslie and me for taking nice things so quickly for granted, and my brother and I would roll our bratty eyes at each other

50

and mouth *nag, nag, nag*. We bickered with and play-hit each other in stuffy aeroplanes that criss-crossed the world. Our parents paid thousands of dollars in order to relocate our arguments and petty grievances across different cities. Us Lows loved each other but seldom got along, even back then. Is every family privately the same, or were we especially negative? Athens, Tokyo, Mozambique. In tour buses, rented cars, rattling trains, we paid no attention to the scenery, blinkered by our freshly funded monstrosity. Leslie kept his eyes on his Game Boy, I on my Tamagotchis.

All these things come back with such clarity and detail in my sleep that first thing in the morning, just before I grope around for my phone, I feel this pit of old time nested in my chest. It's a physical thing. A weight shifting. For a moment or two I think that I'll see my old Backstreet Boys poster on the wall, and I expect to put on my uniform to go to school. All this, even though it's been at least two years since Leslie and I had a genuinely nice time together, just the two of us (I think it was one of those nostalgic big-screen showings of *Hook* at the Old Cathay, when his wife was working late and at the last minute couldn't join us). And next month I'll turn thirty-three years old.

I never dream about my ex-husband. I'm glad we ended it sooner rather than later. We exhausted all our ugliness; we have nothing left to inflict upon each other. I shudder to think what it would be like had we carried on resenting and attempting to bridge our irresolvable differences, over and over, until we were forty, fifty, sixty. At least I've got some youth left in me. Working around twenty-one-year-old interns keeps me feeling trendy. I notice how this generation hold their bodies (slouching, eyes shifty, averted; white-knuckle grip on phone), how they speak (listlessly, favouring texting to vocal conversation) as well as what they wear. The seventies look is back in fashion – bell-bottom jeans, peasant blouses – as well as the Recession Chic of the mid noughties: crumpled shirts, muted florals, interview outfits to sweat in. Vintage hand-me-downs are essential; nothing freshly manufactured. Morgue-Core, it's called. All the same there are entire factories dedicated to distressing new clothing, making it look dirtied and snagged.

Mummy, ever charming, insists that I only notice the stupid and superficial things in life (like clothing or TV shows) and ignore what is important. What *is* important? That is something I would still like to know. Nowadays I catch my mother looking at me with bafflement. As if I turned out the complete opposite to what she hoped and expected. She's gotten more negative in old age. She tells me it is not a big surprise that I gave up on my marriage, because I'm a pathological quitter. She blames me for her gallstones and says I am ageing her. I tell her I can't do that because she's already old.

'You and your rudeness,' she replies. 'I wish I had a sweeter girl.'

She's kept my divorce quiet from most of our relatives. She secretly hopes Jarrold and I will get back together, perhaps go see a Christian marriage counsellor, even though both of us are lapsed Christians, at best. No one needs to know, is her line. That's fine.

Leslie is my mother's ally. He lives with his wife Rachel

in a swish East Coast condo with rooms the size of teacup chihuahuas and a swimming pool that looks phallic from the aerial view. They are the flawlessly devoted parents of two precocious boys whom I find hard to handle; I'm bad with kids. We could not have ended up more different. The freshest impression I have of my big brother is his face contorted into disapproval, while his wife tiptoes around the shambles of my marriage with sanctimonious delicacy, like singlehood is a malady that needs curing.

I am deep into the process of unknowing my ex-husband. Unknowing is as delicate and gradual a practice as its reverse. It deserves the same space and deliberation. Why does a divorce carry so much more gravity and defeat than a break-up? Why do friends quietly judge and feel sorry? Sure, there's the issue of assets, and titles, the naming of things. The people closest to us withdrawing the expectation that we would stay together forever and have fat, gifted kids. That's the pinch. He can keep his boring friends and priority club memberships. I am not sorry. Right now I am at the stage where I'm startled that my ex-husband and I ever shared a straw, a blanket, a flat. I can admit to myself that he was a bad kisser, tepid in bed.

I never dream about the last ten years. I read a list on the Internet that said that some of the most common things that people dream about are:

1. Falling off buildings.

2. Being chased.

3. Animals.

Nothing as exciting as the first two for me. The animals I will come back to. No running or falling in my sleep. Just this sludge of the past. The well-trodden and the has-been. All these old feelings bubble up and leave a thin film over my waking day, like the skin on a soup.

*

I work as a social media consultant. I've been at my company for over four years. When I joined, in 2016, I was twenty-nine and happily married and very excited to be here. Now I'm almost thirty-three and happily unmarried, and on some Monday mornings, sitting in this very room, I feel like if I was stuck on a ship out at sea with these people I would kill everybody. I should find a new job, but I just don't have the energy.

The main account I'm handling is Jolene See's. She is a Channel 8 starlet who is trying to break into the Taiwanese pop market. First stop: Taiwan. Next stop: China. And then: the world. I'll be impressed if she makes it out of South East Asia. She's got a half-decent voice: a forlorn, saccharine soprano, but you just can't force these things. I should know. Her management team are awful but they pay us on time. I end up doing a lot of their work for them, curating Jolene's English language social media content. Every post, every tweet, every mailer. Jolene is seventeen, dewy-eyed and lithe and dumb as bricks, but she's a nice kid.

'Make it cute,' her team instruct me.

'I'll action that,' I say to them.

For at least half my working week this is what I do: paid

ventriloquism. I adopt the voice of a 'cute', kooky, highly relatable seventeen-year-old. My office is open plan; everyone can see my monitor. The sun is coming in strong through the floor-length windows. There must be a word – some German or Inuit term – that describes the stuck, dreadful feeling of disliking a beautiful view just because it is overfamiliar, and synonymous with work and daily boredom. I've lived on this island all my life, and I often forget it's just a speck on a map of the world.

So much is crammed into this city. No such thing as a quiet, empty space around here, unless you count a corporate car park on Sundays. I crick my neck left and then right and take in the crystal ship glint of Marina Bay – skyscrapers of silver and mirrored blue glass, the swoop of a highway, construction cranes lifting container crates. Reclaimed land, all this. Thirty years ago it was part of the sea bed – now it's a tall jagged skyline, hiding a giant sinkhole. By our long windows is the sage-green Feature Wall, so called because it's meant to be a special feature of our recently refurbished office. This colour is meant to be calming. Instead it reminds me of the terrible paint job by the staffroom in my secondary school. Someone needs to change the batteries for the wall clock. The hands are stuck on 6.30, which is just cruel, because no one can leave until our boss says so.

The government is constructing another MRT line outside. **BAY VIEW STATION – READY TO SERVE YOU IN 2023.** I don't see the need for so many stops within such a small radius. Tunnels of marble, steel and Plexiglas, with subterranean magazine stands and incessantly beeping barriers. The stations are so close to each other that it takes less than twenty seconds to get from one stop to the next. By the time the door hisses shut it is time for it to reopen.

I'm writing an email to a painfully obtuse woman in the Joy Management Hong Kong offices. I need to get the tone just right: not too snarky, but firm enough to let her know that if she was doing her job correctly, I wouldn't have to keep asking her for the same stupid things. After two sentences, my focus is interrupted by drilling and the clang of metal. I check the time on my phone. I take a medication called Praziquantal every four hours, after meals. This is a new development, these small beige capsules in a blister pack. I pop the pill silently at my desk, wash it down with fizzy water. I haven't told anyone in the office that I am recovering from a tapeworm infection.

How I picked up a tapeworm in a first-world country like Singapore is a mystery to me, and to my doctor as well. Dr Quah said it was raw meat. Some shoddy hawker not washing his hands properly. Tapeworm eggs are spread through faeces. Somewhere along the line, during the past two months, I must have been too busy to realize that I had eaten shit. I could have eaten shit and died if I wasn't careful.

I know that some people ingest tapeworms in the hope that the parasite will eat them thin. Mine just gave me cramps. I remained the same weight, but developed a little more of an appetite. I craved sharp and demanding tastes: candied orange peel, fried cuttlefish, chilli kangkong, pickled cabbage. It was only when the cramps worsened that I went to the doctor. I was shocked to find that something had taken up a home inside me, uninvited. It thrived, while I clutched my sides and felt dizzy.

Dr Quah prescribed the medicine to treat it. Now I'm killing the sucker, slowly and surely. Poisoning the life out of it. When it gives up the fight I'll shit out segments of its sickly white body. An eye for an eye, a shit for a shit.

I know what my worm looks like. I've seen its little face in my sleep, peeping behind my eyelids. *Cestoda cyclophyllidea*, that's the name for it, which sounds like a thrush medication, or an ugly woman in a myth. My Cestoda is long and slender and moves with purpose. It's not a dumb creature. It wants to sap up the very best of me. All the vitamins and nutrients. All the funniest anecdotes and fondest feelings. Cestoda lives in my intestines but likes to travel around my body, take a gander, have a look-see. I have a meeting in a minute. I squirm in my chair as I feel the worm wandering down my gullet. There is something exquisite and almost sexy about how alone I am with this knowledge. I feel it ripple past my oesophagus, clogging up my voice box, avoiding the heart. Nestling into the atrium of my lungs, down to the belly. Is it the worm, or a bad lunch?

Gordon Cheong, my boss, nods his head at me. I get up and we file into the meeting room, seven of us. Jeanette Kok Hui Ling is walking in front of me; the office babe. I study her ass in a taupe-coloured pencil skirt, her sashaying at once both effortless and practised. I wonder what it would feel like to hold her hips like a jar and rattle them. Jeanette brings back the oiliest meals for lunch at her desk; char kway teow, dripping satay sticks, mee goreng and deep-fried chicken wings from the food court next door. Sometimes she takes the food out of its sweating styrofoam box and lays it on the one square white plate we have in the office kitchen. From the water cooler, I watch her angling her phone camera. After she's uploaded and tagged the evidence, she eats it. Wolfs it all down whilst online shopping, making gobbling and slurping sounds like a cartoon, a frenzy of disposable chopsticks and plastic spoons snapped in staccatos by her ferocious hunger. Where does all that oil and fat go? Does it clog up her tiny arteries? Does it travel out of her body peacefully, like rabbit pellets, or does she take epic, life-or-death shits?

That apocalyptic appetite is the only thing that makes me warm to her. I wonder if she has a worm that she knows nothing about. Maybe they have a one-sided, long-term relationship. Her worm would be inferior to my worm; less selective in its tastes, lethargic in the afternoons.

As if she senses that I am thinking about her, Jeanette slides into the leather seat across from me and glances up. I half smile at her, but she dismisses it. She returns to her tablet. Her nails are violet-coloured shellac. Kiat Ming, Irfan, Carl and Mona assume their seats and take out their tablets as well. Tap, tap, tap. Everyone scrolls to the schedule for today. Carl gawps at Jeanette's cleavage. Gordon clears his throat and starts talking. I look at him and try not to glaze over.

'Look at the screen,' Gordon says. Our gazes follow, like good little sheep.

On the large monitor on the wall a woman's face appears. Her features bear the artificial clarity of digital restoration. It takes me half a second to recognize her, and when I do a lump forms in my throat. The bastard child of a feeling at once both horrified and deeply moved. My stomach shifts. My worm must like that. Plenty to feed on.

I force myself to examine a younger version of the woman I knew. She is half hiding behind a large green leaf, smiling so that you can see the crinkles at the corners of her gleaming eyes. The dark-red painted crescent of her mouth is in shadow. Even though the image has been retouched, the woman is the biggest giveaway that this is an old photo. She has that Peranakan, Nyonya kind of beauty that you just don't see on the streets these days.

'Anyone know who this is?' Gordon asks.

'Never seen her in my life,' says Jeanette.

'Me neither. She's hot,' says Carl.

'I know,' says Irfan, who seems to know everything. 'That's the chick who played the Pontianak in the seventies movie.'

'That's right,' Gordon replies. 'Amisa Tan. If you don't know her name you might recognize her face from vintage posters. Aaron Leow's studio is doing a reboot of this movie. This is a major project. All hands on deck. Thali and Joseph will tell you how hard they had to fight to win this client.'

Carl and Irfan make murmurs of assent. Gordon hovers his cursor over Amisa's face.

'*Ponti!*, 1978. Followed by *Ponti 2*, 1979, *Ponti 3: Curse of the Bomoh* in 1980. Iskandar Wiryanto wrote and directed all three of them. Anyone heard of him?'

Silence in the room. Jeanette is smoothing her index

nail with her thumb. Kiat Ming is checking his phone under the table. Mona is borderline snoring.

'Don't expect anyone will. He never made it big. He thought he was making art-house movies. But these *Ponti* films are camp entertainment. Nobody took them seriously. Anyway, Leow's production company is currently in casting, and they want us to handle the promotion. Any ideas? I want to see you excited.'

Carl and Irfan pretend to be excited. Ming is still texting. Nobody is looking at me.

I remember the first time I saw her: Szu's mother. I never knew her as Amisa Tan the cult actress, the siren from the film archives, doe eyes on a painted poster. Just the jellyfish billow of her nightdress as she walked away from us. Her pale wrists and those sharp features, steely even off guard, too striking for someone's quiet, housebound mother. Amisa had a face that was always lit up with anger, or irritation, or some grown-up, storied sadness she never thought to disguise from two teenage girls.

That first afternoon returns to me in jolts of film. Szu unlocked the front grille and the old beige door. I stared at the nape of my new friend's neck, vaguely repulsed by the beads of sweat forming along her hairline even though I was sweating myself. The moment we stepped into the front room I knew that we had to keep quiet. This was a place of reverence, of a finger to a lip, hushing my jokes. It was an offensively bright day in January, three weeks after we met. None of the sunshine glare made its way in. The air was static and tomb-like.

'Got any snacks?' I asked Szu in a lowered voice.

At that point I was still testing her, aware that I hit a nerve with every reminder of eating. She nodded sombrely. We took off our shoes and padded down the corridor. Szu and I were sixteen, each other's only friends in the world. We were symbiotic in the intense, irreplicable way that comes as part and parcel of being careworn teenaged girls; we wheedled and resented each other in fluctuating measures. I looked around the kitchen. It was so scummy; the dishes on the drying rack faded or soup-stained. When Szu opened the fridge, it exhaled a bad breath of fish and pickled vegetables.

'You brought a friend back, Szu. I'm impressed,' someone said.

Szu turned away from the stressful glow of food, and my eyes followed. A spectacular, spectral woman stood in the doorway wearing a light-blue housedress, and the red plastic slippers you can get for ninety-nine cents from the wet market. Even in that get-up, I had never seen anyone more starlike. I gawked. At this point Amisa was already very ill. I didn't know it then, but of course they did, mother and daughter both; their knowledge heavied the room. From this first time I met her Amisa Tan had less than eight months left to live. She was so thin. She seemed less like a woman made of flesh and bone, and more like an exquisitely etched stencil. Long streaks of grey and white showed in her chignon.

'Um. Hello, Auntie,' I finally said.

'Please. It's Mrs Ng.'

'I'm Circe.'

'Nice to meet you.' She assessed me for a moment. I

felt insufficient in my dark-grey uniform. Her eyes flicked away. 'Well, make yourself at home. Enjoy, girls.'

Mrs Ng didn't ask me to repeat my unusual name; didn't feign any interest. She was so different from other mothers, who would have offered water, or chrysanthemum tea, or layer cake. She had this regality to her movements. She lit a cigarette and made her way to the room at the end of the hallway, and shut the door quietly behind her. I felt something catch in my throat. I had this fawning urge to follow her, but I kept still.

'Well . . . now you've met my mother,' Szu said. 'Sorry. There's nothing in the fridge to snack on. We might have Khong Guan biscuits somewhere, but I don't know how old they are.'

'Forget it,' I replied. 'Can I have a tour instead?'

The house was crawling with large red ants. The walls bore long, snaking cracks, half the paint peeled off in jagged archipelagos. The grilles of the kitchen window were matted inches deep with bird and bat shit. The old bungalow was dim and quiet except for the bubbling of the aquarium filter from the huge fish tank in the kitchen and, from time to time, the sound of low chanting. A man, or a woman with a hoarse voice, muttered in a dialect I couldn't place.

'That's my aunt Yunxi,' Szu said, a little apologetically.

I thought: *Who could live here? What a creepy dump.* Yet at the same time there was a certain aura about the place. I don't know how else to put it. The house was suffused with a strangeness that has stayed with me for years. Its dirty windows and closed doors appear in my dreams from time to time. At the end of my afternoon visits I felt glad to return to the tidy familiarity of my own home, and yet I wanted to go back to Szu's. I looked forward to revisiting that off-white building at the end of a leafy driveway, containing its beautiful discontent. The place was so run-down and neglected that my own mother would have been appalled. It reminded me of the backstage of an ancient theatre in there. The melted-down candles, the orange lamps, the palettes of fine pink powder that I assumed Amisa applied to her smooth, ghostly skin.

6

AMISA

1975

She was all packed. It wasn't difficult. She had not much to take with her, just one bag and all the ringgits she saved from odd jobs: rambutan and cockle picking, button sorting, dishwashing, Campbell Street trade assistant, steamboat dream girl, whatever she could get.

'I'm ready,' Amisa said, and her parents looked up at her from where they sat at the wooden table, and both nodded.

To be seventeen, and so beautiful. Sloe-eyed, fine-nosed, glistening pink mouth like an ang ku kueh. Her father thought: who is she? How did this terrifying goddess come from me and my sweet but plain pudding of a wife? What is she doing here? Over the past three years, frankly, Amisa had made him nervous, and he hadn't been able to protect her from her lascivious uncle and the leering, oily boys from the charcoal factory.

Or maybe he hadn't been able to control her. She had joined a dance troupe at thirteen, and they performed during Chinese New Year and the Mid-Autumn Festival. Amisa moved with a sinuousness and sensuality that harnessed the spotlight and made the older women in the crowd unintentionally draw their hands to their mouths and the men's eyes dart away and then furtively back, flick up and down, oh yeah. Late at night Amisa would slip back into the house smelling of grass and sweat, with charcoal stains all down her arms and up her legs from who knows what, and even her beauty-queen smile felt like a failing. He didn't understand how she could be so unlike her good sister or seven strong brothers who worked hard and laughed easily.

The family borrowed Khim Fatt's open-top truck and her siblings rode in the back with her.

'Do you have everything you need?' Jiejie asked. She had brought her youngest daughter with her. She was never on her own these days.

'Yes, Jiejie,' Amisa said. 'You don't need to worry.' Yet as she spoke she felt a wiggle of fear in the pit of her stomach, the sick certainty that she had really decided to leave them. She didn't know how to phrase her selfish, valid, various reasons. In the house, she was outnumbered. The atmosphere had grown unbearable. Her parents looked at her every day like she might murder them.

As the truck rattled over a bump, Amisa rested her face on her palm and stared at her favourite person. Didi blinked back with an expression of rare focus, tender concentration. His mouth curved into the end point of two neat dimples. Some day soon my Little Ghost will be a heartbreaker, Amisa thought.

He still had that cheeky capuchin demeanour from childhood. Her gaze fell to the vicious laceration on his right leg, a long, raised mark. Didi was the wildest boy in the kampong, and this spring he became obsessed with a used motorcycle, its fender and gas tank a chipped king-fisher blue. How Didi took to it, this sprayed-bright hub, revving the engine till it panicked the chickens. His puckish face lit up over the cowboy saddle. Amisa acquiesced to one ride in the pitch dark. She screamed in his ears and held on to Didi, felt the thrum in his ribs as he whooped and laughed at her.

One week later, Didi swerved to avoid a giant monitor lizard and crashed his motorcycle into a pole. The accident opened his right leg from hip down to knobbly knee. It took six agonizing weeks for him to walk properly again, and now he acted like he had never been injured, despite his telltale hobble.

The journey passed too quickly. The last stretch of road, Didi kept his eyes on the trees, gritted his jaw. Jiejie smoothed her daughter's hair and smiled at Amisa.

At the bus terminal Amisa hugged Jiejie tightly, her brothers one by one, and Didi last of all. She could barely look at him without wanting to cry, so she kept her eyes on the ground. When she looked up, he grinned at her like they were in on the same joke. Maybe I can't go, Amisa thought.

'You'll write and call?' Jiejie said. She was smiling, but still there was a lovelorn shadow, worry tucked in the corner of her mouth. Jiejie's seven-year-old daughter tugged at Amisa's arm. She patted the little girl briefly.

As she boarded the bus, Amisa turned to her family standing by the kerb: her parents with their greying hair and stern expressions; her sun-stroked brothers in their khaki slacks and singlets; her wonderful, serious sister in the grey dress with her lookalike kid. Didi smiled and waved. Amisa took her seat and waved back from the window, her palm coming to rest against the glass.

It was only after the bus crossed the highway and the island shrank to a small green glimmer that Amisa reached into her pocket and closed her hand around its contents. She peered around to make sure nobody was looking before taking out the red cloth pouch, tilting it on her lap so that the jade bangle peeked out. It had been her great-grandmother's and was her first sister-in-law's by right, but her eldest brother hadn't married yet, and it didn't seem like he would anytime soon. Her mother had always said she was a thief, not to be trusted, and Amisa felt it was almost expected of her to take her mother's most prized possession, tucked at the back of the second drawer, right where she knew she would find it.

When the causeway snaked into Singapore she looked out into the concrete expanse, the tall buildings clustered like rows of crooked teeth, HDB flats in stucco textures and half-constructed office buildings. She realized that besides wanting to leave Kampong Mimpi Sedih, she had not given this new place much thought, had not allowed it to occupy any space in her idealizations. And perhaps because of that, she would be impossible to disappoint.

Yellow-top taxis zoomed past along the wide roads, painted with their orderly white stripes; cars and trucks moved in obedient rows. Amisa felt steeled, not alarmed, by the scale of the city, the rubble and scaffolding everywhere.

In Geylang her mute, bald landlord led her up a flight of narrow stairs that creaked underfoot, as if the wood would moulder away at any moment. The shophouse smelt faintly of urine and vegetable oil. At the top of the stairs were two doors so close to each other that they could only open inwards. Up here the air reeked of incense and the sour, bodily smell of sickness. The square between the two doors would only hold one human at a time. The landlord unlocked the yellowed door to the left and Amisa followed him into her new home. The room was tiny, with a bare bulb and water-stained walls, but nobody could enter without a key or a knock. This place was truly hers.

In the early mornings she worked in the wet market, helping Mr and Mrs Lim sort cockles, clams and prawns. Mr Lim was an old friend of her father's, with white bushy eyebrows and an accosting stare that slipped into a bare-faced ogle when his wife turned the other way. Amisa did a little wriggle when Mrs Lim wasn't looking, and winked at Mr Lim, kept him sweet on her but didn't allow any touching. She was the cynosure of all eyes in the market, even at 4.30 a.m. wearing a fish-stained apron, with a face scrubbed of sleep and her hair hidden underneath a white plastic cap.

On her long walk home, men leered and sucked the air through their teeth. Sometimes she didn't even know they were there until they followed her. To distract herself, Amisa filed the leerers into racial generalizations, feeling very much like her own mother as she did so. The Malay men mostly winked and nodded at her. The Chinese men called her *mei nu* and shouted out rude come-ons in every dialect, getting increasingly agitated as she ignored them, and the Indian men stared at her with a leonine intensity, but at least they said nothing. She jutted her jaw and tried to walk quickly, keeping her own eyes trained safely ahead. This city was worlds away from the susurrating shoreline of Kampong Mimpi Sedih with its promise of turtles, its lowlands and marshes, but it seemed that men everywhere were alike in their swampy intentions, no matter how well they disguised it. They wanted to gobble her up. Their hunger was rote.

In the late afternoons and some evenings, she worked in the Paradise Theatre, a small cinema at the junction of Jalan Ubi and Everitt Road. It had only two screens: one that showed Hindi and Chinese films, and another that showed second-run Hollywood movies. Some days she cleaned the toilets and other times she ushered and sat on a hard-backed chair at the back of the theatre.

In front of her unfolded a screen the size of a small world.

Whirring countdown: ten beeping numbers and the final fidgets before the long, darkened room became as hushed and vast as the bottom of the sea. Peace at short last. It was a whole way of being, and for her, it felt completely free. She loved the kung fu movies with their mind-boggling choreography and mulleted young men who never tired; or the Hindi musicals with their flutter-ing romance, lush intriguing girls and stirring scores that surged in and out of bass and bongo beats. Saris swished vivid colour across the screen, every frame pulsing with life that was so much better than life. She even adored *Jaws* with its stupid-looking shark and the choppy threat of American waters. Hollywood seemed incredibly unreal: everyone so blonde, buttery, strong-thighed and somehow cruder. She could have watched films all day, and even without the visuals the sounds themselves were calming: nothing but the soft puttering of the film reel through the projector, the rustle of snacks, and the laboured breathing of an audience either aroused or half asleep. She could live right here, behind them, dwell always in this darkened kingdom of muffled dialogue, muffled intrigue; and she felt a rare kinship, a shared humanity with the silhouetted heads tilted upward, chewing kachang puteh or watermelon seeds.

The young couples amused her. They entered the auditorium primly and, once the lights dimmed, necked with slurpy passion, creaks challenging the folding seats. Sometimes they left a sticky residue, a snail trail of indeterminate bodily origin that she wiped away with bleach. Her manager, a permanently scowling man in his thirties called Pok Hian, instructed her to tap politely on the shoulders of such canoodlers, even granting permission to hit them lightly on the head with a wooden fan if that would make them cease. But mess and all, Amisa let them be.

There was one particular Chinese couple in their early twenties who came in for the Sunday matinees. The girl was ponytailed, plain and slightly pudgy, and the man was of medium height with sloping shoulders and a mildly pockmarked face. The couple would turn up to the theatre holding hands, the girl beaming, nakedly and radiantly in love. The man would stride up to the counter and buy a pair of tickets for the back stalls seats, and as Amisa tore the stubs and handed them to him she felt unsettled and annoyed by the way he stared at her, all the while holding his girlfriend's hand. His gaze always lingered for at least two beats too long.

By the time the lights came on and the crowd emerged from the theatre the ponytailed girl almost always had reddened eyes and glistening cheeks, although Amisa never actually caught her crying. Perhaps she was easily moved even by the ridiculously slapstick Hong Kong comedies. Perhaps she had an eye or sinus condition. But Amisa noticed the couple's silhouettes one time, conferring furiously in inaudible whispers during a fight scene in *Dong kai ji*. Theirs seemed like a terrible and especially boring courtship, doomed to failure. She wondered why the ponytailed girl even bothered, why anyone bothered really with the rituals of love, why they didn't just get down to it the way she had back in the village, barebacked animal fumbles in the tall grass with any handsome body, undeterred by what she might catch or what risked growing inside her. If it happens, it happens, and I'll handle it, she thought, with the same clear-eyed abandon she felt all those years ago. Striding into the forest with no ammunition or protection from the darkening green except a plastic bag containing a dishcloth and a half-eaten watermelon. Maybe her mother was right and she was lucky, charmed even still to exist.

So life went on this way: fondling seafood in the small hours, whiskery grey prawns slipping from her grip, shucked shells and wet floors and the rush and furore of the market before it opened. When her job was done Amisa strode like a samurai past the bucket mountains, the reams of belt noodles and cloth and extravagantly violent, gushing cuts of beef and pork, to go home and shower and take it all off. And then she would have a nap, and turn up for her shift at the cinema. Rinse and repeat.

Mr and Mrs Lim were agreeable enough bosses, although they disapproved of her living in Geylang.

'That whole area got prostitutes,' Mrs Lim said, and shook her head. 'Dirty place. Stay away from the red numbers.'

The numbering of the shophouse where Amisa lived looked like it had once been red, but was now scratched off.

7

CIRCE

2020

Over the next few weeks it feels like a can of Amisa-shaped worms has been opened. I hadn't seen her face in years, but now she is hard to avoid. I get her image embedded in emails. Printouts of her accost me from walls and tables. I get bombarded with Amisa and my thoughts return to Szu. But the memories are time-fogged, static, and badly formed. I keep getting snapshots of Szu's stick arms and her long, dolorous face. I wish I could swipe them both away, clear them permanently from my brain's bin.

Gordon dispatches our team to the Somerset offices for 'Initiative and Leadership Skills-Building Training'. I usually hate these sessions but this time I'm relieved to have a *Ponti*-free day. The instructor is a chubby, oily man named Clarents Goh Bok Tin with a cowlick of greasy hair and a vague lisp. I am paired with Jeanette. We sit on white plastic chairs that resemble the play sets in kindergarten. Every time I shift in my seat my thighs squeak against the plastic. Jeanette is chipper today: newly in love, the rumour goes. Some people are so good at moving from love to love. They make a charmed, easy habit of it. Jeanette's like that. It helps that she is so good-looking. And when she decides the guy isn't working for her, she dusts the relationship off like lint on her shirt, and tries on the next new thing.

When Clarents comes round to our table he is all eyes for Jeanette and I might as well not exist. He instructs us to think of a vegetable, any vegetable, except for a carrot. That old mind trick. Of course all I can think of is a damn carrot.

The bright orange carrot in my mind morphs into Szu's face. She makes me wince. She clouds my vision on the bus home, on the toilet, the next morning waiting in line for the cashier, the evening after, when I'm in dark tunnels willing the taxi uncle to hurry me home. The next day, at lunch hour, Szu's scared and sullen face floats around my brain and I force a song into my head and keep walking forward. I've preserved her as a teenager. Szu floats in the murky brine of my memory, with pimples scattered across her forehead and that furtive, worried look in her eyes that used to both reassure and annoy me. Because it is comforting to know that there is someone similar to you in the world, it helps a person to feel less faulty and alone.

But past a certain point, when there are too many commonalities, this comfort shifts into unease. *Copycat. Imitator*, I used to think. I try and walk her off. I tell myself I will take as long as I need, I will lie that I was stuck in line at the bank. I keep walking. Beyond the lunchtime ambit of my colleagues, past coffee shops and electronics megastores. I head towards a row of perfumed shops that smell like nouveau riche housewives, *tai-tais*. Luxury comforts me. It reminds me of what I took for granted when I lived off my parents. Tai-tais smell like laundered blouses, pomade and three sprays of Chanel No. 5 on pampered but underloved skin. The clichés exist because they are true. In a display window I see a brown Marni bag haloed in sunshine. Something in me tickles. My worm finds this beautiful. Cowhide and handsome handles. It costs S$3,600.00 including GST. It would take me two and a half months of an instant-noodle-only diet to afford this.

Back at my desk I spend twenty minutes daydreaming about how much that beautiful leather bag would improve my existence. If I slung it on my arm I would become a better person. Life would steady itself. Although by the time I paid for that bag all my hair would have fallen out from the preservatives in the noodles. And my nails would have grown chipped and yellowed. And maybe my Cestoda worm would be poisoned to death from monosodium glutamate, rather than my medicine. I would have nothing to keep in my new bag except credit card bills and a non-refundable feeling of disappointment.

Gordon appears at my shoulder. This afternoon I'm meant to be composing a mailer for Jolene. He peers at my screen.

'Very interesting,' Gordon says, which is Gordon-speak for 'What the hell are you doing?' I glance back at his pubic-looking stubble and his striped blue shirt, deliberately unbuttoned in a deep V at the collar.

In the compose field, all I have written is: *The beauty of capitalism = to covet. Too obvious? Marni bag = S$3,600. Rent = 2,600 Misc. = 900.*

'I'm trying out a new angle . . . for Jolene's comms campaign. Moving forward,' I say, feeling stupid even as

I keep speaking. 'It's a game changer. Going from good to great.'

'Can't wait to see the results, then.'

'I'll action that!' I reply, with saccharine gusto.

'Right,' Gordon replies, which really means 'wrong'. I wilt inside in a way that I haven't since secondary school. As he walks away the cloud of his disapproval lingers over me.

*

The week after I first visited her home, I invited Szu over to my place after school. We waited by the concourse for Mummy. Szu fidgeted beside me, a twitchy beanpole. Our silhouettes in the visitor's office window reflected our whole-head difference in height. We made quite the duo: I the small one with the frizzy bob, Szu the tall one with the lifeless ponytail. Out of the corner of my eye, I noticed the Badminton Girls shooting derisive glances our way. I pretended not to care.

Mummy's Porsche pulled up. Everyone noticed. Szu got into the back seat and I took the passenger seat up front, slamming the door for emphasis.

'You're late, Mom,' I said.

'Sorry, Sisi. Traffic. Hello, Szu! Nice to meet you. I'm Auntie Magda.'

'Hello, Auntie.'

'How was school, girls?'

'Going from good to *just great*,' I replied.

'You and your funny sayings!' Mummy chuckled and shook her head.

I got out my phone and started to play Snake. I heard Szu still struggling behind me with the seat belt: the polyester shift and stir, four fails and a click.

When we got home, my maid Josephine brought out a tray full of orange slices and peanut cookies.

'Take it upstairs, thanks,' I said. I followed the torpid turn of Szu's head as she took in our reception area: the peach marble floors, double cupboards full of Swedish glass ornaments, and the Persian carpet Mummy sent for immersion cleaning every year.

'Sisi tells me your mother is a movie star,' Mummy said.

'Um, yeah,' Szu replied. She gulped and looked up from under her eyelashes. 'She acted in the *Ponti* trilogy, 1978–1980. Local horror movies.'

'Ah! I can't say I've heard of them,' Mummy replied. 'Does she still act?'

'Not any more. She's retired.' Szu had on that gummy, bashful voice she reserved for teachers.

'Well, I'll look for *Ponti* in the movie rental store next time.'

'Please, Mom,' I said. 'You never go to the rental store. Nobody uses rental stores any more. It's all pirated VCDs nowadays. From Johor.'

'You young people, I cannot catch up. Auntie is a dinosaur! And what about your pa, Szu? What does he do?'

'Antique restoration.'

'Sorry, dear? I didn't catch that.'

'Antique restoration.'

'Oh! How nice. Our family friend Uncle Meng also—'

'We're going to my room,' I said. 'Come on, Szu.'

77

Upstairs Szu squinted at the Backstreet Boys poster tacked to my farthermost wall. SHOW ME THE MEANING OF BEING LONELY, it read. The Backstreet Boys stood arms crossed or akimbo, all curtain fringes and bleached tips, five set jaws over five pairs of priceless sneakers. Szu crossed her arms and stared down at her own canvas shoes. There was a dejected cast to her hunch.

'Sorry Mummy asked about your dad,' I said. 'She didn't know.'

'It's okay. It's not like he's dead. At least, not that I know of. Anyway, I don't really want to talk a—'

'I can't believe he *won the lottery*! Your family is so random! My dad always said if someone wins the Toto they're not supposed to tell anybody or they'll get murdered for their money.'

'Murdering someone is a mega stupid way to get money.'

'Oh yeah?'

'I don't really care about money.'

'Yeah, right!' I laughed. '*Everyone* cares about money. Just look at our school. If you claim you don't you're either lying or deluded.'

'Can I use your toilet?'

I pointed her towards my en suite. She shut the door and had to pull it twice to lock it. She stayed in there for a long time.

'Why do you use men's shaving cream?' Szu asked when she came out.

'My brother Leslie likes to use my bathroom. He probably just took a shit and shower in there, before he went out. He has his own toilet but he messes mine up because he thinks it's funny.'

'Oh,' said Szu. She sat down, gingerly, on the edge of my queen-sized bed and looked around again. I rifled through my CD collection.

'What do you want to listen to?'

'Anything. I'm neutral.'

My upper lip curled up as I selected a Fleetwood Mac album. 'Neutral' was my term, one of my catchphrases. As the music started to play I shifted up on the cloud-printed covers and flopped down to one side on the bed. When I peered up at Szu she was sitting ramrod straight, hands on her lap, eyes lightly closed.

'Your house gives me a happy vibe,' she said.

After she left I took a shower. When I stepped out and rubbed the foggy mirror to judge my body, I noticed that all the bottles and Kodomo toothpaste on my counter had been lined up straight, turned label-outwards. I pictured Szu taking her time, studying their ingredients.

*

I'm renting a flat in Tiong Bahru. It's been super hip for about a decade, and the cost reflects that. Even the prata is more expensive around here. Sibeh Hipster pricing, I call it. My flatmate is a forty-year-old named Julius (or Yong Ling Kiat on our rental agreement). I met him through an ex-colleague. My only stipulation for a roommate was: not a freak. So far, Julius and I get along just fine. Julius works in advertising and identifies as asexual. He told me this early on, to get any misconceptions out of the way that he might ever have any designs on me. Initially affronted, I've come to appreciate his directness. He is really tall for a Singaporean guy, over six feet, and wears his hair in a greasy ponytail.

'When are you going to cut your hair?' I ask him as I put down my bag. 'It's getting scraggly.'

'Don't boss me around,' he replies. He's making a pot of tea. His mother bought him this transparent teapot from Japan. I watch the grey-green bud unfurl and bloom in the centre of the pot.

'Something in the mail for you,' Julius says.

'What is it?'

'It's on the side table.'

I pick up a thick padded envelope with my name and address scrawled on it in black marker. The ink is running out and so the final line of my address is scratched with frenzied strokes of the marker pen, indents in the paper.

It's mostly bubble padding that has bulked up the envelope. Inside are red sheaves of paper, and when I take them out I see they are paper stencils, the sort you find all over the place during Chinese New Year, of the different zodiac animals. I count eleven of them, my heart quickening in my throat. Only the rabbit is missing. I grope around the envelope for anything else, inspect it carefully for a return address, find nothing.

'Viral marketing,' Julius tells me. 'It's really well done. Looks authentic, like some poor intern actually used a faulty marker pen to take down all those addresses. Maybe the logo is in invisible ink. Chinese manufacturers. Hm, I've got a hunch which agency this is. Give it.'

'No,' I reply. I put the stencils back into the envelope. Thin crêpe paper in my hands, giving off the faintest whiff of dust. I feel the urge to hide them. I know it's not someone trying to sell me something. It's someone trying to *tell* me something.

I remember being eight years old, and an old woman who smelt like dustballs pressing stencils like that into my palm. I picture her sad, inky eyes and shiver.

Later that night, I feel a presence in my room. It must be 2 or 3 a.m. – witching hour to someone somewhere. *Whoever believes it, feels it.* Wasn't that what Szu's crazy aunt used to say? Aunt Yunxi, a proponent of her own personal brand of voodoo.

When I sense somebody in my room, the first and most obvious person that comes to bleary mind is my ex-husband, Jarrold. I might as well say his name now, calm and flat, two words that otherwise mean nothing. Jarrold Koh.

I remember the weight of Jarrold's fading, bony-chested body in bed – how he would dream like a dog, legs tussling and scrambling, twisting the sheets; for a rare, shimmering moment I feel fond of him. This man I grew not to hate but to feel disdain for, total utter disinterest. Which is even more damning than hatred. Towards the end, when we weren't arguing but filling the room with a noxious fog of conflict, he would be the first to start talking. To start trying to explain things to me or accuse me of not listening, and this would literally put me to sleep. My eyelids closing in spite of themselves, I would pinch my arms with the jagged nibs of my nails to keep myself awake. And he noticed, of course he did. Even thinking about it now my eyelids start to droop.

And so I remind myself: I only miss him because I'm lonely. And it's less lonely to do that than to have nobody to miss. Because we no longer have to squeeze into the same bed, and maintain the young-couple charade of sharing our lives. As if life is a jumbo packet of chips. As if you can make odd shapes fit. As if everyone is built for bliss. Maybe Jarrold has a shot. I reckon he's moved on and fallen for someone docile. I can imagine him murmuring endearments to a moon-faced girl with glossier hair and a kinder heart than me. Every sticky step of love, emoji trails and coy conversations, I can picture it. Date night: he'll bring her over some lontong and soya bean milk from the hawker centre near her place and she will beam at him, accept thankfully. And later on they will dim the lights and fuck full of earnestness to Adele or something.

All these details I'll never know, all of it is happening. While I lie here on my own, getting haunted. And this wakes me up a little bit, brings me back to my body. I return to the limp, shea-buttered heft of my limbs on the mattress and all this space around me, blanket all to myself. And then I realize that the someone else I sensed isn't Jarrold but a woman standing at the foot of the bed. Her shadow stretches over my pillow.

Long ago I stopped believing that you can will things, good or bad, to happen to you. But now it seems so obvious, half awake, that Szu should appear to me tonight, because I've been expending so much energy thinking about her. No choice of my own, this sense of someone near me.

Szu is wearing our secondary school uniform. Her scuffed white shoes are the only things catching the slice of moonlight coming in through the slats of my bedroom window blind. Arms crossed. She is lankier and just as angular as I remember. When I put together her shape, facial features a little blurry, I don't even cry out. Why would she scare me? She was never capable of intimidation.

'Circe, what's up?' she says, and she doesn't sound hostile or sad, either. Her voice is so matter-of-fact and familiar, it makes me choke. The tone is a little off-kilter. She sounds like one of those American voiceover dubs on a Japanese animation, slightly out of sync.

My tongue unglues itself from the bottom of my mouth.

'What the hell?' I blurt out. And in a way I am being honest. What is up with me, lately? Answer: a constant state of what-the-hell-is-happening. I don't know if my mouth is moving or if I am saying the words in my head.

I'm seized by the impulse to reach out and grab Szu by her scrawny wrists. I want to hold her shoulders, with the cavalier liberty of the old days, and give her a shake. Ask her what went wrong. The general and the specific.

The Internet can tell me in a millisecond where my old friend really is, but that would give away a game I don't want to be a part of. I don't want to know because to know where she is and what she is doing is to invite the past back as a symptom of the awry present. Our story is done. *I don't care and I don't want to hear it*. It's ancient history.

Szu fades and flickers at the foot of my bed, and uncrosses her arms. Soon my jangling alarm tone will be right in my ears and the birds cawing their outdoor refrains, and the weekday, always the weekday, all over again.

'What a way to greet me,' Szu says, and this time she sounds just like me. She licks her lips. 'Especially after what you did.'

She lets the words settle over my bedroom, like leaves shaken off a tree. My stomach flips. I can't move, can't even flinch. She opens her mouth to speak again.

'Go away,' I say, but all that comes out is a groan and the edges of my room begin to blur.

As I slip into deep sleep I think: I don't want to hear about Szu, or see her ever again. If I run into her I'm sprinting in the other direction. Even if my feet won't comply, I'll force them. I don't want to know if she looks as prematurely worn out as I do at thirty-three, or whether she's glowing; whether she's put on weight, become healthy; whether she's rearranged her face or cut all her hair off, highlighted it; whether she has a Caesarean scar on her body or broken bones, whether she is living in this country or on another continent. Or the darkest thing I fear, whether she's been dead for God knows how long and I was too distracted by my own life to have even the slightest inkling.

*

I wake with a jolt. My left hand flails over the pillow and I gasp for air, just as my alarm begins its polyphonic pleas.

I feel for my phone and swipe it quiet. I had an action-packed dream, before it was interrupted. My client Jolene was running after me; Jolene turned murderous, suddenly terrifying with her pop star perm and the acetate sheen of her skin. I bolted away from her, down a FairPrice aisle with flickering strip lights and shelves full of cereal boxes. I wore shoes with too-thin soles that made me feel as if any moment I might lose my footing.

I get ready to go to work, gulping down an acrid bitterness in my mouth. Two stops away from the office, I remember Szu standing by the foot of my bed, goading me.

When Amisa went into hospital Szu became obsessed with death. *How long do you think it would take for someone to die if they didn't eat, or didn't drink?* she asked me. She made me look these things up on the Internet because she didn't have a computer.

I didn't blame her. It is hard not to fixate on death if it is staring your own mother in the face. Mondays and Wednesdays after school I followed Szu to the hospital, Mount E., a massive complex of aquamarine and wretched beige. We dragged our feet past the circular driveway and into the air-conditioned lobby, took the lift to floor 3 and two lefts on the bleached linoleum that made our canvas shoes squeak.

At sixteen I had never experienced any real death in my family, nothing close enough to touch. But from TV and movies I knew enough to conclude that all hospitals truly look the same. And this uniformity was bare and brutal more than reassuring.

Aunt Yunxi spared no expense. Amisa had her own room, with one glass wall for observation. I tried not to look into the other units on the way there, but I couldn't resist. Everything in the ward was sprayed clean, sterilized to a plasticky shine. Although there were no signposts Szu and I knew we were in the Land of No Hope. We had learned about this place from made-for-television movies but it was surreal to actually be unmoored within it. We had to observe decorum. Stand with our hands folded, our feet close together, heads bowed. The scent in the air was a mixture of disinfectant and disease. The disinfectant couldn't cure the disease; it could only try to cancel out the infectiousness of a surface. A sign on the wall had a diagram that indicated: if you don't wash your hands, and you touch your mouth, unthinking, sometimes this can be enough to make you sick. Left untended, even a small sickness can mutate into something serious. As if we needed any further reminders of this. The air in the ward was heavy, solemn. The curtains by the beds were dark mauve and the other patients looked older than Amisa.

In the Land of No Hope certain words were forbidden. 'Dying', 'terminal', 'unfair'; those are a few examples I can think of. Nothing overt, no expressions of outrage, no alarm. Slack-jawed old men, eyes shut tightly, breathing through a ventilator as their middle-aged children stood by the side of the bed, past crying. Tiny grandmothers with thinning crowns of hair, skin pulled tight and jaundiced, or swollen and discoloured blue-grey from the medication, the expensive drugs entering these failing bodies intravenously. And at the end of the corridor, Amisa Tan.

Her condition had deteriorated over the past two months until it became clear she needed to be hospitalized. Before, while her sickness remained unsaid, it was easy to mistake its increasingly pronounced displays for a doomed, noble fragility. I'd come into the kitchen at 3 p.m. to the sight of her delicate profile tilted towards the kitchen window, peaceful for a moment. When she looked back at Szu and me she had this expression of futile anger, as if we were bailiffs come to seize her furniture. Amisa turned her nose up at me with undisguised contempt, but this only made me want to win her favour even more. Back then I was too unformed to feel insulted. But the way she looked at her own daughter was far worse – she would flick her eyes from Szu's messy black hair down to her feet, and grit her teeth, as if to say, *Why her, why me, why all this?*

Amisa was like this almost every time I encountered her. I derived the guilty pleasure of Schadenfreude, watching the mother be so brazenly brutal to her own child. Szu kept her head bowed, hunched her shoulders until she was almost my height, and never challenged her mother's hostility. Even I knew things weren't so simple as that, and that there would be no empowering denouement to the daily insult of her bullying. Amisa affected Szu more than any of the taunting girls at school.

By the time Amisa entered the Land of No Hope, I had developed an intensity of feeling towards her that hovered between a crush and intimidation. She was incorrigible and out of this world: this beautiful woman who broke her daughter's heart every day as much as she continued to fascinate us both. Isn't this what magazines mean by star quality: that ineffable thing, charisma? No matter what we say we humans are fundamentally shallow, it's encoded in our eyes and monkey brains. I have never met anyone like Amisa Tan. She had a brand of bruised yet appealing insouciance that I wanted to grow into one day myself.

It was the wrong time to think that, to gawp at the object of my grotesque private adoration. All colour drained from her face, cheekbones so badly sunken. She was dying; it was plain to see, although nobody would say it. I can't forget how she looked, towards the end. Dark hair with streaks of grey fanned out on the pillow, chest rising and falling like a small bird's. Increasingly often, when we visited, she was asleep. Yunxi never came with us; she told Szu she had to stay in the house, attending to the roster of clients. After all, they had to keep up the business.

One afternoon when we visited Amisa was sitting up in bed. Her blue hospital gown was bunched up all around her and she looked like a china doll nested in crêpe paper. Her face was swollen and waxy. She blinked as if she had something in her eye.

'Hi. How are you feeling today?' asked Szu.

'Hello, Mrs Ng,' I said.

'Go away,' she replied. I flinched. And then she turned to her daughter.

'I bet you're happy to see me like this,' Amisa said. Her voice was so hoarse and I could tell it was an effort to exert herself, to project it with such vehemence. 'You've cost me.'

'What?' Szu asked feebly, even though Amisa had spoken loudly enough that we both heard. 'Why would you say that?'

I started backing out of the door, my hands cold, hurt and shame tracing my ribs.

'Because it's true,' Amisa said.

*

In 2003, the big haze lingered. Severe Acute Respiratory Syndrome had broken out in Guangdong the year before and coughed and hacked its way around the region. People had died from it. Everyone was afraid of getting infected. Some wore stupid-looking hospital masks but Szu and I would rather have been caught dead than join them. We drifted around Heeren like a pair of angelfish, giving boys the discreet side-eye. Our long black hair trailed like fine, wispy tails. Our bubble voices echoed in the atria of shopping centres – Takashimaya, Far East, the Heeren. *How cute is that. How does this look? Too expensive. Cheaply made. Perfect for a hot date. What hot date? Ha ha.* This chit-chat of commerce. We were the target demographic, spoilt teenage schoolgirls with a proclivity for bored buying. We were more powerful than we realized.

Five months into our friendship, Szu and I developed a manic obsession with Japanese skincare. Rather, I led the way and she followed. Some days, after our hospital visit, we made a trip to Wisma. We lingered in the tiny Sasa store that lay at the foot of a giant escalator, scrutinizing poorly translated labels until the shop assistant with the rebonded hair and false, spidery eyelashes told us to leave if we weren't getting anything. Rolling our eyes but secretly glad of the excuse, we bought things. Even whilst taking out our wallets we knew these products wouldn't work on us;

they were geared toward Japanese girls from a cooler climate, fed on a diet of miso and sashimi, with fair poreless skin. In Singapore, three seconds is all it takes for a slick to form over the forehead. Szu and I dabbed at our T-zones frantically with oil blotter papers, and drew our hands away ashamed and disgusted by the film of oil on the previously matte blue surface. The subtle scent of linen oil and fear. Would we always be like this, buying and worrying?

During teenhood all you know is all you know, which shouldn't be discounted. You have this one narrow window on the world, the stakes smaller but no less deeply felt. Teenage heaven was marble shop floors and neon signs along the sides, behind glass railings. Perfumed, safe world. Things to buy with leftover pocket money. A blouse, a hair clip, a tube of overpriced lip gloss that I knew, even while unwrapping it, wouldn't make me any more attractive. Just a strange glittery oil slick gluing my mouth.

'My mother has some amazing collectibles from the film sets, but she keeps them locked away, or I would show you,' Szu liked to say and I would nod; I liked to hear it.

It didn't matter to me that Amisa was nowhere as famous as Szu made her out to be. Or that Szu was vague about which well-known admirers had bequeathed crushed-pearl compact mirrors and exorbitant jars of cream to her mother. At the time it didn't even occur to me: what sort of admirer would give a woman night cream as a present? I didn't want to actually watch the trilogy in case it was terrible, and shattered the illusion. The truth is Szu and I told half-fictions to each other. We were complicit in our mutual exaggerations. Besides, I was fascinated by Amisa's brief but alluring movie star career, a frame in which to hang our fantasies of fame, the shared suspension of disbelief. Szu's voice took on a reverential tone when she spoke about the three movies.

We lounged in her room looking at magazines and together we coveted expensive radiance creams and glimmering eye shadow palettes themed after black-tie balls we would never attend. When Szu and I weren't spending money we dreamt about the things we would be buying to make us feel prettier, stronger, inoculated against the world.

*

When I leave the office it's pelting, and I think of acid rain, and whether it is corrosive. Skin cells getting damaged. My worm within me recoiling. I'm five minutes away from the MRT when the sky gives way to a proper downpour, so punishing it's personal. Thunderstorms scare the shit out of me. Slapped by rain, I quicken my steps. Without an umbrella, I have no choice but to scuttle like a chicken towards the station escalator. My feet are too close to the edge of the silver stair and I feel the sickly wet on the back of my calves. How many times a week do I imagine what it would be like to fall all the way down? Would I die or just hit my head in a damaging way? I board the train and the doors beep shut. Under the unflattering green glow of the carriage everyone is looking at their smartphones.

I must have the only stupid phone in the city because it's been acting up lately, lying that I have missed calls, and sounding out notifications for nothing. I check the vibration in my pocket; another false alarm, no one seeking me. I rub my eyes and steady myself, gripping the handle on the train. A tiny somersault in my ribs. Cestoda, fluttering. I'm spacing out when I spot the top of her head. The shock feels like a mini heart attack.

Szu is standing on the other side of the glass doors. Rush hour blur of aunties and ah bengs around her. She has her hair in a low bun but she still has the same sleepy teenaged profile. For a moment I think I'm mistaken. But she turns towards me sharply just as the train is pulling away. We lock eyes for a moment. Dark-brown iris to dark-brown iris. That unmistakable, maddening look. And then she's gone.

8

SZU

2003

After we have pumped Slurpee-blue sanitizer onto our hands and tiptoed down the corridor, Circe presses the lift button as if our lives depend on it, this hasty escape. I wonder for a second if she thinks that all this dying around us is infectious. But when the doors slide open I feel it too, the urgency and relief, as if a weight has been lifted. I am just as glad as she is to descend into the lobby, where an auntie with a red-curled perm is pushing a wheelchair. Any forward motion, however slow and however slight, seems hopeful compared to the bedside tableaux that we are now so used to.

Seated in the wheelchair is a man with liver spots on his face and milky eyes. He looks a little bit like an actor who used to play the angry patriarch in the 9 p.m. drama serials from the late nineties, a scheming gambler wreaking intrigue in some family business. His stare follows Circe and me out of the corridor and into the reception area.

As we step out into the sunshine, Circe says, 'The Land of No Hope was okay today. The machines were beeping peacefully. The air smelt like banana-flavoured cough medicine.'

I don't encourage her, just move my face into something like a smile. Circe insists on calling Ward 12A the Land of No Hope. We rewatched *The Land Before Time* in Circe's living room the other day, on a scratched VCD. The frames froze and jolted sporadically and we pitied the baby dinosaurs with their faded pastel skin and dulcet voices, trying to make it safely across the treacherous plains to find their parents. That's where Circe got the idea for the name. I don't want to let it catch on, for these visits to become another ingredient to her anecdotes, even though that's what I've started calling it too in my head.

That makes my mother the Queen of the Land of No Hope. Look at her propped up on her throne, surrounded by scratchy pillows, wearing a paper gown with an IV drip for a sceptre. She's reigned for three weeks. If she is Queen, isn't it unlikely she will ever leave? I don't want to think about it. All I can do is watch the monitor with its impersonal *deet-deet-deet* and the lines of her breathing. And when I leave the ward I can't get her stretched, shiny face out of my head. *Please just get better and look normal again. Just get better and let me hate you in peace.*

Circe and I walk out of the automatic doors and the sun makes me squint. I think of how cold the ward is, and the mother I left there dozing in bed; that's it, a perpetual half-doze, never a deep sleep, because of the beeping and her pain.

It's almost 4 p.m. and sun reflects off the white concrete driveway straight back into my eyes. Maybe I'll go blind. Part of me envies the depressed Icelandic postmen I read about in a magazine article in the waiting room, doing their morning rounds during the winter solstice. Having only four hours of daylight could drive you sad, cycling on creaking bicycles in the dark and the bitter cold. Imagine dreading life because you have a Vitamin D deficiency, having the clarity of knowing that the only thing you are lacking is sunlight.

'Come on,' Circe says, beckoning me towards the bus stop. 'You can't keep standing there.'

Lately I have recognized that this is what I do: I freeze stock-still because it takes so much energy to steer my thoughts into something bearable, and I forget the basics of locomotion.

*

This weekend it is Valentine's Day and our classmates are in a flutter of anticipation. The Available girls, ourselves excluded, fret and wonder if the mawkish boys they know will ask them out, last-minute, in an artfully flippant text or meandering stream of late-night instant messages. The Taken daydream about their boyfriends with renewed fervour. Their ponytailed heads tilt like flowers dense with nectar. Faces pressed to palms during the mid-afternoon period, Geography or English Lit, nothing learnt, eyes blinking so slowly as if to close, with a sticky, sugar-glazed sheen to the lids. This peripheral increase in oily complexions is something Circe has also noticed, florid smatterings of acne across the flushed cheeks of the Taken.

Taken girls have the following other unmistakable characteristics: they wander about dazed, inattentive, in the always-throes of their rapture; they insert their boyfriends' names, or the prefix 'my boyfriend', anywhere in conversation. Before assembly and after school they clump together and compare relationships. They let out a smug, secret sort of giggle, a tribal sound of a particular frequency that only their own kind can decode and appreciate. It irritates the ears of everyone else. Even the teachers and cleaning ladies whip their heads around in barely concealed annoyance.

Sarah Choo is the worst. From what I've heard she's been with her boyfriend for all of a month. They met at church. She can't stop talking about him. She puts her hand over her mouth and hunches her shoulders up, like a bad actress playing the part of Giggling Schoolgirl. Circe rolls her eyes at me, and I shrug. Overheard phrases: 'How far?', 'Everything but', 'Not yet', 'We agreed on soon. Very soon' (giggle).

At recess time the line for the drinks stall is slow and snaking. I rattle my small change in my pocket. The coins feel sweaty and meagre in my palm. The girl in front of me keeps bringing her bracelet up to her face and biting the star-shaped charms on its chain.

'You can just smell the hormones. It's disgusting,' Circe mutters behind me.

'Everyone's so horny it makes me sick,' I reply, lowering my voice at 'horny'.

The girl in front of us glances back with a slight frown.

'On Valentine's *evening* that's when everyone humps like dogs,' Circe continues, in a ribald whisper. 'That's when Sarah Choo will cook up excuses to go over to her boyfriend's house. He will make sure his parents are out for dinner, so they can be as loud as they like. I bet she has some special panties she's saving—'

'Ugh, stop it.'

'Frilly, fuchsia. Like a cliché.'

'You're disgusting,'

'Leopard-print pink,' Circe says, but she's already losing interest in this routine, so clearly inspired by the bawdy, goading frat boys in the teen movies we've been watching. If high school in America is exactly like *American Pie*, then everyone is obsessed by sex, thinking about it maniacally, breathing it, dreaming it, bragging and plotting and speculating endlessly. The boys all have perfect teeth and chiselled jaw-lines. They fist-pump each other and whoop almost like they mean it. The girls flaunt tanned abs and honey-coloured highlights, and proffer an endless supply of double entendres and witty comebacks. Everyone seems to have a more expert grasp of the performatives of teenhood than we. It's depressing.

We turn to look at Sarah Choo, who is settling down with a tray at a crowded table nearby. We take in her thick ankles offset by that Buffy-the-Vampire-Slayer button nose. We try to picture the fabled boyfriend. Is he a big fan of Buffy? Does she drive him crazy? Neither of us says a word but I can tell we are thinking the same thing: *What has she got that I haven't (besides that nose)?* Simultaneously: *What is wrong with me?* Both of us know that the answers to these questions, if they exist, aren't quantifiable.

Circe and I have never had boyfriends, have never had to construct elaborate ploys or rickety alibis to be alone with somebody in some shuttered place where we shouldn't be. Circe's parents pay only minimal attention to her and I would be touched if my one remaining parent made such a socialized assumption of me.

Circe told me she exchanged a couple of clumsy kisses with two underwhelming boys, one a year younger and the other the same age as us. She no longer talks to either; the kisses and fumbles took place within the pockets of two dreamlike afternoons. By 6 p.m. and the exeunt hiss of the 177 bus, all associations had ended.

'One of them smoked,' she said. 'He tasted like lung disease.' I winced at her choice of words.

She met the boys in the dingy pool hall by Peninsula Plaza and on floor 2 of MultiLeisure Arcade respectively. I am 70 per cent sure these boys exist. Like amateur criminologists, we have revisited the scenes of passion, scoping out the gel-haired ah bengs in a manner that we hope appears insouciant and charming, two intrepid French coquettes imported straight out of a Godard movie, instead of a pair of Singaporean convent schoolgirls with sweat patches on the back of our uniforms and rings around our ankles from scratchy socks. The arcade smells of vomited popcorn butter and toilet bleach. Seduction tactic: we balance our spines against stained, sticky walls, breathing slowly, taking in every single thing. Isn't this the mating call of seaweed, of anemones? No response, not even one glance at our chests or faces. No signs of feeling life; just the whirring of ventilators, the rattle spin of a cue. I try the charm machine twice, can't win. I am a girl-ghost, an imitation of what a girl should be.

'There was something in the air, last summer, for me,

and now I'm sixteen, and over the hill. Past it,' Circe says, joking in that half-gauche, half-worldly way of hers that, when I attempt it, only comes off as overly sombre.

She calls it her Summer of Love. At the time I thought, I don't know how much she can claim to know about love. But I can't say I know any better. I am vague about my experiences. I told Circe I kissed a boy over the Christmas holidays, a visiting Indonesian, a friend of a friend. She's never pressed me further (what other friend, for example), maybe out of courtesy. All the same, I told her he was very rich and very quiet. Oil, jewels. I said he complained that the great Sumatran haze that is still clearing from our shores clogged up his lungs and made him spit blood in his sleep. I knew that was a bit of a stretch, but Circe has never caught me out. If pressed I am prepared to mention some grave diagnosis, the smoke and copper tang of his tongue probing my teeth. And it's the truth, if I think very hard I can sense that phantom kiss, the wet and reach of it.

Some days he is eighteen. On other days, an unimaginable twenty-three. He is taller than me, smooth nape of a neck to tuck my worrying head in. I modelled his face after Benson Chen, one of the *Star Search* semifinalists perpetually on television, hawking skincare. Benson Chen is pale as a snow skin mooncake, and equally translucent. He has long dark hair spiked up like cake icing around his gamin features. Circe knows I've got a crush on him. What I never mention is how much he reminds me of her brother.

Leslie Low is two years older than us, which means that after he sits his A-level exams he will get conscripted for

National Service. It is hard to imagine Leslie in army fatigues with a shorn head, wielding an assault rifle. He never seems to leave his room within the Lows' spacious, parquet-floored villa. He is like a stalemate chess piece. He mumbles in his own lonely-boy language. I have run into him by the winding staircase four times.

Circe guards Leslie like a dagger. He calls her Sisi sometimes. Throwaway, but some ancient in-joke. She always refers to him by his proper name, Leslie. When she mentions him she bristles a little, with unmistakable pride.

*

The two pathologically prettiest girls of our level float by the canteen. Trissy and Meixi are their names. Everyone else screeches across that newly retiled stretch of floor, but their white canvas shoes make no sound at all. The mid-morning light casts their long, smooth braids in a glow, graces their figure-skater shoulders. I cannot imagine them growing old, or any better-looking. There is no limit to this soft sort of envy; it makes a wistful, gawping owl of me. I crane my neck to watch them leave.

Trissy and Meixi have nineteen-year-old boyfriends: handsome twins. Neither of the girls are virgins. In the Whampoa Convent of the Eternally Blessed, news like this doesn't just rustle down the grapevine. What we have in place is a virile beanstalk, all errant stems and curling leaves. It's impossible to ignore the whispered-down stories.

Trissy resembles a sexy Korean actress. She has a face that looks both knowing and like she doesn't care about anyone or anything. Sometimes I think that she can tap into whatever power my Aunt Yunxi has access to, only Trissy is instead some kind of social, cool-girl psychic. Fierce, kinetic secrets spark and spread from her like wildfire.

Lee Meixi has legs that go on and on, and a heart-shaped face made to be admired. I have never seen her sweat. I have never seen her look anything besides serene. What goes on in there? *Something*, her eyes say. *But you're not good enough to get it.* Beauty is an armour. For as long as I've known her, my mother acted invincible because of it.

My mother and I watched a movie called *The Bride with White Hair* on TV once, when I was about eight or nine. In the film, a gentle, gorgeous woman gets falsely accused of killing people and her lover turns against her. Lin Ching Hsia, who has impeccably outraged eyebrows and a beautiful cleft chin, plays the woman. When she gets wronged and rejected she becomes so mad that her hair turns Marilyn-platinum and very long. She looks amazing in her new incarnation; 'murderous' is a mode most becoming to her. She goes on a rampage. The clang of swords, the swish and grunts of choreographed fighting. I remember little else about what happens in the movie, only my mother clutching my arm until her nails dug in, leaving bloodied crescents on my skin. She was quivering. Her jaw was set, mouth pursed. Her eyes watered slightly, as if allergic to what she was seeing. I remember being scared to know exactly what was going through her mind, but being able to guess, even at that age, how she must have felt to see another much more famous, beautiful monster wreaking havoc across the screen.

*

I leave for home at that point of the day when I don't have any choice left. Remedial classes are over. Circe is busy with choir practice. Two terms in, she's gotten more involved with her choral section. She drops the names of the girls she sings with casually: Rong En and Angela. I know of them but I don't know them. Late afternoon, the workday ending, cars pull out of the curved road. The concourse is almost cleared and the security guard at the gate gives me a disgruntled nod as I finally leave.

Walking home from the bus stop I feel like I have stones in my chest. I pull open the rusty gate and it screeches like a small dinosaur. I drag my feet down the long driveway. Just as I'm walking the sky darkens from milky brown into an inky blue-grey, with the flick of a switch. This city is so full of neon lights, beaming off the blocks of HDB flats, the high-rise office buildings. You can't see the stars, too much glare. I have never experienced proper night-time, never left the country. The idea of a holiday is foreign to me. Real skies are the stuff of stock images: stars spread out in dizzying constellations. None of that here. Too much artificial light.

I turn the key in the lock, step into the entrance hall. Now that my mother is in hospital the house is even quieter. It's not like she made much noise when she was awake at home, but now it's as if a muffler has been lifted and you can hear everything within the walls. Pipes and plywood exposed, ugly old clanking. The lizards scamper behind the plaster. They seem to come out more now that my mother is away. Now they seem unabashed, unafraid.

I help Aunt Yunxi set up for an evening appointment.

Today she is seeing a woman whose child has a hole in her heart. I dust the altar. Everything must go in precisely the spot my aunt dictates.

'You look so unhappy,' Aunt Yunxi says to me. I put down a plate of betel nuts and turn towards her. She's just been meditating and looks drowsy. She's been old for as long as I can remember but now she is an ancient ruin. Her features are so wan and crumpled. I wonder how many years it will take for my own face to fold this way.

She comes over and presses one cold finger under my right eye, gently. 'You look like you need more sleep. Don't worry, ah girl. Why not have some fish soup? Auntie can set up on her own.'

'I'm okay.'

'It's hard to see your mother like this,' Aunt Yunxi continues. 'For me, too. A long time ago, I told her it was bad luck to put on white clothes and act like a bad thing. And now what.' She stops talking and exhales sharply.

'Now what?' I ask. 'Will she get better? Can you divine it?' I sound like one of her clients.

Aunt Yunxi takes my palm and squeezes it. Her hands feel dry and cold. I search her eyes but she looks at my throat instead.

'We can pray and wait, Szu,' she says in her plain, real voice. 'I can't force things.'

9

AMISA

1976

It was her eighteenth birthday tomorrow and so what about it. When she arrived for work at the Paradise Theatre, she watched her manager Pok Hian strutting around instructing everyone to call him Rocky. He was feeling especially brutish with his new name and made her scrub a diarrhoea-conquered toilet; she didn't even get to catch the tail end of a screening.

When Amisa got home that evening the woman who lived in the room beside her had left her door open. Her name was Yunxi and it was impossible to place exactly how old she was. She came from Fujian province, near the mountains, and had moved to Singapore twenty years ago. They spoke in Mandarin. Yunxi had a thick Fujian Wuyi accent that sounded so much better and more refined than Amisa's; it was the way she intonated. Her hair seemed to change colour, going from pitch-black to peppered with white and grey. On some days, Amisa thought she could pass for twenty-five. On others, she looked twice that age, and so hollow-eyed and exhausted that Amisa didn't even try to speak to her.

Yunxi was a slight, wiry woman who banged shut the

kitchen cupboards and went about her day in a buzz of energy. Although they had never explicitly discussed what it was she did for a living, Amisa had heard the stream of mumbled male voices that filled and left her room all night and into the early hours. Now Amisa was surprised to see Yunxi lying prone on her hard wooden bed, with her grey blouse ridden up to expose a strip of jaundiced, waistband-imprinted flesh, strangely obscene.

'I'm not feeling well. I think I've been poisoned,' Yunxi said. 'Food poisoning,' she added. 'Dirty meat. Old bones.'

'Can I get you anything?'

'Just some tea.'

Amisa boiled some cheap black tea and brought it to Yunxi. She perched on the edge of her bed because there was no other chair in the room. Amisa thought of Yunxi's visitors, the men who snuck in late at night. She couldn't help but feel sorry for Yunxi with her sunken cheeks and skinny arms, blowing the tea to cool it. Who knew what she had been through?

'How are you, Xiaofang?' Yunxi asked her.

'It's my birthday tomorrow,' Amisa replied, eyeing up the small altar in the corner of the room, which had a joss stick and a painted squatting figurine she didn't recognize.

'How old are you?'

'Eighteen.'

'You're just a kid,' Yunxi replied, and drank her tea. 'You have so much ahead of you, you won't even believe it.'

Two hours later, Yunxi had a visitor. Yunxi referred to the woman as her mother to Amisa, but called her Laoshi to her face, in a deferential tone. The old woman had visited only twice before, which led Amisa to think that Yunxi was suffering from something serious; she wasn't the type of person to call for help otherwise. Laoshi wore brown linen and a beleaguered expression, and was as wordless and shrunken as a dried shiitake mushroom. She hunched by the stove boiling a bloom of sickly fungi and thickly coiled black herbs.

'Do you need help?' Amisa asked.

Laoshi turned around. She smiled to reveal a set of small, perfect, greyish teeth, and shook her head. Amisa went back to her room to try and sleep between shifts. But she kept hearing Yunxi's hacking cough at intervals, and even after Laoshi had taken the pot off the boil the pungent medicine filled the narrow corridors with its smell, as heady as paint thinner, though hard to place definitely, disturbingly more animal than vegetable.

Hours later, Amisa woke for work. She shuffled out into the kitchen. She peered into the pot and decided to wash it for Yunxi. She tipped it over the drain. The remaining herbs clogged the drain hole and reminded her of gigantic strands of pubic hair.

'Don't do that – I was saving the herbs,' Yunxi said, in a broken voice. She rubbed her eyes and came over to the sink. She wore a thin nightdress with yellowed stains all over it. As Yunxi peered into the sink at the herbs, Amisa noticed the florid insect bites and tracks of bruises down her arms.

'Sorry,' Amisa said. 'I had no idea. I was trying to help.'

She tilted her chin out, expecting the harshness of a rebuke; that familiar, accosting look her mother gave her that indicated stupid behaviour was all but expected.

Instead Yunxi sniffed and shrugged at her. 'That's okay. Thank you, Xiaofang.'

When she came home after her shift, Amisa found a bottle of plum wine outside her door with a note wishing her happy birthday. She knew Yunxi would wave her away if she thanked her. Alone in her narrow room, Amisa toasted the mirror with practised braggadocio, just like Amisha, the arch-browed bad girl from *Lomari*. Amisha strutted around in her sari unapologetically, refused to follow her father's instructions, and stole every musical number she participated in, finally eloping with the painfully handsome stranger who turned out to be a crook, a scoundrel, a love rat. By the end, they had stabbed each other and died. It was a huge flop but Amisa loved it.

She cocked an eyebrow seductively to no one, before she took a glug from the glass. Even though it tasted disgusting, the wine was a still a gift, so she decided to finish it all at once. She swigged straight from the neck like one of the weathered, nicotine-stained gamblers who scared her on the way to work. It was her first time drinking a whole bottle of alcohol. She was glad it was small. The burn and the cloying sweetness almost made her sick.

She lay back in bed and stared at the ceiling. The grey water stain above her bed seemed to bloom and lengthen. Eighteen years. Childhood was this long, murky pool that she had only just climbed out of. Her body still ached from the effort of escape, and every day, even from the first moment awake, she already felt tired. She would send money home when she had enough to go round. She would return to Kampong Mimpi Sedih to visit one day and bring Didi back to Singapore with her. But so far she had been putting off calling home. She had accomplished nothing yet, and it was easier for her family to speculate in the silences. The distance between where she was and the glossy point where she wanted to be stretched and stretched.

From the left wall came an insistent thudding. One of Yunxi's clients. She had thought Yunxi would be too ill to receive anyone. Amisa never caught the men coming up the narrow stairs and entering the room beside her, never heard anything from Yunxi herself; only the clients, who often sounded like they were sobbing, or trying to reason in unintelligible dialects. Amisa couldn't make out what languages they mumbled in, only that the indistinct, pleading male voices brimmed with sadness and shame. She hadn't been with anyone since she moved to Singapore, and the hot, moreish memory of body to body that had so consumed her over the past few years had loosened its grip. If this was what desire sounded like, she was happy not to reacquaint with it.

Still, when the men left, Amisa tried to catch a glimpse of them, even just their backs. They retreated so quickly – doleful shadows trailing downstairs and out of the door, swallowed whole by the muggy evening air. She sensed their weight and presence, heard them, but never saw them. Sometimes she worried that they were a figment of her own perverse imagination, or she wondered if Yunxi was actually alone in the room beside her, rattling the wooden bed frame against the wall, bouncing on the creaky springs, playing garbled voices from a damaged tape recorder.

*

The next morning she wanted to die. She couldn't imagine how old, frail men like Ah Huat, her long-dead neighbour, had made a pleasure and a pastime out of heavy drinking. Standing at the stall, her chest hurt and her muscles tightened, as if the market heat had crept inside her ribs and wrung her heart dry. Everything was unbearable. She just had to try to keep on breathing. One breath at a time. That's it. The smell of shellfish made her so nauseous she wanted to retch.

'What's wrong with you, ah girl? You're green in the face,' Mr Lim chided. Mrs Lim looked up from the piles of cockles and tutted.

'That won't do. Look, why don't you go home early,' she said.

'I'm fine,' Amisa replied, and put one gloved hand in front of her mouth as she felt bile rising in her throat. Her head pulsed as if there were worms thronging her brain, threatening to push her filthy thoughts out of her ears.

'You look like you've seen a ghost,' Mrs Lim said. 'Go home, lah. Wait got your germs go into the seafood. We will be fine on our own for the rest of the day. Get some rest.'

Amisa took the 985 back home instead of walking. Every time the red-and-white bus went over a speed bump her head felt like it would explode. Amidst the tumult of her hangover she felt the niggling heat of eyes on the back of her neck. She turned around with a scowl.

'Miss, are you okay?' a man asked in Mandarin. He stared from a row behind, across the aisle, head cocked like a concerned Alsatian. It took her a second to recognize that pockmarked face inscribed with rude lingering longing. The young man wore a striped short-sleeved shirt with a crumpled collar, and chinos. He looked less ugly than she remembered. His expression was softer, more lidded. Amisa glowered at him. She wondered about the ponytailed girlfriend; it had been a while since they had come to the theatre.

'Sorry to disturb you, but you don't look well,' the man said. He seemed shy, couldn't hold her stare as he spoke. 'This might be strange, but I remember you from the Paradise Theatre. You work there, right?'

She pressed her temple and considered telling him he was mistaken, but it would be more of a hassle to deal with his protestations. They had crossed paths too many times for any doubt about it.

'Do you need a doctor?' he tried again.

'I feel fine,' she replied. She didn't need help, and even if she did, it wouldn't come from him. 'This is my stop,' she said, glancing out of the window. 'Nice to see you. Bye bye.'

She was about fifteen minutes from home but she could manage the walk, if that would rid her of him. She stood and steadied herself on the metal bar of the seat, but when she let go her legs crumpled with a speed that alarmed her.

Her right kneecap hit the floor and sharp pain sang. The man rose quickly and gently hoisted her up, hooking her arms around his shoulders. She still couldn't speak as the doors hissed open and he helped her off the bus.

'Let me walk you home, you're not well,' he said. It was around 7 a.m. and the sun had just emerged, dominating the blunt grey clouds and jagged skyline. She said nothing and leaned into his arm as they walked down the boulevard of HDB flats and a row of tyre shops, the coffee-and-crockery clatter and chatter of kopi tiams.

'I still got time before work,' he explained. 'It's along the way.'

'Mm-hm.'

'It's nice to see you again.'

'Yep.'

At the overhead bridge, he turned to her and said, 'I'm Wei Loong, by the way. What's your name?'

'Amisha,' she replied. The kohl-lined eyes of the girl in the movie swam behind her own.

'Amisa?'

'Yeah. Fine. Amisa,' she said. It was easier to pronounce. If that dumb bastard Pok Hian could rebrand himself, why couldn't she do the same?

She spent the remainder of the walk in a dreamy, satisfied stupor, turning the syllables over and over in her head. Amisa felt original. Amisa felt shiny. Her hangover lifted itself above the scaffolding and dissolved into the crisp bright air. By the time they reached her door she had agreed to meet Wei Loong at the Kallang Theatre for a movie later on.

10
SZU

2003

Time seems to pass in fits and starts. It breaks into a sprint before stumbling to a halt. The first Wednesday in March is the day of our school excursion. I had to fill in a depressing little consent form and get it signed by my aunt. It seems so ridiculous to me that our level is still sent on school trips. Surely at sixteen we are too old to be packed into a coach and given the morning to wander around an educational site with cartoonish signs and an activity sheet.

Everyone knows Haw Par Villa. Everyone loved it once, but would never admit to it. Most of us visited as children, keen and bug-eyed, back when it was a big deal, in the early nineties. The brothers who owned Tiger Balm designed and built it. They had millions to spare and so they decided to create a dream space. I first saw the photos of the newly reopened grounds in the newspapers. The bright colours, the lacquered statues, a log flume in the shape of a smiling dragon. I begged to go and eventually my father took me. I was only six. It took a long drive to get there, about thirty-five minutes, which I consider lengthy because Singapore is so small that you can walk from one end to the other in half a day.

Haw Par Villa was shrouded in trees with its spires sticking out, like a badly kept secret. The entrance was gleaming and gigantic. I held my father's hand as we walked up to it. The gateway was an elegant pagoda, painted in orange and red and dark grey. I was glad my mother had stayed at home, although I didn't say so. I could imagine her calling the place tacky, bringing up some other park in some other city that she'd maybe been to as a young actress. If she came out that day she would have been wearing a scarf, a hat and sunglasses, and cooling her night-creamed face with a paper fan.

There were a few other families milling peacefully, but the place wasn't too crowded. The paint on the lacquered wood still smelt new.

'Don't breathe in too much, Little Bunny,' my father had said. His old nickname for me, derived from the White Rabbit Creamy Candy that I used to love: cream, blue and red wrapper. 'The fumes give you brain damage.'

The fresh paint on the scalloped walls and engravings gleamed, highlighter-luminous in the afternoon light. At the centre of the gate was a roaring lion. Even the ground seemed to shine. Later on my father bought me a stuffed toy, a small tiger with a pink tongue. I think I left it on the bench of an MRT station or on the back of a bus, at some drowsy point over the years. From time to time I wonder where it is.

Now the coach pulls up in the car park with a hiss and our class files out of it. A cluster of clouds shift to reveal the sun, which renews its scorching and makes the ground blind-white. I drag my shoes along the concrete. My throat feels so dry. I haven't been able to form sentences all day.

I stand to one side as Trissy and Weili, the swim stars, stride before me towards the park entrance. I look at their tanned, shapely legs, immune to mosquito bites. I marvel for a split second at the unfairness of genetics, mysterious spirals of DNA coiling and cohering into life sentences: *You will be plain. You will be beautiful. You will repulse mosquitoes. You will have an iron gut. You will be sickened by crabmeat.*

Circe takes my arm and pulls me along, and I allow her to steer me towards the park. The once-grand gate looks small and shabby. The paint has faded and flaked away in unpleasing shapes. The avenue the entrance opens out into is broad but flanked by green dustbins and half-dead patches of grass. Everywhere, the chirrup of crickets and the low machine-hum of power generators. There is no one else around in this sad, shitty place.

'No one stray too far off,' Mrs Tay says. She is a young-ish new mother with bushy brows and dark bags under her eyes.

We file off in pairs. Circe keeps on making sarcastic comments about the figurines scattered around the park in half-neglected dioramas, re-enacting morality tales, Chinese legends. I half listen. I can tell that Circe is enjoying herself, despite her protestations.

Twenty minutes later Mrs Tay comes to find me by the pagodas. She advances with such severity and purpose that my first instinct is to flee, but she locks my gaze. She has her Nokia clasped in one hand. She is frowning.

'Circe, do you mind giving Szu and me a moment?'

Circe and I exchange a look but she does as she is told and steps aside to stare at a plaster statue of a mermaid with her arms thrown up in the air. The sun moves behind a veil of viscous white clouds. I feel faint and a little cold. I narrow my eyes to try and focus on Mrs Tay.

'Szu, I'm afraid I've received a phone call,' Mrs Tay says. 'It's about your mother.'

I feel like someone on a television show. This is a scene I have watched unfold many times before in Channel 8 drama serials. I'm playing the part of the young girl with the quivering mouth and the eyes already welling up with tears. My face feels hot and unreal yet my hands are freezing.

'Your aunt just called to tell me. Your mother has passed away. I am so sorry,' Mrs Tay says.

It occurs to me right then that when people say 'passed away' it implies that we have just missed them. As if they passed by on their way to another errand.

Mrs Tay keeps her voice flat and calm but I can see that she is trying to control her expression. She wants to scrunch her features up. Pity is upsetting. For a moment I feel more sorry for her than she must do for me.

I keep staring at her, in that bovine, blank way that I know usually irritates other teachers, but Mrs Tay's gaze remains soft. I feel a mosquito land on my right arm. Its snout pierces my epidermis and sucks my rare Type AB blood out. All of a sudden I can hear every cricket in the park, little green bodies hiding amongst the reeds and in the crevices of the gaudy, plastered statues.

115

'I am so sorry,' Mrs Tay repeats, and I can tell she really means it. 'You poor girl.' She shakes her head and comes over to me, pulls me close for a hug. I wilt like a soggy cabbage. I stare at Circe over Mrs Tay's shoulder. Circe's mouth hangs open and her hand rises up and lands at the base of her throat.

'Do you want to call your aunt back?' Mrs Tay says. She releases me and my arms flop to my sides. I shake my head at her.

'Um, no, it's fine, please, no, it's fine,' I finally reply, and scratch my neck as I lower my head. I don't want to look at her. The pavement is turquoise with a pattern of swirls, an imitation of the ocean, only the cracks have gathered so much dirt over the years that the surface seems muddied.

'When did it happen?'

'Forty minutes ago.'

Why did the news take so long to reach me? What timing is normal? How am I supposed to know what to do *a)* now; and *b)* ever? One hour ago we were boarding the huffing bus and I had one foot on the step. I was thinking of why some steps are built so much broader and harder to climb than others. I was also thinking of my mother lying in the hospital bed. I had started to picture her perpetually, habitually, that image of her waxy, sleeping face stuck fast to the back of my mind like a fly poster. I made a list of possibilities:

— *Maybe my mother is one day from getting much better, and when I see her tomorrow she will be sitting up in bed. She can be healthy and bitchy again. Maybe she will snap at me as she applies rouge to her cheeks. Maybe she will demand a cigarette and for me to fetch the younger doctor, Dr Ngoi, with the chubby char siu bao face, and the eunuch voice.*

— *Maybe my mother will slip into a coma, and come out infirm, vegetative. And then I could spend the rest of my life taking care of her, being so admirably nice.*

— *Maybe she will really go (and to where, or nowhere, I do not know). But only some time in the future, after we've grown close and entered into the realm of moving conversations, parting pearls of wisdom. Love in spades and blankets, easy love.*

My fantasies were similar to how they had been, even before she fell ill. I hadn't sensed anything different. I hadn't paid enough attention, or I would have known.

'You are free to go if you need to, Szu,' Mrs Tay says. I shake my head.

'I'm fine,' I say. 'I'd like to stay here but I need to be on my own.'

'Of course.'

I feel trite tears welling up. I try to think of my eyes as small basins, holding water.

'Can I go?'

'Yes, but I might come to check up on you. If your

Aunt Yunxi wants you to go to her, I'll let you know. But for now you take your own time. Just as long as we re-assemble by the main gates in two hours. Are you okay?' She reaches into her bag, brings out a tissue packet.

I take it from her. The packet has a design of a small yellow bear holding up a balloon on one side, and the plastic is all crumpled from days in Mrs Tay's bag. The bear makes me want to cry.

'May I go?'

'Yes, Szu, of course.'

I march off as quickly as I can, past Circe who starts to follow me but I shake my head and put out my arm like I'm holding a sword in a samurai film, tilting the hilt downward, elegantly. Last week Circe and I tried to watch *Rashomon* because sophisticated film buffs seem to love it, but we ended up snoring on the sofa instead. I remember the samurai in the film, so strong and stoic. So I pretend I am a stalwart Japanese warrior and keep on walking.

I go past the figure of the crab with a man's head and past the sculpture of a village at work: figures toiling, wielding sickles and balancing bamboo sticks across their peeling plaster backs. I walk further and further into the park, away from everybody, until I arrive at a cave flanked by two figures of a bull and a horse, both dressed in finery for battle: chain armour and bold turquoise-trimmed robes, boots for their hooves, clutching sceptres. I'm out of breath even though I hadn't been going that quickly. My inhales are rapid and ragged.

The Chinese sign above the figures reads: THE TEN COURTS OF HELL.

I've been here before. Seeing that dead-eyed horse stirs up the faint embers of memory. The cave entrance looks so much smaller and shabbier than I remembered. Why do the dimensions of real life always disappoint me?

My father was standing right over there, eyes downcast, forehead furrowed grey. He looked deeply sad and angry at the same time. Like a man that had just been slapped with a prison sentence. There was so much depth in his face it was like staring into a chasm. I remember thinking: is this what adults do, brew their frustrations inside their heads? Does anger charge up like batteries? Later that night, my parents mumbled like thunder, and one of them knocked a pot of pu'er tea off the table and it shattered. Sometimes I wished I were blind and deaf. Maybe six was the year that unhappiness started to cluster like spores of mould in our household. Maybe I'm just speculating. I plugged my ears with my fingers and lay still as my parents clamoured next door. I longed for a thick, soupy silence, calm walls behind which nothing hateful happened.

*

Circe finds me huddled in the Third Court of Hell, sitting beside a figurine getting his heart pulled out by a man in a yellow mask. His small, pinched face has an expression of quiet anguish, made even sadder by the paint peeling off in flecks, giving the illusion of a skin condition. She comes across me with my mouth slightly ajar, like a frog catching flies, and my eyes glazed and watery. It is humid in the cave, and its interior seems to stretch on and on, illuminated by orange, low-wattage bulbs. There are even more mosquitoes in here and they bite me in awkward places, the fold of skin behind the knee, the shin.

'Hey,' Circe says, and sits down beside me. Water drips off the cave ceiling and onto the crown of my head.

'Are you okay?' she asks. I don't say anything, just pick at a scab on my knee and offer her a small smile.

I hope that she cannot see, in the dim orange light, that I have been crying. Circe looks unsure of herself; she doesn't seem to know what to do with her hands. She looks so much younger when her face isn't contorted into a sardonic sneer. She could be thirteen. Maybe it is the lighting, but her eyes are slightly pink. Perhaps she, too, has been crying.

'Mrs Tay told me to look for you, and of course now everyone else knows,' she says, staring into her lap.

'That sucks.'

'I know.'

I let out a long sigh. The thought of mumbled condolences and forced smiles makes me so tired. Even Trissy Kwok and Lee Meixi possess the capacity to turn suddenly, and fashionably, feeling. I dread the soft focus of their empathy, the awkwardly kind gestures that will fade once the tragedy isn't fresh.

I've seen this happen before, with Nancy Lau, the girl with severe eczema who everyone ceased to tease for the brief few weeks after her grandmother passed away. During that time Nancy was treated to warm smiles at recess, shared textbooks, invitations to Lido, until the unexpected morning when Trissy and Meixi resumed calling her 'Lizard Legs' during PE, chanting it with increasing speed.

This was their declaration that her period of respectful mourning was over and they were done with feeling sorry. Nancy slunk away from the netball line. Mr Toh, the PE teacher, picked me to fetch her. Nancy had hidden out under the farthest rain tree, where she hugged her bare, shamed legs and cried like a baby. I brought her a tissue but she waved me away, infuriated by my fellow pariah's pity.

'I don't want to go out there,' I say.

'Don't worry, we don't have to,' Circe replies, and glances at her watch. It is a glow-in-the-dark Swatch and I have often envied it. It is not something my mother or Aunt Yunxi would allow me to have.

'We've got until 4.30. It's just past three now. Plenty of time.'

'Good,' I say. I don't know how to tell her that I want to be on my own, and even then, the impulse changes from moment to moment. A drop of water falls off the ceiling and onto my bare arm.

'This place is just as weird as I remembered it,' Circe says. 'Leslie and I played hide and seek here once, when we were kids. I fell and scratched my knee. There was a man with claws for hands and, like, a globe strapped to his back. That gave me nightmares.'

'Who even comes here?' I look at the display in front of us, the painted figures with their suffering faces – pulled black commas for eyebrows, downward jellybean-shaped mouths. A demon with gaudy yellow hair grips the sides of a man's chest and rips it apart. The man's shiny little organs threaten to tumble out of his stomach. I read the sign:

CRIME:

Ungratefulness

Disrespect of Elders

Prison escape

Drug addicts and Traffickers

Tomb Raiders

PUNISHMENT:

Heart cut out

Tied to red-hot copper pillar and grilled

'Which would you rather?' Circe asks. 'To have your heart cut out, or to be grilled?'

'Heart cut out.'

'Yeah, it's more poetic. Who wants to be grilled? Like a sotong or a piece of chicken? No dignity,' Circe says, and laughs, but there is something forced in it.

A chill enters the cave; long shadows flicker over the entrance. We can hear some other girls coming up. Whispers. The shuffling of canvas shoes. A peal of laughter echoes, and then it ceases, like an audio file that has cut out. We wait. After a few moments they go away, but now the cave seems darker than before and the figures being tortured seem a little more lifelike, as if they might actually move when we aren't paying attention. I look down at my hands. I can almost see the energy flowing out of me like a cartoon life force, something to pillage a planet for, a glowing green substance that evaporates into the stupefying air.

'Um, Szu?' Circe says. 'Don't you have to go? To see Aunt Yunxi, or to the hospital, or wherever.'

'No.'

'Are you sure you want to just sit here? I'll go with you, to the hospital – we've got permission.'

'I don't know. No.' I can feel the tears welling up again and making the sight of my hands blurred and misty. My tears keep falling into my palms, hot fat drops that I can tell alarm Circe just as much as they embarrass me.

It is so exposing and unpleasant to be watched crying. Even babies bawling on public transport know this, which is why they always look so stricken.

'I'm sorry,' Circe continues. 'Look, I'm really sorry, Szu.' She pats me on the back, gingerly. Her bony hand taps in time to my sniffles. Like Mrs Tay, she's trying. I'm not used to all this effort made around me. The spotlight is unnerving. I can tell from Circe's strained posture and her Serious Voice, which is so different from her normal one, that she is out of her depth as well. It feels like we are acting but we don't know our lines.

'I feel so—' I gulp.

'So?'

'I – I don't know. Like I want to vomit.'

'Are you okay? Do you want me to get you some water?'

'No.'

'Aw, man. Look, do you want to get out of here? Mrs Tay said you could go.'

'No. I kind of – I kind of like it in here,' I say. 'I don't really want to leave.' The last thing I want to do right now is to see my mother's body laid out clear and plain for all it finally is: a body. It's both too much and too obvious.

'Okay,' Circe says.

'Okay.'

'Hey, you know what?'

'What?'

'I'm kind of in shock too, you know. Your mom and I were never cl—'

I put my hands up over my face and that seems to stop her.

'Sorry,' Circe says in a small voice.

'You don't need to keep saying it,' I reply, even though I feel a knot of anger gathering in the back of my gullet, like a furball or the beginnings of a sore throat. After all, right until the end Circe had made such a joke out of the hospital visits: the Land of No Hope. She was right, there had been no hope, but she shouldn't have kept on reminding me.

Hours pass, or what feels like hours. There is something comforting about the boredom, something novel about the silence. Usually we prattle non-stop. Instead we just sit there as if we have known each other for decades, and not just since the start of the year. I feel this grand exhaustion in the tightness of my throat and in my joints: now that my mother has died I have aged irreversibly over a single afternoon. The distance between now and before seems to stretch into infinity. There is so much I have left to say to her. I think of the last few frenzied, other-peopled months that got in the way of me and her and Aunt Yunxi. I think of the oncologist with his clipboard and the radiologist with the painted nude nails and the jaw specialist with the soothing voice – they had indicated to Yunxi and me any day now with every flicker of expression, every glance in the other direction.

We sit there until our bums are sore from the ledge and the mosquitoes have bitten each of us twenty times. And then we hear Mrs Tay and Mrs Yeo calling for us. As we walk to the coach Circe links her arm in mine. I lean into her, stooping slightly to accommodate our difference in height. Everyone is watching but they make no snide remarks this time. I feel like a shamed celebrity. I feel like I'm walking down an aisle or a gangplank.

*

When I get home it is a quarter to five and shadows dapple the bright sunlight on the kitchen table. Aunt Yunxi is out. She's left me a hastily scrawled note in Chinese: Settling things. There's soup in the fridge.

The soup lies in a blue china bowl covered in cling film. The fat and oil has congealed into a thin, murky scum over its surface. I know for a fact that Aunt Yunxi slow-boiled this fungus soup two days ago. It stank up the kitchen with an odour like armpits and expired chicken. Could it be said that this soup that smells like death has outlived my mother? Things look just the same as they did yesterday. Every object in here seems dishonest in its fixity. The house has the static air of a furniture showroom after hours. As if the walls are made of plywood and everything is held in place by Scotch tape and safety pins.

The water in the fish tank needs changing; it has turned

sickly green and a dark sludge has started to form along the glass. The mouldy damp aquarium smell puts me off food, even though my stomach is rumbling. I suck in and shudder. Three saddle grunts with their yellow scales and cold, unquestioning eyes continue their perpetual loop from one side of the tank to the other in languid synchronicity. My favourite, the milkfish that I'd thought was dying over six months ago, is still going strong. I had been wrong about him. The milkfish has grown new, shimmering scales over the fissures in his side and he avoids my gaze with his flat, impersonal fish eyes. I think of some of the things that have happened in the brief time between my pronouncement that he was doomed and today.

Last week it rained so heavily that the huge monsoon drain on the main road overflowed and a tree broke and fell halfway across, a long, peeling trunk sticking out of inches of rainwater so muddy it looked like gallons of Milo. Traffic was congested for ages, cars marooned on the wide, sloshing roads. For seven days I had weak sleep, empty of dreams.

Last month the Sumatran haze came back and the Pollutant Standard Index measured above 150, but instead of panicking and keeping their children indoors everyone just grumbled, because it had happened so many times before. I coughed up a giant ball of phlegm the size and colour of a baby chick.

Earlier this year, just after my birthday in January, I made a best friend and she talks a lot. Circe can be bossy and really irritating but I am grateful for her. Aunt Yunxi lost two clients because a reporter from the New Paper came to see her and accused her of being a scam medium. The annual Star Search competition happened and I didn't follow it. A new shopping arcade went up on Orchard Road called the Hive. A fire broke out in a shophouse three streets away and one month later the Urban Redevelopment Authority tore it down.

It was only ten months ago that my mother first went to the doctor. It wasn't her hacking, smoker's cough or perpetual tiredness that drove her there. Much like her functional alcoholism, those things had been constants for many years. But her shoulders had started to hurt so much that some nights she couldn't sleep. She said it felt like a cast-iron hanger bearing down on her nerves. Her groans, which I heard through the paper-thin walls that separate our bedrooms, made me wince. She put the pain down to the exhaustion of being a spirit medium, channelling or appearing to channel the harsh, reticent voices of the dead. One day, her right eyelid started to droop and would not reopen to its normal shape. I would never have dared to tell her she looked kind of funny; that now there was something loopy about her beauty. She went to the polyclinic expecting to be referred to a cosmetic surgeon, but instead she had one doctor referring her to another, and finally another, gathering opinions. A specialist with a dyed-red chignon and a consultant so old he resembled a carp with whiskers and an oncologist who looked worryingly young, as if fresh out of NUS med school, with acne battle scars across his cheeks and a prominent Adam's apple. They recited these labels that meant nothing to her: ptosis, miosis, presentations of Horner's syndrome, Pancoast syndrome, eventual paraesthesias. They showed her the broccoli-bloom X-ray of her lungs where, at the top of the right side, was a grey shadow, so faint that we had to squint.

'Are you sure it's there?' my mother asked the radiologist with a voice both plaintive and angry. He didn't even nod. I looked away and at my Aunt Yunxi instead. She was staring out of the window with a glaze in her eyes, fixed upon the car park and the rain trees. She had the same expression she took on during a seance, when she was trying to make urgent contact beyond the room. Was she wondering why she hadn't sensed something was wrong? I thought of Aunt Yunxi pressing her palms on the bowed backs of clients, on a hopeful head, but this clinically well-lit room did not seem to hold the promise of some hokey, mystical healing.

We thought it was just one lawless tumour but the problem was bigger than that, and it moved with such vicious speed. My mother was a semi-famous monster and I thought she'd live forever. Could I have warned her months, years, a decade earlier? Could I have had the foresight to tell her: stop living complacently? Did I have the guts to phrase it, and would she have listened?

I am sixteen and a half and beginning to realize that life sometimes happens like this: quickly, with no further allowances. You think you have decades ahead of you and all of a sudden there is no time left.

11

AMISA

1977

Six months after they started courting, Wei Loong took Amisa to the Satay Club. While he went to order she sat on a wooden bench overlooking the river and stared out at the water, dark as oil. Her arms and legs ached. It wasn't just the long shifts at work; increasingly, she found it drain- ing being around other people all day. To think that she had grown up in a crowded kampong and now the only serenity she felt was in a darkened theatre. She was only nineteen. With age, would her misanthropy worsen like a chronic condition? She felt separate yet shamefully like the other girls who sat on adjacent benches waiting for their beaus, smoothing out their skirts, adjusting the buckles on their patent shoes.

Wei Loong came over with a paper plate piled with satay. Amisa took a stick and tore a nub of burnt mutton off with her teeth. She chewed with cowboy consternation. Smoke from the charcoal grilles wafted over.

'Did you call home this week?'

She wiped grease from her lips. 'Yeah, Didi wasn't around. The auntie down the road taught my Jie how to make kueh tutus and now she's obsessed. She can't stop making them. My second brother has a girlfriend. Everyone else is the same.' In truth, Jie was the only one she spoke to. Her parents hardly ever came to the phone, and when they did, the conversations were stilted and brief. She had a lingering, guilt-borne worry that they would ask about the bangle she had stolen.

'And what about you?' she asked. 'Have you heard back?'

Wei Loong shrugged. 'You know how my brothers are,' he said, even though she'd never met them. 'Ah goons and ah sengs, all of them. Only want to borrow money, now that Ah Luat gave me promotion.'

'Money then talk,' Amisa said. She felt full now, and a little nauseous. She moved her tongue around the inside of her mouth and dislodged a piece of gristle from her left molar. She didn't want to appear unladylike so she swallowed it.

*

Later in bed, Wei Loong twirled her hair in his hand. She fidgeted out of his grasp before leaning back against him. There was a very tall, ancient ficus tree that she could see from his sixth-storey window. At 10 p.m. its long branches were backlit by the amber squares and punctuations of people at home. The tree was considered sacred, with a shrine underneath its boughs. She liked the look of it, grand and incongruous against the skyline of scaffold and construction cranes.

'Move in with me, Amisa,' Wei Loong mumbled into her hair. He said her name like an exotic fruit. Sex cast a particularly soporific spell over him. He had the long, low drawl of a sleep-talker.

'Maybe,' she replied in a syrupy voice. 'I'm so tired. I can't believe I've got to get up at three.'

'Quit the seafood stall.'

'I can't just do that,' she laughed.

'I can't, I can't, I can't,' he mimicked.

She laughed, a little less enthusiastically this time, still staring out of the window. She heard him draw his breath.

'Marry me,' he said.

Amisa turned towards Wei Loong. He was serious. She took in his softened eyes with their deep epicanthal folds, his pockmarks and sharp nose. He was so good to her that it felt traitorous to recall her initial repulsion. She pressed her mouth against his in intimate panic. He put his arms around her, tilting her fully towards him, and reached for her breasts. She felt his tongue part her lips and slide around, this fat tender worm stubbed to a stem. She thought of Humphrey Bogart and Ingrid Bergman with their close-lipped kisses, crisp shifting profiles, the epic idea of epic romance. And then, incongruously, she pictured her own mother back in their dingy, herb-scattered kitchen, wondering about what disrespectable deed her daughter was up to, if she even wondered at all.

*

The next afternoon there was a fire scare at the cinema and it had to be evacuated. Besides the time she had fallen ill after her birthday, Amisa was never free at this hour. As she walked home, light on her tired feet, she jangled her keys

131

in her dusty pocket. Outside her house, she saw a middle-aged woman standing in the street. The woman clutched a young boy by the shoulders. They stood apart when Amisa neared. The boy looked about eleven, knock-kneed and with a pale, rabbity countenance and a chapped mouth.

'Excuse me,' the woman called out, as Amisa reached her front door. 'Does Datuk Aunt Yunxi live here? Is this the right address?'

She showed Amisa a piece of paper. Amisa nodded.

'Yes. Are you her family?' She studied the woman's wan face. She bore no resemblance to Yunxi.

'Oh, no,' the woman replied. 'I've come to consult her, about my son.' The boy stared at the ground.

'Um, sure, I'll show you in,' Amisa replied. She frowned as she led the visitors up the narrow stairs, floorboards creaking in protest at the footfalls behind her.

At the top floor she showed the woman and boy into the kitchen. They waited gingerly by the hanging wok and a garland of onions.

'Just give me a second,' Amisa said. She stood outside Yunxi's door and leaned in. She heard a mournful, gravelly chanting coming from inside the room. It frightened her.

'Yunxi? Some people are here to see you.'

The chanting stopped. When Yunxi answered the door she was wearing a dark-grey samfoo fastened by toggles. Her face was flushed and full of deepened lines that Amisa hadn't noticed so clearly before.

'Yes, of course. Please show them in,' Yunxi said, her voice echoing out onto the cramped landing. Her Chinese intonations sounded almost oratorical.

Amisa went back into the kitchen and ushered the woman and boy towards Yunxi's room. The woman shut the door behind the boy. Amisa poured herself a glass of water and gulped it quickly. She wasn't hungry, just sleepy, as usual. She was taking a break from Wei Loong this evening. Betrothal felt like a strain in the arms. What did it really mean: to be engaged? She walked over to her room and shut the door. Lying on her tiny bed in half a daydream and dirty clothes was her favourite thing to do. The pictures behind her eyelids were infinitely better than the cobwebs across the beams of the ceiling or the sooty shutters. She listened out but could hear nothing through the walls.

Her thoughts drifted to a bow-tied blouse, mauve-coloured and made of silk, that she had seen an elegant woman wearing on Havelock Road. The woman's hair was flipped out at the corners. Amisa imagined being that woman, getting into a yellow-top taxi with a casual, privileged grace – one stockinged leg piled delicately after the other.

After an hour the door next to hers opened. Amisa kept her eyes shut but her ears peeled.

'Goodbye, Laoshi,' the boy said meekly, his voice cracking. Perhaps he, too, was older than she thought.

'Thank you, thank you,' the woman said in Hokkien.

After they had gone down the stairs Amisa couldn't take it any longer. She got up and peered around the corner into the kitchen. Yunxi was taking down the wok.

'Hello! I don't usually see you home at this time,' Yunxi said in her ordinary voice.

'There was a fire scare.'

'Ah. Of course. You are an Earth Dog, aren't you?'

'Excuse me?' Amisa asked, rubbing her eyes.

'You were born in 1958, the year of the Earth Dog. Today is an unlucky day for you.' Yunxi began chopping an onion, working deftly with the little knife.

'I never asked you what you do for a living. I assumed—'

Yunxi looked at her patiently.

'With all those male clients—'

'Ah. Hah!' Yunxi said, the blade clanging staccatos on the wooden board. Instead of anger, her face erupted into a grin. 'I can't believe you thought I was selling my body like that.' She laughed, a bawdy, throaty chortle. 'You could say I am using my body, but in a different way.'

'How so?' Amisa asked.

'I have always had a gift, but my Laoshi helped me to refine it, many years ago.'

'I don't understand.'

'I am a medium. I get possessed by the spirits of the dead, the gods of roadsides, anthills, trees. Those men who visit are desperate – just not in the way you assumed.'

'Ah,' Amisa said.

Yunxi nodded at her and smiled. A slight breeze wound its way through the accordion window. Amisa thought of the boy who had just left, knock-kneed and very thin. She wondered what haunted him.

*

The next week she quit her job at the wet market. Quitting was so easy when it was presented as an option. Mrs Lim handed her an ang pao. Mr Lim smiled gingerly.

'Good luck and take care,' he said, and turned back towards the piles of prawns.

'I will do,' Amisa replied, staring at the pink, pitiable eyes of a sardine in front of her.

She took off her cap and stained apron. Her ponytail lay flat and greasy against her skull. She handed the things back to Mrs Lim and walked away from the stall, smiling and waving to the uncles and aunties as she went by. She untied her hair and teased it up with her fingers. She felt like punching the strung-up bunches of Chinese sausages as she passed. Outside, the rest of the city was just warming up. A paper mask seller pedalled past her with his trishaw loaded full of craft masks and puppets. Mickey Mouse, a donkey head and an operatic male face with upward-slanted brows bobbed away from her. She got out the ang pao from her pocket and opened it. Inside was S$20.

The next day she went with Wei Loong to Fort Canning. At the marriage registry she signed her name in shaky characters and watched as he followed with his own. *Ng Wei Loong.* She was an Ng now, too.

Their wedding took place three months later, on 9 July 1977. It was a small and simple ceremony, without fuss or fanfare. On the day it rained, but she thought nothing of it, wasn't superstitious. Yunxi and Laoshi attended, and some of Wei Loong's friends, inoffensive childhood classmates with meek wives of their own. She kept a peaceable distance from them, a faint smile on her face.

'Your friends are boring,' she whispered to Wei Loong.

'Yunxi looks like scrap wood,' he replied.

'How dare you say that?'

'Fine, she looks like a violin. A priceless collectible.'

'That's better.'

Amisa wore a blood-red qipao stitched with little flowers. It was tailor-made in Chinatown and Wei Loong had saved up for it for months. When she emerged into the void deck wearing it, he looked like he wanted to cry.

'*Mei nu*,' he said, and she winced inside, because he sounded just like those awful men in the alleyways. 'I am so lucky. I could stare at your face forever.'

Amisa contemplated her new husband. She couldn't picture him any older than thirty, nor herself, either. Youth felt expansive, bulk-bought, and useful, like an endless supply of tissue paper.

She wrote to her family after the fact to tell them: guess what, I'm married. He's a nice man. He makes a decent living. He doesn't hurt me. Be proud of me for once, and trust that I won't ruin everything. She asked after Didi. A letter arrived back from her sister: Didi was working in Genting Highlands, and had taken up a gambling habit at the grand old age of sixteen. Everyone was in good health, and happy for her. Parents sent their regards, Jiejie said.

Two days after the wedding she packed her things to move out of her room. Yunxi helped her, even though she had very few belongings.

'Do you think it is strange, or unlucky, that I didn't ask my family to attend?' Amisa asked.

'You have your own reasons. They understand,' Yunxi said in the tiny space on the staircase landing.

'Yes,' Amisa said doubtfully. A pair of cockroaches

scampered away out of the corner of her vision, into Yunxi's room.

Yunxi pressed a small, greenish medallion into Amisa's hands.

'This is for good luck and a happy marriage,' she said.

'I'll still see you?' Amisa asked.

'Of course,' Yunxi replied, and fixed her with a small, warm smile. 'You know where to find me.'

'Thank you,' Amisa replied, embarrassed by how moved she was. 'I'd better go.'

*

Wei Loong's flat, and now hers, was in Toa Payoh, near to Geylang and a busy public housing town, bordered by eight old Chinese cemeteries. There was a wide parched plot of grassland opposite their development where on some nights secret society gangs staked their turf. But it was still more of a family area than Geylang, full of maciks and their grandchildren, fabric stores and coffee shops, and most mornings the smell of fresh otah and kopi o gifted the air.

When she woke up every morning the first thing he did was kiss her on the nose and then hungrily on the mouth before she could catch her breath. He mauled her lovingly like it was his last day on earth. He told her over and over how lucky he felt. He said this so many times the compliment lost its meaning. He filled in Toto tickets every week with her birthdate, 23081958, and bonus numbers for the date they got together: 190476. He doted on her, his lucky little lottery number. When he sensed her annoyance he

137

went out to the market and brought her back breakfast, lunch or dinner: little baos or kueh lapis, nasi lemak, chicken chok, ban mian, murtubak, whatever she wanted.

Seemingly overnight, Amisa gained five kilos and felt appalled, but even she had to admit that the new weight made her look even better. Her hair acquired a glossier sheen. She became invincibly beautiful: the clarity of her cheeks, her little ankles, and the lucid poetry others projected onto her blank expression. People stopped by the box office just to catch a glimpse of her. She was locally legendary, at nineteen: something mythic, this unendurably lovely girl in full bloom. Even stray dogs and children smiled at her, but she didn't return the favour.

Wei Loong worked as an antiques restorer in Bartley Road. The workshop smelt of earthy fragrant teak and varnish. The first time Amisa visited, the four other men working there put down their tools and looked from this goddess to Wei Loong and back, gawking with incredulity.

'Wah lau, you're so lucky,' they said to Wei Loong, right in front of her.

'Don't I know it,' Wei Loong said. Amisa bristled like a peacock in her orange-patterned shift dress and go-go boots.

Orphans together, both of them. She could be happy this way, as long as nothing changed; as long as they never grew sick or old and nobody burnt or burgled the largish room with a laundry pole poking out of the window, the unmade bed, and the beige walls. Wei Loong wasn't rich, but he wasn't dirt-poor, either. He wasn't a stud but he wasn't a little anchovy, either. He wasn't interesting, but he wasn't totally boring, either. His unhappy childhood had taken care of that, and it was a spite they shared, something that stung and bruised them in similar places. His father had walked out of the house when Wei Loong was seven, a philandering sailor. His brothers were in prison or left a contraband trail across the neighbouring countries. She could have had her pick of literally anyone but it took less energy to remind herself: at least he had plucked up the courage to talk to her.

If love was someone real who treated her like a princess then this was clearly it. Wasn't a good marriage the jackpot for traditional Chinese girls? It was nice to be held. Checked up on, asked after. Amisa felt as if she could relax into such an existence. The sex was decent. They were careful. She didn't want any children yet, and he didn't rush her. They drank together some evenings at the nearby hawker centre. He made for better company when slightly intoxicated; he became surer of himself and more witty and animated. He toasted her and cracked rude little innuendoes until a glow rose up in her cheeks and alcohol swirled through her veins and made everything softer.

12

SZU

2003

It's been one day since my mother died. Excused from school, I spend all morning lying in bed, overhearing traffic and the birds outside changing their tunes. In the afternoon Aunt Yunxi gives me instant permission to stay over at Circe's house. She is too tired and busy to quibble. My aunt has always been made of sterner and more mysterious stuff than me. We both know I am flimsier, that I can't bear the sight of my mother's bedroom one door down from my own, with its oval mirror that questions the hallway and the slight indent in the memory-foam mattress from where she folded her slim body.

I go over to Circe's house and flop down on her bed. Circe puts the Kinks' album on really loudly even though I am getting sick of them. When I tell her this, she ignores me for three songs and then switches to *The Velvet Underground & Nico*. The CD has a graphic of a banana on the cover that we both want flattering T-shirts of. We love this album. We want to wear our love for it across our chests and for imaginary indie boys to think we are cool and datable because of it. But today the chords and gentle voices coming through the computer speakers sound far too wistful and mellow, at peace with an airbrushed sort of world. I don't want music but I can't stand the silence, either. We sit in her yellow room willing the afternoon to melt away, flipping magazines and trying to make it seem as if nothing is different.

That night, I have a terrifying and obvious dream in her Ikea double bed. In my dream I am strapped to the deck of a sinking ship and my mother appears at the prow looking younger and more hopeful than I have ever seen. She's far away and everything is rocking but I can hear her perfectly.

'It's not your fault I am me,' she says. 'And it's not my fault you are you.' I want to reply but I can't speak. I wake up shivering and with wet eyes and cheeks. Circe snores lightly beside me.

Just then it starts to storm. I wriggle on the sheets, feel my cold toes uncurling. Above us slow rumbles. I picture thunderheads spread out across a stark raving sky. I think about how big the sky is, how it enfolds all of us impartially.

A gust of wind rattles the steel pipes on the roof. I remember the mynah birds that Circe, her maid Josephine and I had watched hours earlier, just before dinner time. Bobbing creatures perched on the telephone wires, so delicate and small.

'The littlest ones get eaten by cats,' Josephine said. 'No hope for them.'

I worry where the mynah birds are hiding. I get a sinking dread about their well-being. I open my eyes and peer into Circe's face. She looks calm, almost beautiful. The darkness in her bedroom is inky and tinged with cobalt blue. The air fizzes like television static. Circe mumbles and draws me towards her. She breathes on me, my mouth no more than three inches away from hers. She smells like Kodomo lion toothpaste and Gardenia bread. I know from this moment that these two things will always remind me of her, with a flinch, an ache. And maybe because of this, over time I will learn to avoid them.

Her perfect, unknowable brother Leslie is in the other room. Just six feet away, this quiet boy right now probably dreaming with his mouth open. Half asleep, I wonder if to kiss one sibling is the same as kissing the other; if my love for them both will be revealed if I kiss her, like an inkblot on white card, a marking, a patternation. I can't pin down the nature of this tangle in my chest. It could be good, or bad, or in between. Maybe one day it will mutate into something deadly, and there will be nothing I can do about it.

I hold my breath and lean forward. But just then Circe turns away and pushes her back to me, almost forcefully, like an admonition. I roll over onto my back and stare at the ceiling. The wind howls hurried nothings at the roof. At every fidget the mattress creaks with my treachery, my cowardice. From the wall beside me, Leslie's mattress also creaks. Perfectly naturally, and with no shift in her breathing, Circe hooks her legs into mine so that we are loosely tangled at the knees and shins. It feels both uncomfortable and calming. My skin is hot and sticky, but every time I try to move she keeps me in her grip. Eventually I fall asleep.

When Josephine switches the light on at 6.15, our legs are still half tangled but the cover has fallen off the bed.

From the corner of my eye it looks as if a poltergeist has swept through the room and flung off the pillows and blanket. The crumpled pastel pile looks like a discarded *Sesame Street* costume. All the blood has drained from my lower body and my legs are entirely numb. A thin film of sweat clings to my clammy forehead and under my arms. Circe and I are like Siamese twins conjoined at the legs. I don't mind my immobility. My mother is dead. It's still hard to say it. It feels good to be held in place, to be anchored to earth.

*

I've got four more days off school for bereavement. So I put on a tatty T-shirt and shorts while Circe grumbles and buttons up her uniform. After breakfast of kaya toast (I watch, too sick and shy to eat, as Leslie and Circe wolf their bread down, and end up giving her my untouched square), we get into her father's shiny Lexus. He's giving me a lift home after he drops Circe at school.

On the way there's a traffic jam snaking along the Pan Island Expressway, a veil of residual haze settling over the lamps and treetops. The air conditioner blasts on my knees. Circe frowns out of the window. I guess she's jealous because I don't have to go to school and there is an e-Maths test at 11 a.m. that we both haven't prepared for. She acts as if everything is normal but also slightly my fault. I can feel her irritation in the stuffy car air. She's good at this, these pendulum shifts from warmth into unkindness.

When we drop her off she slams the car door and doesn't look back. I crane my neck and watch her shuffling through the school gates. She lingers half a step behind a trio of girls sleepwalking in tandem, with their French braids and linked arms. As the car pulls away she hitches her blue backpack up on her shoulders. It is so disconcerting to really need someone, is what I think. My only friend gets smaller and smaller until I can't pick her out in a sea of uniforms. For once I wish I was joining her, partaking in the horrible comfort of routine.

Driving me home, Circe's father doesn't quite know what to say. I've never been in the car alone with him before, now that I think about it. It's mostly Circe's mother, Magda, who gives me lifts. He switches the radio on to YES 93.3 and we sit there acutely aware that the DJs are speaking too cheerfully. After one intersection he switches the station to classical music. Sombre strings replace chipper Mandarin. I picture Victoria Concert Hall and elegant girl prodigies from the SSO, dressed all in black with violins balanced under their focused jawlines.

We're driving through Queensway. Big green trees and shoals of schoolchildren by the roadside. Circe's father met my mother, once, when he came to pick his daughter up from our house. My mother smiled at him as he stuttered his name. Low Ghim Teck, the import–export businessman.

'How wonderful,' she said in her actressy, Channel 5 English. 'Well, I'll know who to call for imports and exports.'

He didn't seem to notice that she was being sarcastic. She had that effect on people. I don't think I ever met a man of any orientation who didn't find my mother beautiful, who wasn't affected by her in some way. It was always harder to read what women really thought of her. Cashiers and shop assistants used to back away, as if cowed by her beauty, or simply put off by the disdainful way she asked for things or ordered them around.

After I get dropped off, the day blurs out into its corners like a watercolour painting. It starts to rain and the overcast sky makes the house go dim. Aunt Yunxi has instructed me to 'generally tidy' the reception area, kitchen and toilets as we will be having visitors for the wake. I've never been good at tidying. I lack thoroughness. I flit around with the brown feather duster, smudge every surface with my fingerprints. I swirl dust around with the wet rag cloth. Dust and dirt beget even more dust and dirt. There are long strands of hair all over the place. My own, Yunxi's, my mother's. Aside from the front room that the clients see, the rest of the house has always been pretty grimy. Behind the sink, I find two dead cockroaches the size of mini staplers. They have one antenna entwined, almost braided together, and as I tip their bodies into the bin I imagine they are an incarnation of immortal lovers who have passed on into yet another doomed, doubled life. So long Romeo and Juliet, Yang Guo and Xiaolongnu, Sid and Nancy.

That night, Aunt Yunxi doesn't come home. I feel strangely unworried. I go to bed listening out for movement in the walls, something bigger than the lizards. Now that she is gone I think of my mother constantly. She preoccupies me so much that it seems inevitable that she will reappear. Hasn't my mother's young face been scattered across my dreams for years? It seems impossible that she is gone for good.

I peer out of my window before I go to bed. I stare through the curlicued grilles into the garden with the bird's nest ferns and clusters of dark trees. The long, wet grass doesn't move. I listen out with senseless superstition for the sound of a baby crying. If you can hear a baby crying loudly from somewhere in the vicinity, the Pontianak is far away, willing you to get nearer to her. If the crying is distant, that means the monster is close.

But if my Pontianak is now a ghost, she is a very shy ghost. She doesn't want to make herself known. I wake late at night supernaturally sure there is a flutter by my ear, only to find the insistent normality of my bedroom. Warm air and the crickets in the garden reminding me they are out there. But not here, not her.

*

The next morning I get woken up by the big, insistent beeps of a lorry reversing. Aunt Yunxi comes in just as I've sat up in bed. She's holding a mug for me.

'How are you, ah girl? The lorries are here to set up for the wake,' she says. 'I'm closing the business for nine days. No clients. Just visitors.'

I nod and rub my eyes. My aunt offers no explanation for her absence the night before, and I don't ask. She passes me the mug. It is full of steaming Milo. I think of the milk solids and sugar inside this chocolate malt, comforting and corrupting. I take a small sip and set it on the table beside me.

Aunt Yunxi gets out a square of white cloth from her pocket and hands it to me. The badge of mourning, of being felt sorry for, of being sorry. Something so small that makes it all so real. For a moment we sit opposite each other dazed, parched and wordless. In this light my aunt's skin looks wan, veiny, almost translucent. Grief makes ghosts of people. I don't just mean the ones lost, but the leftover people. After a while my aunt pats my hand and gets up.

'Szu, you must be prepared,' she says on her way out of the room. 'Think about what you have to say to your mother. Hold it in your head. Don't tell anyone. Especially not your friend with the big mouth. This is for you. It's important.'

What do I have left to say to my mother? We never arrived at what we really meant to each other. When she was well I was so sloppy with my ill feelings. I slapped my anger around my forehead in bold, crude strokes. She was only forty-five. Right now her body is being drained and filled with chemicals.

On my thirteenth birthday, my mother told me I was a happy accident. I had just gotten my first period the day before and I was inconsolable. My mother, Aunt Yunxi and I were sitting around the marble table. My mother held a knife that wavered like a question mark over a small green cake.

'Your stupid father and I aren't like other parents,' she said. 'We never needed or wanted a child. And I was getting too old for that, even by the time I had you. So you weren't really meant to happen, but look how far you've

147

come. It's great, Little Bunny. Happy thirteenth accident!' she said, and sliced.

She hadn't called me Little Bunny for a long time. It was an expression of endearment, and she had long ceased to be fond of me. That's why this moment stuck out for me. I knew she meant to be comforting and maybe even funny, that the word 'happy' matched 'accident', but all I could focus on was 'accident'. Its syllables stung like freshly scraped skin. I ate in silence, masticating the pandan chiffon until it was a flavourless mush in my mouth. I tried to think of other happy accidents but all I could picture were cars careening into balloon stands, clown bouquets exploding, cartoon figments of the imagination: unwelcome, abstract, implausible.

*

The wake will be held in our driveway. There is so much to do today. Soon I'll have to leave the messy safety of my room. I look out of the window and watch a white van and a blue lorry pull up. Seven men pile out, all wearing the same ugly purple polo shirts. They bring out folded chairs and tables from the back of the truck and pile them against the wall. Two of the men haul out steel poles and start putting up a striped yellow awning. One man calls out directions to another in Hokkien. They start positioning a row of buffet tables.

I suck the air through my teeth and my stomach makes a sound like rolling rocks. Nowadays I feel lighter on my feet. I pin the square of white cloth to my right sleeve. The wake will last for three days. I have no idea who will show up. As far as I know, my mother had no friends. My grandparents are all dead, and I don't know where my mother's other siblings are.

I met my maternal grandmother only once, eight years ago, just before she died. I remember a small, stooped shadow in the doorway, and my parents' surprise. They invited her in, my mother shuffling about the narrow hallway, suddenly ungraceful. Grandmother was very old and very scary. She reminded me of the Empress Dowager. She wore her years resplendently; decades of bobby pins stuck around her head, holding her thin white hair up in an imperfect bun. Even her hands, which fidgeted on the teak curve of the sitting-room chair, were ancient, speckled with liver spots and textured as tree bark. She eyed me suspiciously, beady eyes finally settling on indifference. I was eight years old and ugliness had already found its way into my features. By then, my face had started to lengthen and narrow, growing from hamster-cute into rat-gross. Regardless of how I looked, I didn't matter. What mattered was whatever lingered between my mother and her. Grandmother seemed to drain the sitting room of sunlight, leaving it airless and eerily calm. She didn't even give my father a second glance. He dithered by the door frame before retreating into the wild, scorching garden outside.

My mother sat opposite my grandmother with her mouth pursed. I didn't know that this would be the first and last time in my life that I would see them together. There was little to no family resemblance. The only thing they seemed to have in common was anger. They were like two cats with their backs arched and their fur raised. And then they began, hissing under their breaths, spitting out occasional phrases. They were arguing in Hakka. I understand Hokkien but not Hakka, so I had no clue what they were saying. Both of them sounded mad and sad. It seems to me that except for a select few, people only ever felt one of two things about my mother: livid, or in love.

At one point my mother got up and went to her bedroom. And then she stormed back out to the sitting room. When I peered around the doorway I thought I saw her throwing something at my grandmother. It looked like a small red pouch, but I couldn't be sure. Grandmother left shortly after that, before my father could perform the hospitality of offering her something to eat or drink. She hobbled down the driveway in a hurt huff, and that is the last I ever saw of her.

By the point that I met my grandmother for the first and last time, my parents had already started their own blazing, tired battles. There seemed to be neither end nor purpose to their continuous disagreements. It was plain ugly habit.

One morning in early September, even the air seemed to flinch. I woke up with a bad feeling in my brain and ribs. An awful silence filled the house. I cowered under my peach-coloured blanket. I heard my mother slam the door to the master bedroom. And then my father called for me. His voice sounded strangled and subdued. When I met him in the kitchen he looked all pallid and googly-eyed, like one of the cling-filmed pomfrets that stared from the second shelf of our fridge. I followed him to the front door, where he turned around and hugged me gingerly.

'Daddy's got some things to do in Ghim Moh. I'll pick up some fish porridge if the stall is open. I'll be back soon,' he said.

I didn't believe him, even at eight years old, and he knew it. He wouldn't look me in the eye. He slung a heavy duffel bag over one shoulder, adjusting its weight as the strap slipped. I followed him to the gate, though no further. He walked stiffly all the way out to the battered Honda Civic with my Little Twin Stars and Lisa Frank colouring books strewn across the back seat. He started up the ignition and kept his eyes on the dashboard and the Courtesy Lion charm hanging off the rear-view mirror. That ugly lion had started out as a shared joke, a free gift that became a fixture. I watched him manoeuvre the car out of the cul-de-sac. It swerved left and then joined the everlasting, anonymous conveyor of cars and lorries along the main road. As if on cue, my mother barked for me to come in.

'*Szu! Szu! Szu Min!*' She had a sore throat from arguing and her voice sounded monster-harsh. By the time I re-entered the house she had retreated into her bedroom again and shut the door. She didn't even want to see me, she just wanted to make sure I was still there. I stared at the peeling wallpaper in the hall. We were marooned together, my mother and I, but for the first time in my life I felt truly alone. It was an aloneness that seemed greater and more grown-up than my body, even bigger than a country could hold. Oh, this solitude was continental. I went into the kitchen and made myself a cup of Milo.

Days passed. Weeks. Months. Not a phone call. Not even a scribbled word. It was hard to believe that my father had quit us and hightailed it to some untraceable pocket of the island. I didn't think he actually meant it when he threatened my mother with that. I thought I was the one who should have done the running away, me, the restless eight-year-old, not him, forty and knowing better.

'Your father is a crook,' my mother said. 'Nothing better. He's an ah goon, an ah seng. He comes from a long line of crooks, nobodies and nothings and he's gone back to the rubbish dump, right where he belongs.'

I couldn't swallow her bitterness. My father was better than trash, even if he couldn't stand us any longer. Maybe we were truly insufferable, and he'd had enough. My mother, an occasional smoker from her acting days, now took up the habit full-time, rapaciously. She started drinking like a cliché, favouring dark liquors that made her breath smell like an old, cantankerous man's. She was always hung-over and in a horrible mood. I forgot what she looked like when she smiled and how to enjoy her company, although I never lost the pathetic desire to please her. I loved her so hatefully; around her I felt disloyal, disgusting. Secretly I wondered if it would be more fun to live with nobodies and nothings than with a former horror movie actress. Maybe being somebody and something was overrated.

All that year, I kept hoping it was a misunderstanding, that we'd simply thought the worst of him. Any day my father would come back down the driveway bearing a faultless grin and two plastic bags fit to burst with fruit and snacks. Sour-plum candy, my mother's favourite.

I played his departure over and over in my head until I

confused myself as to what actually happened and what I'd gotten wrong. Every single detail mattered. If the morning before I had gone left instead of right on the main road, if I'd eaten my vegetables, if I'd followed his every word, perhaps the outcome would have been different. In any case I didn't really want fact. I wanted to tell myself things could be reversed, even if I didn't believe it.

13

AMISA

1977

Now that she was newly married, Amisa worked at the
Paradise Theatre six days a week. Rocky promoted her to
full-time box office and usher, no more dirty toilets. That
week, a Hollywood picture opened which astounded her
with its popularity. It was called *Close Encounters of the
Third Kind*. When she described it to Wei Loong, it
sounded like a bad, drunken dream.

The film centred on a man who was obsessed with
UFOs. He became obsessed with the vision of a mountain,
tried to recreate it in mashed potatoes, his madness escalat-
ing until he built a huge clay structure that overwhelmed
his family and his living room. When the aliens revealed
themselves, Amisa found the creatures unimpressive and
vapid, their pushpin heads backlit in soapy light.

Still, the queue for tickets snaked all the way outside.
Everyone wanted to encounter aliens. She was busy all day
at the box office, issuing tickets and with no time even to
move, until her bottom was sore on the plastic seat. Just
before the 8.30 p.m. screening on the Thursday, a man
rushed up to the ticket booth. He was middle-aged and
had a craggy, tanned face above which rested a thatch of

black hair that resembled a toupee. He had a moustache like a gothic caterpillar. He bought a top-tiered ticket: S$3.50. As she handed it to him he looked at her straight on. He had a hard, arresting stare, direct yet not impolite. When she glanced up in annoyance, he did not even blink.

At that moment she remembered watching eagles swoop over the lowland marsh with Didi, five years ago, and Uncle Khim Fatt pointing at a shrewd-looking bird roosting on the bough of an oil palm. It had a dappled brown plumage and a white-tipped crest.

'That's a Wallace's hawk-eagle,' Uncle Khim Fatt said. He scribbled something in his notebook.

'Who is Wallace?' Amisa asked. The bird stared at her.

'Probably some rich white army man,' Didi replied, crouching beside her. His small, rough hand rested on her shoulder as he craned his neck to look. 'I've seen this sort of eagle around before, but this one is mighty! Like a bird god.'

They turned their heads at the same time as the eagle shifted on its perch. It spread its wings, showing off their russet span. And then it opened its mouth and called out 'yik yee, yik yee' in a shrill, haughty tone.

Afterwards, they made the long trek in silence back to Kampong Mimpi Sedih. Didi was eleven then and held her hand with a cavalier carefreeness, only letting go when they neared the houses.

The man in front of her bore a remarkable resemblance to that Wallace's hawk-eagle. Stupid moustache aside, the likeness lay in his hooked nose and yellow eyes. Even more astonishing was the complete lack of lust or attraction in

155

his gaze. Maybe he was a homosexual, she thought arrogantly. He was sizing her up as if she was withholding some great wisdom, an answer to a question he had pondered for years.

'Can I help you? Popcorn and kacang puteh are on the other side of the hall,' Amisa said.

'Incredible!' he said, and kept staring. 'Sorry. I can't get over your face,' the man continued. 'It's like the perfect mask.'

She frowned and blinked slowly at him.

'Yet it also unveils,' he said. 'I've never seen a face like yours, not in Singapore, nor all of South East Asia. In Kazakhstan or Tibet, maybe, high up in the sacred passes, but certainly not around here. You're so beautiful you make me slightly sick, if you don't mind my saying so. You probably get this all the time.'

I do, Amisa thought. She crossed her arms.

'I can assure you I am not a pervert,' the man continued. 'I am married and have a small child of my own. But I know the real deal when I see it, and you, young lady, have a face made for film.'

'Er. Thanks,' Amisa replied. She didn't tell him that he looked like a hawk-eagle. He spoke like someone out of a movie. Someone who was sure of himself, even if he was putting on a voice, a South East Asian imitating one of those early American talkies: more than a little affected. Still, her cheeks reddened.

'What is your name?' he asked.

'Amisa.'

'Amisa. I want to work with you. Please can I give you

my card?' There was an odd, curt roll to his 'R's. She wondered where the man came from. He looked Malay but spoke English with an accent she couldn't quite place.

She shrugged as he slipped out a name card from an elegant silver holder.

'Now if you'll excuse me, Amisa, I've got to catch this show. I see great things ahead for us. I have an offer for you: be my star.'

She stared back at him, squinting a little. 'I don't know what you're talking about.'

'It's simple. I'm presenting you with an opportunity, because I think you're special. Take the running time to consider. Let me know what you think when I come out later on.'

She took the card from him as he turned on his heels toward the auditorium. After he had disappeared into the darkness she flipped it over. It was printed on off-white layered paper stock with raised lettering.

ISKANDAR WIRYANTO

VISIONARY · FILM-MAKER · AUTEUR

2 3 0 8 5 8

His phone number was the same digits as her birthday. What are the odds, Amisa thought. She knew what a film-maker was, but the other two words sounded pompous and unfamiliar to her. Maybe he could help her become a fashion model. Maybe he knew people that could put her in touch with people. Was a visionary someone like Yunxi, conjuring messages from the ether?

She didn't sit in on this screening of *Close Encounters*, she'd seen quite enough. Instead she got out a little compact and examined the split ends of her hair, took a diffident shit in the staff toilet, flushed and made elastic, horrible faces at herself in the bathroom mirror. She felt light-headed, a little giddy from this man's compliments. Somehow, they bore a more stately quality than the usual.

135 minutes passed. She watched the door. The Malay families streamed out first, mothers chiding their crying children, followed by the Indian and Chinese teenagers throwing popcorn at each other, the every-raced young couples glazed in each other's juices, the married people trying to keep it together or thinking about work, the lone wolves pondering the universe, and finally Iskandar Wiryanto himself. He strolled out of the theatre with his hands in his pockets, and came right up to her counter. She pretended to be busy with the ledger.

'What a film,' he said. She didn't reply. 'My mind is blown. Well, Amisa?'

She shrugged, uncharacteristically gormless. She couldn't hold his eye. He was staring at her with a candour and familiarity as if they had already known each other for years. After a moment she got out the card from her uniform pocket and held it up.

'You want to work with me like how?'

'Be my lead actress.'

'Is this a joke?' Amisa muttered in Mandarin, before repeating it in English. She cleared her throat and studied the card again. 'Mr Wiryanto, I'm not an actress. I sell tickets only.'

'I know,' he said, smiling so that the wrinkles at the corners of his eyes deepened into creases.

'And I'm married, by the way,' Amisa continued. 'If this is some sort of sleazy offer I am really not interested. If you bother me I'll call my manager over. His name is Rocky.'

'Easy. Calm down,' he said.

She glared at him, her mouth a straight, luscious line.

'It's not like that, I promise. You don't need acting experience, I prefer someone unpolished for the role. And scary, like you.'

'Scary?'

'Yes,' he said. His eyes twinkled. 'I want you to play a monster. A powerful Pontianak, a really big role, bigger than most debut actresses get offered.'

'Pontianak? Why do you want me to act like a ghost? Isn't it bad luck?'

'Ah, at least you're considering it,' he smiled. 'Why, are you superstitious?'

'Not really,' she admitted. 'Where are you from?'

'I've lived everywhere,' he said, with an enigmatic pause. 'But I'm originally from Kota Pontianak, Indonesia.'

'I've not heard of that. Are you making it up?'

He laughed. 'You're funny,' he said. No one had ever called her funny before. 'Of course I'm not making it up. The city sits right on the equator. It's real. I can bring a map and show you.'

She waved her hands in front of her and shook her head. Rocky strolled by, shooting a quizzical glance at her. She checked the clock.

'I don't understand your name card,' Amisa said hurriedly, holding the card up to the light. 'What is an *auteur*? What is a visionary? Why can't you just say it simple?'

'Because it describes me,' Iskandar said, simply. 'Well, what do you think?'

'I'll think about it. Thank you,' Amisa replied. But she noticed him noticing her put the card back into her shirt pocket.

'We start filming in six weeks,' he continued. 'I can't budge on the schedule. However. Call me crazy, but if you're suitable, I'll fire my lead actress. I wasn't very happy with her anyway. She's got nothing on you.'

'Really?'

'Really. If my instinct is correct and you are as great as you look, I'll say the word. I have a really good feeling. I won't be able to sleep tonight.'

She crinkled up her nose and scowled.

'Don't make that face. I'm really excited about you. Please consider.'

'Sure,' Amisa replied. 'See you. Bye.'

'You have my card, Amisa. I hope to hear from you. Goodbye.'

At the double doors Iskandar turned to admire her one last time, then he saluted her and walked off into the humid evening.

You have a face made for film; the real deal; you're perfect; lead actress. She kept on recounting what he said to her, repeating it over and over in her head. At dinner she was dazed, a small dreamy smile playing on her mouth. His praise was like a new dress waiting at home, in a nice carrier bag, in the cupboard. She picked at her noodles but didn't attack her plate with her usual lunchless workday vigour.

'Are you okay?' Wei Loong asked. 'Did some ah beng bother you at work again? Got show him your ring finger? Tell those bastards you're a married woman and I'll wallop them.'

She shook her head slowly. The hawker centre was hot and crowded and families chattered around them, but she felt like she was in another world. The pristine, sweat-free world of the rich and famous. She pictured the man from *Close Encounters* floating up into the kueh tutu-shaped UFO. She basked in an alien spotlight, and it was delicious.

'I met someone interesting today,' she finally said.

'Huh, really?' Wei Loong glanced up at her and then back down to the plate of char kway teow in front of them. He funnelled a piece of fishcake into his mouth and chewed.

'Yes, he's an Indonesian director called Iskandar Wiryanto. He gave me his card. He said he wants to work with me . . .'

Wei Loong took the card and turned it frontwards. A shadow flickered over his face.

'He's making a horror movie. About a Pontianak. You know, the ghost,' Amisa said. 'He offered me the lead role if I come in and audition.'

'Do you think you'll do it?' Wei Loong asked.

'Well, why not?'

He studied the card once more and handed it back to her.

'Imagine how much money we'd have,' Amisa continued, 'if I became an actress? All the shiok things we'll be able to buy for home. All the nice furniture. He's talking about making a trilogy, even.'

'Singapore where got film industry?' Wei Loong asked, waving his chopsticks. 'Last time I know got Melayu movies, but didn't all the studios close?'

'He's financing it himself.'

'How did he find the cash? This bugger sounds shady. Also, P. Ramlee already made Pontianak films a long time ago and they did so well. This one how to fight?'

Amisa shrugged and bit her lip as Wei Loong stared off into the distance, considering something.

'Also, isn't a Pontianak a bit old-fashioned? Hong Kong already got so many ghost story movies – who needs more? Everyone is crazy now about *Star Wars*, and aliens.'

'Yeah, yeah, I get it, it's a stupid idea,' Amisa said. 'And I'm an idiot for suggesting it.'

'I didn't say that,' Wei Loong replied.

Amisa put down her cutlery and grabbed her drink.

'Don't you always tell me I should try more things?' she muttered into her sugar cane juice. 'Now when this comes up you are so doubtful about it.'

Anger crouched on her shoulder like a vulture. *You should be so lucky I'm with you. I can do so much better. Maybe I can be a star, make it all the way to Hong Kong or even Hollywood*, she thought, staring daggers. Wei Loong shifted on his stool. Silence stretched.

'I guess you should try and audition, if it makes you happy,' he finally said. 'You might not get it, but no harm to show up since this big shot asked you. Maybe it will take off.'

'That's what I thought,' she beamed, and the air shifted. 'You never know, right?'

'Yeah. You never know,' Wei Loong said tentatively. 'I think I should go with you, though.'

'Why?'

He sniffed and wiped his nose. 'In case it's something shady.'

'Huh.'

'Like those sleazy photographers who want to take naked pictures of you and sell in JB—'

Amisa let out a loud, equine sigh and pushed bean sprouts around her plate with a plastic spoon. 'I'm not stupid. I can take care of myself.'

'I know.'

'So?' She stared him down and he looked away.

'Nothing, lah. Forget I said anything.'

'Sure.'

After dinner they trudged back to their block in pall-bearer silence. Wei Loong followed her into the cramped blue elevator with the speckled board unpeeling from the wall and shut the accordion door behind him. She reached across and jabbed the button for the sixth floor.

'You don't need to keep pressing it,' he said. 'We're already moving.'

Amisa ignored him and watched the floors rush past upwards through the little window. She remembered riding the old funicular from her childhood, creakily ascending the steep hill – hill and railway both now likely refurbished to a state of gleaming slickness. She saw it happening in this city all the time, the crooked and old being knocked down to make way for the relentlessly new. The city was changing at breakneck speed and she knew Penang would be no different. You either kept up or got left behind in the dust and dereliction.

Wei Loong got the house keys out of his pocket. They heard their telephone ring. He opened the grille and then the main door as the phone kept up its shrill and insistent tone. She stormed over and picked up the green receiver.

'Hello?'

'Xiaofang? Hello? Xiaofang?' It was Jiejie, and she was sobbing.

Amisa cradled the phone closer to her ear. 'I can hear you. Jiejie, what's wrong?'

Her sister was crying too hard for Amisa to make out her words.

'What happened, Jie?'

'It's Didi,' Jiejie said, quickly. She sounded the way she used to as a young girl, hitting her knee hard on something and gulping back tears.

Amisa felt the sugar cane juice rising back up. She could taste it in the tightening chamber where mouth met throat.

'What happened? Did he get into another accident?'

She heard her sister's drawn-out exhalation. Amisa had been perched on the wooden arm of a chair and now she extended the phone cord and sat fully on the seat. Wei Loong hovered in front of her, but she shook her head and waved him away.

'There was a landslide,' Jiejie said. 'This morning it was so rainy. Didi got on his motorcycle anyway. He was going towards the Kuala Lumpur–Karak highway when it happened.'

'What time?'

'Just after ten.'

Amisa tried to remember what she was doing right then. She was probably filling in the box-office ledger in her looping, wayward script, eyelids drooping.

'A tree trunk fell across the highway,' Jiejie continued. Amisa drew her breath. Her sister's voice was a rambling monotone. 'Didi got trapped. All these cars also, and a tour bus. The rescue team took two hours to get to them.'

'Is he okay?' Amisa asked, even though she already knew.

'No,' Jiejie muttered. 'No.'

Amisa's hands were ice-cold. She imagined the deep failure of slopes, debris piling in a matter of seconds. Slurry of muddy water and rocks as they slid, toppled and flowed. Marsala-coloured gushing dirt. It happened like that. She gripped the receiver. It was warm, and hurt pressed so close to her ear.

She started to cry. She thought of the last thing Didi must have seen as he navigated the curve of the road: tangerine horizon and all of a sudden earth rushing to earth rushing to earth. She hoped he hadn't been trapped in the darkness for hours, feeling scared and alone as mud filled his ears, his mouth, his lungs. That his end was quick and painless. She wished she could have done something, anything at all. Changed the weather, stilled the soil. Rung home more often and insisted he come to the phone. Tried to get hold of him yesterday. Told him Didi, please, please, just stay at home. She doubled over, ragged gasps coming in waves. This sadness was so big and savage that she felt she would burst. Didi didn't deserve to die. He was only sixteen. He was her Little Ghost, birdwatcher, braggart, cheeky little shit, and her favourite person in the whole world.

Jiejie sniffed on the other end of the line. Amisa didn't want to hear any more from her, didn't know what else to say. She thought how ridiculous it was, that they were making the same feeble bird sounds from their throats.

After she put down the phone, Wei Loong wrapped his arms around her, but she pushed him off like he was a towel that had fallen from a rack. She went and lay on their bed with her clothes and shoes still on. She interlaced her fingers over her stomach, staring at the ceiling, her mind full of Didi's face when she last saw him. He waved at her from the kerb with the rest of the family, a crooked smile playing on his mouth. What was he thinking? She imagined him now, crushed and still.

She heard her husband enter the bedroom with the tentative steps one would take towards a wild animal.

'Just leave me alone,' she said.

14

CIRCE

2020

The day after I see Szu at the station I can't concentrate. I squint at my screen all morning, wavy lines in my vision like phantom tapeworms swimming. Just after lunch, Gordon calls me into his office.

'How's the *Ponti* promo going?'

'Great,' I reply, and even as I smile I feel the strain in my cheeks.

'You're going to have to be more specific,' Gordon says. He has been staring at me the whole time since I came in. The light from his monitor illuminates the sunspots and greying stubble across his face. He looks like he needs an eye-mask and ten years' sleep.

It has been years since Gordon has addressed me in this slow and reproachful tone. Usually we are chummy. The small hairs on my forearms bristle. I pull my black Baleno cardigan a little tighter over one shoulder and clear my throat.

'Well, we've finished the social media audit. I finalized the overall strategy with Mark and Yihan; we're going for the kitsch old-school Singapura angle. Like the brief called it: "analogue horror for the digital generation". So that's the direction I've taken. I sent you the revised marketing plan last week.'

'Yeah, I've got it up here. Let's see.'

He makes no effort to tilt his monitor towards me. Instead he stares at it with the slack-jawed intensity of a football spectator, as if willing the document to score at any moment. Finally, he turns back to face me.

'I don't know how else to put it,' he says.

I blink at him.

'All this is *blah*, Circe. Pages and pages of *blah*. It doesn't pull me in. We need to be great, not middle-of-the-road. You get it?'

'Yes,' I reply. I feel my stomach tighten. The tapeworm was poisoned out of me a month ago, the X-rays proved it, but sometimes I feel like it still lives in me and I don't know whether I am disgusted or mildly comforted by this.

'The problem is, I just don't think you're engaging with the brief,' Gordon says. 'Listen, Circe . . . you and I, to put it bluntly, we're not super young any more. We have to work even harder to think outside the box. You know what I mean? The world has changed even from when you joined till now, it's moving at such a rate.'

I'm not comfortable being lumped into the same group as him. I'm thirty-three. Gordon is in his mid forties, with expensively highlighted hair and a short back and sides that makes him look more forced than trendy.

'I hear what you're saying,' I reply, in the practised, conciliatory tone I reserve for difficult clients. I try to smile but feel my stomach flip.

'Look, Circe,' Gordon says, but this time his voice softens. 'I know things are not easy for you right now. With the divorce. It's a lot to take on.'

'I'm handling things fine,' I reply. 'To be honest, I got a stomach ache.'

'Okay,' Gordon says. His face clouds over. 'Then I'll get straight to the point. Is it true that you haven't been to any of the archive screenings? You haven't seen *Ponti!* or *Ponti 2* or *Ponti 3: Curse of the Bomoh*? Not even a *single one* of these, when our client explicitly asked us to link the promo back to the original movies? What is going on? Wake up your ideas, Circe! This kind of stuff is *basic*! If you were an intern I'd fire you straight away.'

'I'm sorry,' I say, meaning it.

'It's not like you to act like this. Are you sure everything is okay?'

I nod. I don't know how to explain it.

'Okay. What do you do when you're promoting a remake and you don't have the rough cut of the film in question?'

'You watch all the source material.'

'I shouldn't have to tell you this.'

'I'm sorry.' I feel like an asseverating little mouse.

'You know what to do, then.'

I gather my papers and tablet and leave. I bet Jeanette is the one who ratted on me. Jeanette, with her perfect ass and impeccable flirtatious timing. Two hours later, outside the screening room, she glances up from her phone and says, 'Oh, it's you,' as if she hadn't been expecting me.

The lights have already dimmed as we settle into our seats. I lean back into the plush chair and feel my cheeks flush with a swirl of anxiety and adrenaline. I always refused to watch the films. I preferred to hear Szu's accounts of their grandeur, imagine Amisa in them rather than familiarize myself with the actual footage, diminish her power. Especially after Amisa died, they became ghostly relics. I have a heavy feeling in my throat, like I'm being judged, like I'm disrespecting the dead.

Every time I shift, the chair creaks. The screen flickers on and the title credits appear: *PONTI 2*, unsteady white words across a canopy of brown and green. The sound of strings gives me a sense of rising dread. The camera pans out from a quiet dirt road into wet green paddy fields flanked by traveller's palms with their parched, fan-like leaves. The shot keeps broadening until it takes in the entire landscape of sparse houses with thatched orange roofs, sheds of rusty, corrugated steel, and the odd silo, joined together by thin, snaking roads. Was this the sort of place Amisa grew up in, I wonder? Broad, sun-parched stretches of nowhere. I glance to my right. Jeanette has her eyes glued to her phone.

A rattling truck appears, white and blue, coming down the dirt road. A handsome man frowns in the driver's seat. He squints and grimaces all the way to his destination. In the village he strides through the shadow of palm trees and a cluster of Malay villagers gather around him, wearing tengkoloks and baju melayus. When one of the men starts to talk, he is dubbed over in a gravelly American voice.

'We need your help!' he tells the hero. 'There is a Pontianak terrorizing our village. She's claimed so many of our men's lives. If we're not careful, we will run out of men. She looks like a beautiful young woman, but don't be deceived.'

'I know her,' the hero replies, with a determined set in his jaw. It turns out his brother was murdered by this same creature in *Ponti!* before.

How to defeat this spectral interloper? How to set things right? Thirty-five minutes in, the hero trundles through vegetation, carrying a parang for safety, a frown clouding his handsome features. He has been warned about how dangerous this monster in the trees is. She's worse than a typical Pontianak. She's Ponti! with a shriek, an exclamation mark. She is furious because she will never find peace. She got her heart broken from a stillborn child and her husband cheating and beating her. She's unreasonable and crazy and every womanly wrong.

The hero searches for her past the tranquil fallow, deep into the untidy, sloping greenery that borders the banana plantation. Telltale musical cues: strings swirling. I squeeze my eyes shut for a moment. I can't bear to look. Cut to silence. A pause.

'Did you come here to find me?' a voice asks: sweet, inquiring.

The man whips his head around. The banana trees rustle. It is dark in the clearing, and he looks confused as to where he should be searching. And then. There she is, standing calm and coquettish in a pool of moonlight, as if she's been waiting there all along. Amisa is the most expensive-seeming thing in this cheap movie. She looks so young it makes my heart hurt. She smiles and her eyes are bright and playful. It strikes me hard for the first time: film is such a deceptive fiction. Here is a woman back from the dead – only she doesn't exist any more outside of this screen, her body rendered in slightly blurry footage.

The last time I saw her she was the opposite of larger than life: so real and impossibly small. She lay in bed, lightly shutting her eyes. She was in constant pain and her body reflected it, her skin both waxy and dried-out. Her cheekbones were too angular, tipping off the knife-edge of sleek straight into ghoulishness. She wore a blue wrap around her head, a vestige of pride or even vanity. And she looked very, very old. Isn't that a sign of humbling maturity, realizing that the people I dismissed as impossibly ancient at various times of my life weren't actually that much older than my present self? She was only in her forties. Amisa on screen looks no older than twenty-one. She's in the prime of her beauty. Her hair goes down to her waist, and even with powder dusted on her to make her look a little undead, she gleams.

'Who are you? Have I met you before?' Her mouth moves just out of sync with the American voiceover artist. The dubbed voice has that antiquated, mid-Atlantic English diction that sounds nothing like Singaporean slang.

I can't place my finger on what else is so uncanny about watching Amisa on screen – and then I realize. It's because she looks so *happy*. She beams at the actor like she's in love with him. She lays one hand gently over the other, crossed in front of her body, ladylike in her white shroud dress.

She was nothing like that in real life. Whenever she entered the kitchen or the sitting room, I couldn't take my eyes off her because she was so glamorously sad. Always something heavy to ponder.

The hero sprints back through the lalang fields as fast as his feet can carry him. He wants so badly to warn the neighbouring villagers – although, when did a plan like that ever work? Nobody will believe him.

The beautiful young woman saunters down the street, makes a right, heads into the hero's patio. She takes her time. The tracking shot takes us every step of the way, focusing on the leisurely sway of her hips, the loveliness of her supple shoulders in a white floral dress. Once she's invited inside, the camera pans out and we see her face. Amisa smirks. The hero's good wife gasps. The Pontianak reveals her true, hideous nature, and thunder claps. She looks garish, deranged, red-lipped; monster make-up caked on like papier mâché. With a flutter like a sheet being aired out, the Pontianak flies away. The body of a plantation worker is revealed under the fronds of a nearby tree, blood-ied and bruised. The camera zooms in on his face with one eyeball sucked out, the socket a gelatinous prosthetic pulp, like splattered raspberries. She's torn his stomach open. Blood everywhere, slightly too pink to be fully convincing, but it's sickening to look at. All too much. I cover my face with my right hand, peer through my fingers. A piercing scream and the sound of frantic drums: shot of the good wife hunched in the dirt as an old woman hurries to comfort her. The drum beats to the quickening of my own pulse. Dizzy angles. Shaky cuts. Something about the knowing set of the old woman's face and her skinny limbs reminds me of Aunt Yunxi.

I met Yunxi for the first time when I had been going over to Szu's house for a little over a week. She came up behind me and tapped my elbow lightly: this tanned, very skinny woman whom I'd previously only heard murmuring and rummaging within the locked room behind the darkened antechamber. That particular area always reeked of incense merged with something much harder to pin down: sweet, and a little rotten. If I had to place it, it smelt most like frangipanis – old, pungent flowers left to wilt in the rain – mixed with armpits.

'Circe? I've heard so much about you. Szu has told us such nice things. Let's have a look at you,' Yunxi said in Mandarin.

I stood frozen in the corridor, eyes darting around the room as she regarded me from top to bottom, left to right, and back again.

'You've got a robust constitution, a stable family, not much to atone for . . .' The old woman's voice was as low as a man's with a sore throat. It was a voice that seemed to rise up from the floorboards.

'You're not mourning anybody . . .' All that was true, so far. Szu, who was in the bathroom, had told me about what her aunt did for a living. Her clairvoyancy made me nervous.

'There's nothing to be nervous about,' Yunxi said. I started.

'You've got a special energy,' Yunxi continued, smiling to reveal a row of small, straight and yellowed teeth. 'But you've got to be careful about your behaviour.'

'What behaviour?'

The walls of the four corners of the room seemed to narrow in over my head, and a dark, heavy feeling began to plume within me, like ink in water.

'Circe?' Jeanette is staring at me intently. The lights have come on in the projector room and one of the spot-lights shoots straight into my pupils. My head and limbs feel heavy, as if my body just shut down.

*

After the screening I cut through Haji Lane on the way to Bugis MRT station. It's 4.45 p.m. and the buildings and branches are tinged in rose gold, skyline gleaming like a credit card commercial. Walking down the stretch of manicured shophouses with their candy-hued accordion windows, I come across no fewer than four different teen-age girls posing against blank, white walls. Their friends or boyfriends stand opposite them, taking shot after shot with phones or angling DSLRs. Each time after the camera clicks the girls strike a minutely variant pose. Each girl seems primed for some sort of pagan desert apocalypse: wide-brimmed hats, billowing vests, and bandage-like leggings impractical in the tropical heat. I guess this is what is in right now: the same ugly shit only the beautiful can pull off. They are either fashion bloggers, or blogshop models.

The last girl before I round the corner is the prettiest. She commands attention. She is far too thin. Some things don't change – I remember my convent-school days: girls pretending to subsist all week on small green apples, then relenting into cup noodle binges; the soft Japanese-horror-movie retching that emanated from the farmost cubicles.

This girl is the goal of all that lunchtime crying: ragdoll limbs and satin spar skin, blunt fringe framing her hard, lovely eyes. There is something so barbed and familiar about her. The past rises up like the heat pimples that itch along the scalloped neckline of my top. And then it clicks. Clara Chua: one of the beautiful, bionic mega-bitches from school. I can't believe I still remember her name.

The girl notices me watching, and juts out her attractively pointy jawline. Her gaze is both challenging and entreating. Clara Chua dissolves.

Her boyfriend stops clicking the camera and shoots me a stare. In the ruthless world of teenagers, anyone above thirty is either cool or creepy. What am I but some weird watching frump? An office drone in Mango slacks. I hasten away into the tree-lined neutrality of North Bridge Road. At least I haven't come across a Szu clone today. They seem to be teeming the city suddenly, but then I did just spend eighty-four minutes being forced to watch her late mother terrorizing people.

Out now in the late afternoon heat I feel overcome by this weighty, gluttonous sensation. I feel it in my skin and my soul and the shame of being caught admiring some gorgeous, stupid teen. I check the time on my phone. I've got to catch a train to Outram for a meeting.

I reach the traffic lights at Ophir Road and when the green circle shifts to amber I spot them. Just on the other side of the junction, waiting. They are standing beside another couple, or another pair of people. I recognize Jarrold immediately, the way a dog knows its owner, or an owner knows her dog. There is no chronology or politics to this moment of recognition. It just is. No labels of 'former' or 'husband' attached to what I see. I'm just a darting pair of eyes, hoping he hasn't noticed me. I take a step sideways and try to blend into a group of university students.

It's been one year and maybe three months since Jarrold and I met to finalize our separation and any outstanding matters around the sale of our flat. Even though we actually had things to talk about, stuff to settle, that meeting was s o maudlin and uncomfortable that the memory of it still makes me cringe. In all the time since we've managed to avoid each other, maintaining our safe ambits. Jarrold likes to have work drinks at Dempsey, so fine, that's a no-go zone. He knows I've conquered Verdi, that amazing Italian place on Duxton Road. I guess we never bothered to apportion Bugis and its surrounding area.

My soon-to-be-ex-husband turned thirty-seven in May. He's gained a little weight around the jowls, and is wear ing a pale-blue office shirt with a starched collar. Entirely nondescript. But he looks good. Healthy. Happier. He's talking animatedly to a girl who appears a little younger than me. I give her the once-over from behind the safety of a stranger's shoulder. She has long, straight hair and wears a white sleeveless blouse and black skirt. So far, so boring. Is she his girlfriend? Colleague? Friend? It's hard to tell. They are standing close, taking the liberty with each other's personal space that conveys some kind of intim-acy. She laughs mid sentence. I can't hear her, but I hate her already. The light changes and I stick to the students, manage to avoid Jarrold and his companion entirely. I'm so angry and alone I could kill someone.

I hurry to the mouth of the MRT station and even though we've gone in opposite directions I get this prickly paranoia that they have turned around and are walking the same way as me. I don't dare look behind me.

15

SZU

2003

It's the first day of the wake and all the tables and chairs are set up, both fresh and artificial flowers arranged to distraction. They delivered the body this morning. Two men wheeled out the coffin from the back of the hearse. They set it up with the perfunctory tact and calm of professionals, across two long wooden stools with her head positioned towards the entrance of our house. *That's my mother's body in there, there and not in her room or the hospital bed.* I kept disbelieving, right until they opened the expensive walnut lid to let us have a look. They call it a half-couch lid because it doesn't expose her legs. I mean, why would anyone need to see her legs? Just her face and hands. I think that even the term half-couch sounds disrespectful. Couches get sat on.

Aunt Yunxi explained what would be included in the package from the funeral parlour, the cosmetic work, but I wasn't ready for the result. My mother barely looks like herself. Her skin has been lacquered yellow with two huge blush marks to lend her some colour. Her mouth is painted a rose pink that she would have hated: too sweet. Her small, delicate hands are folded stiff.

My aunt is dressed in black, her mouth pinched into a half-smile, half-scowl. She keeps wringing her hands, and doesn't mind if I notice, but if one of the men from the funeral home glances over she puts them down. She looks even skinnier than usual, as if she'll snap like a twig if she moves too quickly. I feel skinny too. Secretly I am deriving a loose and tiny joy from feeling thin. I wonder if Circe and the other girls at school will notice and quietly agree that I look improved. I haven't eaten much this week. Just a couple of slices of fishcake and the plain, clear bone broth in a huge vat in the fridge. My appetite has flown out of the window, the same way as routine. Right now our existence is centred on my mother and the small squares of mourning cloth pinned to our right sleeves.

A car door slams and I turn to look. Two men are coming down the driveway; one tall, the shorter one hobbling. Their features are obscured by the shadows from the trees and when they get close I don't recognize them.

Our new visitors pay their respects to my mother, bowing thrice. I parrot out my lines: there are refreshments in the cooler; plain water over there. Hot tea on request. Peanuts on that table.

'Thank you, Szu,' the taller man says. I'm startled by my name. 'We're okay.' He sits down and the plastic chair creaks. 'Your mother was a good actress.'

'You worked with her?'

'Yes,' he replies. 'And my brother also.' He gestures to the man on his right, who has lit a cigarette. 'Ah Choon over here was the electrician. I was special effects. We worked with your ma for *Ponti!* and *Ponti 2.*'

Hearing him name the films I feel a drop in my chest. Somehow it was easy to forget it was a collaborative effort and not just all about her.

'Your mother was wonderful on screen,' the first man continues. 'Anyone who watched her can't forget that face. She had real star quality, she was a *ming xing*. We loved working with her.'

'Thank you,' I reply, my voice tightening.

The second man smirks through his half-finished cigarette. His brother shoots him a look.

'Szu!' Circe calls out. She's coming down the driveway, closely followed by Mr and Mrs Low. Just three steps behind them, shuffling his feet and with his eyes glued to his phone, is Leslie.

'Excuse me,' I say to the two visitors. I go up to Circe. We exchange a limp half-hug. I haven't seen her in a day. She seems twitchy, excitable.

'Where's your aunt?' Circe asks me.

'Somewhere close by. Probably busy.'

'I'm so sorry, Szu,' Circe's mother Magda says.

'Hello, Mr and Mrs Low,' my aunt calls out in her clipped, accentless English.

'My condolences, Auntie,' Magda says.

Leslie looks up from his phone; glances at his parents busy talking and then at me. I can't hold his gaze for more than a second.

'I never met your mother,' he mumbles. 'But I'm sorry.'

'It's okay,' I reply. I can feel Circe's eyes on me. Her stare is electric. Like one of those charged, humming insect killers I sometimes see in outdoor coffee shops. I'm filled not just with worry but the actual belief that she can read my mind. I cross and uncross my arms, shift my weight from left foot to right and back again. Time is taking time. More strangers shuffle up and then back down the driveway, a dreary conveyor of condolences and muted smiles. My aunt keeps collecting white envelopes. Why have I never seen any of these people before?

'Your mother knew a lot of people,' Circe says. 'I thought she didn't go out much.'

'All these people are from her acting,' I reply. 'Actually, I just met these two men over there who were part of the crew—'

'But do you recognize anyone? And have you met, like, anyone famous?'

'Circe, don't be kaypoh,' Leslie interjects. 'Why are you interrogating her? It's none of your business.'

'I'm just curious.'

'It's cool,' I say, trying to be cool. 'I don't know anyone. They're all randoms.' I sound apologetic, in spite of myself.

'Wakes are like that, I guess,' Leslie says. 'Can I find any of your mom's films online?'

'Nah, nothing online.'

'What were they about? Besides Pontianaks.'

'That's about it. Just the one Pontianak.'

'Oh.'

I remember the first and only time I tried to show *Ponti!* to Circe, just nine months ago. She had started to fidget after ten minutes, checking her phone, and we stopped the tape when Josephine knocked and called us downstairs for dinner. And all the time as I chewed the Lows' white rice and the Lows' steamed pomfret and stir-fried garlic chai sim, I thought of how their food tasted brighter and saltier in my mouth, better-tasting but worse for me, even if my aunt had cooked with the same ingredients. I felt a slow, icky shaft of shame spread from one side of my face to the other and funnel down into my bad stomach as I recalled the part of the film we'd paused on: the village doctor shouting a warning, his mouth a dubbed, boring 'O'. After dinner we went back up to Circe's room and I took the tape out of the VCR. I never tried showing her the films again.

*

'Can we go to your room?' Circe asks. I shrug and look for my aunt. She's busy talking to Magda, who has her arms crossed over her tummy, head tilted attentively. Mr Low stands close by, eyes to the floor, with his hands in his chino pockets. I lead Circe and Leslie into the house, down the vanilla-coloured corridor with its outdated geometrical wallpaper and the cracks in the ceiling.

We file into my bedroom and Circe pulls the door shut behind her. My room is too small for three people. Circe sits on my bed and the springs creak. I sit down beside her and the soft mattress makes our bodies sag into each other.

Leslie moves towards my green swivel chair but Circe gestures to the space on the other side of me. I feel a welter of disappointment and relief when he ignores her. I panic about whatever I've left exposed and scattered across my desk. Jotted-down lyrics. Pieces of foolscap paper, filled with inelegant, incorrect sums.

'Do you want water or something?' I ask them.

'Nah, we're fine,' Circe says. She picks up a book from my bedside table and flips through it, squints at the blurb on the back.

'*We Have Always Lived In The Castle*. Sounds creepy,' Circe says. 'Is it about knights and stuff?'

'Not really.'

'Is it scary?'

'Kind of.'

'Hmm.' She flips through it fast. It's a thin volume and she is damaging the spine.

'Kor, have you heard of it?'

'No, Sisi, I haven't,' Leslie replies. 'Don't be annoying.'

'I'm not annoying,' Circe says, but she stops talking.

Leslie sighs deeply and stares into the small, blank brightness of his phone. I wonder whom he's messaging. I've never actually been in the same enclosed space as both of them before. I pick at a scab on my left arm, a tiny half-circle of dried blood from where a mosquito bite became unbearable. I wait for them to make conversation, but the silence drags on. Every few seconds I adjust the position of my feet or scratch my arms or the back of my neck.

I hear the faint murmur of people outside the window. Voices, new and low. Everybody is a solemn stranger, and they all seem to love my mother. Their worship and affection for her makes me uncomfortable. They are all too late. Where were they two, four, six months ago? Years back, when she stopped leaving this house on a regular basis? I want to wave my arms around and say, look! She wasn't even that nice or perfect! Where were you when she was in such agony she had to be injected with morphine? And when she couldn't even speak, or eat, or use her jaw, even though her eyes told me she was hungry, and she had so much to say. I'm a bad person because I haven't let go of how she crumpled me up like a ball of paper my whole life, and now that she's gone I don't know how to get the creases out. I wish these people would stop pretending she matters so much. Stop acting, is what I want to tell them. That's what she did. Leave it to the professionals.

'Your mom and your aunt—' Leslie begins. He looks unsure of how to continue. Circe puts down the book and stares at her brother.

'Do they really do – spirit medium stuff – or is it, like, for show only? If you don't mind me asking.' Leslie puts his hand to his neck, glances up at me sheepishly.

'It's for real,' I reply, and look at Circe, but her eyes flick to the floor and don't meet mine again.

'Ah, must have gotten confused,' Leslie says. 'Sorry.'

'It's fine,' I say.

'It' is so many things I'm not sure I believe. 'It' is the silence that descends upon the triangular space between us, thick as corn syrup, and just as artificial. Tucked politely away is a hint of judgement in the air. I can sense it. Circe sighs and brings her right hand to her mouth, observes her cuticles.

'So, uh. Do you believe in it? Spirits and psychic stuff?' Leslie asks.

'Sometimes,' I reply. 'What – what about you?'

'Hm. It's hard to tell. I don't think so,' Leslie says. 'But you never know.'

'Yeah, I know what you mean,' I say, and nod.

Circe makes a sound in between a snort and like she is blowing her nose.

'Gotta go pee,' she says. She gets up so quickly that she knocks my knees as she goes past. And then she's out of the room, pulling the door shut behind her.

Leslie glances around my walls, because there is nothing else to see besides my desk or me. My cheeks redden at the torn-out magazine page stuck beside my mirror. It's a Neutrogena ad and the model looks possibly French and no older than nineteen. She has chestnut-coloured hair up in a chignon and her two hands have come to rest on either side of her jaw. I stuck the advert up over a year ago. She stared out smack from the middle of the April 2003 issue of *Seventeen* magazine. I felt both sickened and arrested by her bare, impossible beauty. No amount of New and Improved! Deep-Clean Cream Cleanser could make me look like that. She faces the camera dead on with the steely boldness of a charmed being.

Leslie Low is another of the charmed ones. He is nineteen and glaringly cute, and next March he is getting conscripted for National Service. Circe says that he will vanish into the forests of Pulau Tekong for infantry training, and the trees will spit him out nine weeks later – near-bald, profane and unrecognizable. The Internet at school tells me the word Tekong means obstacles. Supposedly the island is filled with obstacles and hungry ghosts.

Boys go missing, and the next day their remains are found bundled up neatly along the route-march trail.

Leslie clears his throat and stares out of the window. My palms are cold and I feel a strain in my neck. I've pulled the net curtains shut so all we can see is the blurry outlines of people, like shadow puppets, moving with dreary and orchestrated purpose.

'You got a cool house,' Leslie says.

'Thanks.'

'Yeah, it's got a lot of character to it. I like the garden.'

'Thanks.'

I could ask him about NS, I guess. How he is finding it, whether he's ready, how he felt about his A-Level results, what he will study at university. (Economics and Accountancy – I know this already.)

'It'd be nice to have a—' Leslie starts.

'Do you like shoegaze?' I spit out. My voice crackles with the effort of bravado. I clear my stupid throat. 'Sorry – what did you say?'

'Oh. It'd be nice to have such a big garden,' Leslie says. 'What were you saying?'

'Just – it's. Do you like shoegaze?'

'Huh?

'Shoegaze,' I say, my soul wilting. 'You know, shoegaze music. Like Ride and Slowdive and—' The blank look on his face stops me continuing.

'Dunno what that is,' Leslie replies. 'Sorry. You and Sisi are always into the most random things. Like your cheem foreign films. Or all that old-school, old-man music from the seventies or whatever, way before we were born.'

'Then what kind of music are you into?' I ask him.

Before he can reply I hear a snigger just on the other side of the door.

'*What kind of music are you into?*' Circe repeats, in a saccharine, modulated imitation of my voice. She enters the room with a smirk.

'Jay Chou and Taiwanese R & B,' Leslie says with not a trace of diffidence. Circe sits on the opposite side of me from before.

'You're so cheena,' Circe says to Leslie. She turns to me with a sneer that makes her resemble an evil twelve-year-old. 'My brother is such an ah beng. He secretly wishes he were a Taiwanese pop star. Just like Jay Chou.'

'What's wrong with Jay Chou?' Leslie asks, unabashed. 'I bet Szu doesn't know about the crap you play when you think nobody is listening. All that indie is just for show . . . when you're not around, Szu, Circe listens to Britney and tries out all the dance moves . . .' He grins as he spills this and I notice his big, crooked teeth for the first time.

'Bullshit,' Circe replies.

'Phoney,' Leslie says.

Circe glares at him for a second, and then she shrugs and says, 'So what if I like Britney? People are entitled to like what they like. Isn't that right, Szu?'

'Guess so,' I mutter.

I remember all the times she's made fun of Clara Chua for idolizing Britney Spears, because Britney is pure bubble-gum and isn't even the latest thing. Right now people are more into the punkier Avril Lavigne. Clara is steadfast in her untrendy adoration and Circe calls it pathetic.

It is so much harder to detest your only friend in the world when *1)* it is like deciding whether to pick the sole option on the menu or to go hungry; *2)* her hatefulness comes and goes like a rash or a fever; *3)* the memory of her kindness is so fresh that it encourages forgiving; *4)* sometimes her slights are so slight I wonder if I imagined it and I'm the one being mean, undeserving.

Just two nights ago I escaped from this house and Circe tucked me into bed and let me curl up against her back like the grandest snail. I don't know what I would have done with myself, when the walls of my own bedroom seemed to bear down on me. Every tile and turning was a reminder that these spaces are the same but my mother wouldn't be. I spent so much time detesting her. Now that she's gone my sadness feels murky and unearned. How to make sense of it? Circe didn't press me to explain. She patted my hair and put me to sleep. Now she's like a different person, this hard little Grinch scowling beside me.

16

CIRCE

2020

By the time I finish my meeting and come home I'm starving. My flatmate Julius is still out and I'm grateful to have the place to myself. I change into my dreariest, comfiest pyjamas. I'm too lazy to cook so I have four slices of Gardenia bread for dinner instead. One spread thickly with kaya and butter, two with strawberry jam, one with plain butter and white sugar. My tongue goes numb with too much sweetness and my gut will complain later, even without the treacherous worm. I hear the neighbours watching television through the left wall and I wonder if they resent me as much as I resent them for the noise of their living.

I glare into the bathroom mirror as I wipe my eyeliner off. It's the same face, all right; I'm one of those people who has looked eerily unchanged since childhood. I've remained constant in my nondescriptness. I pull at my skin; the flaws I started noticing in flickers from my mid-twenties have decided to stay put and pronounce themselves even more strongly on my face. There are three lines on my forehead, stretched across my skin like guitar strings. I try to smooth them and they disappear for a moment, but only a moment. There are crinkles at the corner of my eyes, and shadows. Pigment spots where the sun hits.

Magazines, with their phoney advocacy of self-love, say that you learn to enjoy being yourself the older you get. In spite of your decrepitude, your decreasing worth. Be a peacefully deteriorating woman; covet, but also accept your lot. Believe in cosmetic products and their promises of preservation. You are supposed to celebrate, not to complain; to ripen like a bottle of wine, not a banana; to thrive, not to rot. You are supposed to hold a hairbrush and lip-sync with gusto to Abba or Beyoncé with your sisters and girlfriends. You are supposed to buy tickets for movies that feature montages precisely like that. You are supposed to hand over your money and embrace the straitjacket of who you are and your ageing. Even in this stifling city, where so many interminably young girls on the street seem to be made of porcelain and no matter how many bowls of mee pok they wolf down in food courts, they still seem to fit into their blogshop skirts.

I'm too young to say I'm too old for this. I'm too pasty for someone who lives near the Equator. I finish washing my face and turn to my hands. I can see and feel my worry all over, and it doesn't make sense because I've built nothing valuable from this worry, and in my head I still feel as confused as I did at twenty years old.

The front door creaks open and then slams. It's Julius, coming back from a work event at some edgy new bar in Jalan Besar. I wonder from the clumsy way he's putting things down if he is a little drunk. I towel dry my hands and make my way to the living room.

'Hey, Circ,' Julius calls out. His face is a little flushed.

'Hi,' I mumble. Julius is standing in a radius of yellow light under the living room lamp and he too looks old. Bloated and faded at the edges. I wonder how much longer we will live together. Our lease runs out in November, and it's already August. This year is already a leathery leaf curling out at the edges.

We sit and drink jasmine tea at the kitchen table.

'Well?' Julius asks, after some time.

'Well what?'

'How was your day?'

'Fine. I'm really tired.'

'You look sad. Are you okay?'

'Yeah, of course. Why would you say I look sad?'

'It's all over your face.'

'How was your night?'

'Same old lah.' He cocks his head to one side and scrutinizes me with drunken exaggeration. 'Are you sure you're okay? You seem bothered.'

'I'm fine,' I reply. 'I told you already.'

'What's with the attitude? Relax.' Julius frowns and I look away.

I've always thought that telling people to relax only makes them more rigid. The muscles at the back of my neck tense and ache.

'Just asking because I'm concerned,' Julius continues, drumming his too-long nails on his ridged porcelain cup. 'I didn't mean anything else by it.'

'Look, Julius, I'm sorry,' I say. 'I just had a really long day. Work is a headache.'

'Okay,' Julius replies.

We sound just like a tepid, long-married couple. Both of us seem to realize this at the same moment. Julius clears his throat. I don't know how to fix the awkwardness that wafts over the table like a fart. I picture Julius naked for the very first time; get a glimpse of his long, untoned body. As if he can read my mind, he gets up in an exposed scurry. His chair scrapes against the kitchen tiles.

'Guess I better sleep soon, got an early start,' he says, and yawns.

I can see the greyish-pink of his gums and gullet and it reminds me of my tapeworm and the way it abseiled audaciously down my throat, months ago. Just a faint memory now: unfunny how pain acquires a foggy, second-hand patina in order for us to endure its inevitable repetition. I wonder if I could call the tapeworm a form of pain. It didn't actually hurt. Yet the invasiveness and disgust I felt from its parasitic thievery – the outrage – pained me.

Julius gathers his things and gets up.

'You know, it wouldn't hurt you to be nicer,' he blurts as he leaves the room. 'I was only trying to help. You shouldn't take things out on other people.'

He's right, and also drunk. Before I can reply he shuts the bathroom door quietly, click and lock. Julius always takes forever in the bathroom and he's deathly silent during the endless minutes between entering and the hiss of the shower. Sometimes I wonder if he goes in there to meditate. Even the gruesome, echoey plop of a turd hitting the toilet would be demystifying. It's reassuring to be reminded that we are all full of shit. It makes me feel united with my fellow humans.

I make my way to bed. As I smooth overpriced night cream on my face, I marvel at the irony of it: how I left one HDB flat and a marriage to move into a more impersonal, rootless dwelling – dimmer, sparsely furnished, no strings attached, no baggage – only to have the same thing happen. Tense, arid evenings, a stalemate of two, a man telling me to be kinder, better, to try harder; giving me advice I don't want to hear, instructions. When did I become so weak and easily upset? When did I switch from doing to being done to?

*

Jarrold and I met at university, during the first week of my first year in NUS. He was a third-year orientation leader, or an OL as he would call it (he was very fond of acronyms). We met at the Ice Cream Bash for the Faculty of Arts and Social Sciences, where he was handing out cups of ice cream. He looked as happy and buoyant as a Labrador. I went up to him and asked for mint chocolate. He gave it to me, double-scooped with a smile. I ate in front of Jarrold with a cutesy shyness, licking the neon-orange spoon like a kitten. I'd noticed him earlier and already knew his name but asked for it anyway, and introduced myself as Circe. Like most people, he stumbled on how to say it.

Jarrold Koh. Jarrold Koh Kok Yang. J.K.K.Y. I still remember the solar haze that once gathered around his name when I thought about him. Back in 2006, JK had fashionably floppy hair and the carefree demeanour of a young man who believed he had everything ahead of him. Even better, my friend Aishah told me that Jarrold used to be severely overweight, but the rigours of national service converted him into literally half the man he used to be. I really liked that. Later on, when he showed me pictures of his teenhood, he looked like an indistinct version of his current self. It had the effect of making him seem more tentative. At the time, how I admired his discipline, loved the idea that he had condensed himself so that he would occupy less space in the world. There was something poetic about that.

Eleven years later, after our relationship had grown big and strong and placidly devoured our twenties, things simply collapsed. The evening that my husband broke down at me, we were stranded in City Hall, the station buzzing and agitated as a hive full of worker bees. Jarrold's face was two wet eyes, an unremarkable nose, mouth formed into a downwards cashew shape.

Crying emasculated him. I felt bad and backwards for thinking so, and this feeling bad didn't redeem or negate my meanness, it worsened it.

'Sorry, sorry,' I kept muttering under my breath. 'It's gonna be okay,' I said, though I didn't mean it.

Over time, unwittingly, I had come to perceive him as someone I worked with but didn't know very well and would never consort with socially. Someone who 'um'ed and 'aah'ed, who apologized so incessantly that it was irritating. Every evening we talked over each other in circles and absolutes, casting desperate blame spells and general-izations like a blanket over a dying animal. By that point it was *you ALWAYS do this* and *why do you ALWAYS do that*. Everything we did together was fraught and boring. I developed a new-found appreciation for walls and doors and the socially acceptable distraction of my device screens.

Above us the announcement ticker kept on changing just a millisecond before I could focus on what it read. An impersonal voice called out that the north-bound train was arriving in two minutes. When I looked up the air around Jarrold seemed to fizz with finality.

'Sorry?' he said. 'Wah lau. Don't you have anything else to say? Is that all you've got? "Sorry?" Ten years and that's it?'

Eleven years, I thought. I shook my head at him. I looked around at the aunties rushing to trains with their herds of kids and sloe-eyed young women texting as they walked and hair-gelled uncles and NS boys with their green caps and heavy rucksacks – everyone brimming with unremarkable purpose. How I envied their detachment. I shivered.

'To be honest, I don't know what else I can say, Jar-rold,' I finally replied.

It was all I could think of to respond, and even as I said it I thought of how the phrase 'to be honest' has always seemed to me to draw attention to a default of dishonesty. We were standing on either side of a semicircular marble bench. Jarrold gulped and began to speak in a choked, testy voice that made me fidget with the fear of being over-heard.

'Listen,' he said. 'I know I'm nothing special.' He kept on staring at me imploringly, trying to catch my eye. 'I know you could get on the MRT right now or you could glance around the CBD and see ten other guys just like me.'

He was right: by that point, in my dreams, he was always a shadow or a series of shadows, not even a real face to pin my frustration on.

'Circe, are you even listening?' Jarrold asked. 'Because you're not being fair, or very nice to me. I'm no CEO, obviously, I'm no stock trader. I don't have a lot of money or any special skills. I know that you don't take my job very seriously—'

'That's not true—' I interrupted.

'Wait, let me finish—'

'I don't know where you got that from,' I said. 'You can't just accuse me of things with no basis. I *like* that you work for Chan Brothers. It fulfils you. We've gotten some amazing travel discounts. I've never said I don't take it seri—'

'That's not the point, Circe.' he said, and his face was all red.

'What is the point, then?'

'Look. I love you. And isn't that something? I care about us. I still think we can work. But it won't happen if you don't try as well.'

I squirm internally at *love* and *us* and *we*. I didn't know how to tell this husband-shaped human that I had been trying all my life, and at just thirty-one, I was sick of it. Standing there, in a split second I ran through our entire shared history: tentative first love at university, being coupled together, BBQs and pot-lucks with other couples, nobody discussing their sex lives openly, hand-holding as if life depended on it. Sentosa Beach. Triple dates to the cinema. Cell groups. Long-term safety. Short-term smugness at how sorry our shy single friends seemed. Applying for our HDB flat together. Tepid in-jokes. Culinary classes after work. Couples' aikido. Packaged diving holidays. My aunts and uncles smiling benignly at me, looking hopefully towards my tummy. Spiralizers. Five-year schemes.

No more of that. Even thinking about it now I feel squeezed. I knew I'd rather be alone than keep on pretending. Who my true self is, I'm not even sure.

Maybe my sanctimonious brother Leslie is correct: I'm shallow and mean.

*

The following Monday morning I find a brown envelope on my desk at work. Made out just to Circe, handwritten in childish black Sharpie pen capitals, with no return address.

'Did Miki put this on my desk?' I ask Irfan. Miki is the intern who sorts out the mail.

'Dunno,' Irfan replies. 'I just got in. Why. You got love letter?' His goofy smile offers a flash of his perfect teeth, and I'm reminded of the fact that he could be cute if he wasn't so annoying.

The envelope is padded with bubble wrap, extremely crinkled and roughly the size of a greetings card. I already know what to expect. It's the stencils again, three this time.

Made of dark-red crêpe paper, somewhat unevenly snipped at the edges, forming crude shapes: a wide-eyed rabbit, huddled sideways, a grinning monkey with soup-cup ears, a coiled snake with a raggedy crêpe tongue. I smooth out the crumples on the snake stencil. Its body curls through itself like a paper pretzel, ending in two lopsided eyes and a shred for a tongue. It reminds me of my tapeworm. I keep the paper-cut-out Cestoda flattened out carefully by my scroll pad and put the other two stencils away in their envelope, back on my letter tray.

I crack my knuckles and open up my emails. There's a progress report from Koya, the marketing wunderkind in our Novena office. At the end of the document is an attachment. A younger version of the Amisa I knew pops up from the left of the screen, in a white dress with a high neck. It resembles a cheongsam collar. She looks like a wartime ghost; haunting and haunted. She has one hand held up against her throat and she stares coyly over her right shoulder towards the camera, lips pursed into a line with a slight, forced curve. She could be Madame White Snake, or a fox spirit, a forlorn liar, a trickster.

Beside her is a better-quality, practically luminous photo of the new Pontianak. *Ponti 2020.* The studio has just cast a Eurasian model/influencer/singer named Eunice Prinze after online scouting and two rounds of auditions. She's adopting the same pose as Amisa but she is zero ghost and 100 per cent tastefully sexy woman. Gaze towards the camera, hand resting on throat. Artful cleavage. Mouth slightly parted. Eunice has really built a profile over the past couple of months. I've seen her pulling her sleek chestnut ponytail and winking from the cover of *Cleo* magazine; grinning like a healthful sunbeam in a probiotic yogurt ad on TV. She is half Indo-Chinese, a quarter Dutch, a quarter Polish, and has that wide-eyed, ethnically ambiguous (mostly European) look that we know will make her massively saleable internationally. Someone like Amisa would never get anything beyond the bit part of a dim sum waitress now; she looks too Chinese and too foreboding, and that's how it is.

But Eunice is familiar yet exotic: white enough to fit in, desirably foreign enough to stand out. Nineteen and gorgeous and invincible. I click on the link and watch Eunice's mini showreel. She's even prettier in motion. Some girls (Category A) have a warm, inviting beauty; others (Category B) possess the sort that shuts other women out and makes them regret their spells of comfort snacking. Eunice is beautiful in an infuriatingly endearing way that makes you think, what a nice, chill girl, too lovely to hate. Let's call her the rarest hybrid, Category C. Marketing gold. Queen of Buyable Hope. Conqueror of multiple demographics. Her voice is a dulcet, transatlantic drawl that dips in and out of reality-star vocal fry. She has that whole long-limbed, languid Bambi thing going.

'What do you think?' Jeanette asks. I turn around. She is standing behind my chair holding a coffee and wearing some kind of jumpsuit that would not look out of place in a Bond movie. Definitely Category B. I shrug at her.

'Yeah, she looks good, I guess. Very slick promo image. I thought they wanted lo-fi? I prefer the original actress.'

'Hmm,' Jeanette says, tilting her head slightly at the

screen. 'You like the old one, ah? She passed away. Nothing we can do. Unless she has a daughter who looks just like her.'

'Yeah, too bad,' I agree, to quell the jagged alarm I feel.

Amisa's funeral: sixteen years ago, in August. Just before the Hungry Ghost Festival. I attended all three days of the wake. It felt everlasting, those humid strip-lit nights full of muted strangers and Szu beckoning me over, pale and clingy and desolate.

'Anyway,' Jeanette continues, 'I think they meant lo-fi in an edgy way. Says so in the brief.'

'I know, but she looks like . . . superhero-movie slick.'

'Well, that goes with Leow's rewrite. You know, the redemption story arc. He wants to make it arty but all action. Like Wong Kar Wai mixed with Quentin Tarantino.'

'Wow. Good luck to him.'

In the original *Ponti!*, which I finally watched recently, the monster has no redemption. She never says sorry. Not over her dead body. She wreaks havoc until the bitter end. After the hero hammers a nail into her head, she wails and screams and refuses to transform into a docile wifeling. Instead, the earth rises up and a big banana tree engulfs her with a violent rumble, a caterwaul of rushing earth. It's left ambiguous whether she is vanquished or has merely found a way to escape from the good witch doctor, the hero, and the brave villagers.

'I mean, her look is completely off-brand,' I say, peering at the screen. 'This new girl's not even scary.'

'If you watched the original trilogy carefully,' Jeanette

says pointedly, 'it's not meant to be scary. It's B-horror, sexy entertainment. Besides, it's a reboot, not a shot-by-shot remake. So.'

'Thanks for explaining, Jeanette. I really appreciate it.'

'No problem. Anyway, Eunice Prinze has enough social media followers for a small kingdom. She's a real influencer. That counts for more than being scary.'

'Hm. Okay.'

I swivel my chair and turn back to my screen. After a minute I get up. In the office pantry I put the kettle on and lean against the counter. I take tiny sips of green tea. Everyone and everything gets old and outdated in time. One day the shitty corporate mug I'm holding will be somebody's antique, and design plans of construction cranes will be displayed in robot museums. People will no longer need to speak. We will swipe and intuit everything. And I'll be long dead and gone, just like Amisa Tan.

After a minute or two I walk back to my desk. My monitor screen momentarily startles me. From a short distance away it's like one of those freaky optical illusions – no matter where I'm standing, the eyes of the outdated woman on the left seem to follow me.

17

SZU

2003

It is the second day of the wake and I have spent the last few hours, as the sky begins to darken, greeting the steady stream of guests. Right now I'm sitting in a plastic chair on the veranda, spacing out so much that my eyes are going blurry. The yellowed ceiling fan swivels in place with slow precariousness.

I take a break and go to the kitchen to gawp at the open fridge. A tub of tofu has split and drooled brine onto a huddle of cloud ear mushrooms on the shelf below. Disgusting: all these dead plants, dead meat. I don't want any of it inside me. I get a rag to wipe up the mess. As I wring it clean under the tap my aunt calls for me.

'Your friend is here,' she says.

Circe pokes her head around the kitchen door frame.

'Hi.'

'Oh, hey,' I reply.

'Thought I'd come by to see how you were doing,' Circe says. 'Have you smelt the haze?'

'Smoky.'

'I'm choking to death.'

We wander out to the driveway. Aunt Yunxi is sitting by

the side of the coffin speaking in low, hushed tones to a sobbing woman with a cropped haircut. It is Lian Ying, one of my mother's long-term clients, who was crying dramatically yesterday too. We take a seat on two plastic chairs just out of earshot.

'That weirdo is here two nights in a row!' Circe says. 'Who even is she?'

'It's your second night here too,' I reply, and instantly regret my bluntness. I hate the doglike apology in my smile, my aching cheeks.

'What's your problem? I can go if you want,' Circe says, unsmiling.

'No, sorry,' I say. 'Don't go.'

'Fine,' says Circe. She sounds pleased.

'I wish I never had to go back to school,' I say, to change the topic.

'You'll get over it,' she replies. She is still watching Aunt Yunxi and the attention-seeking crier. 'Oh,' she adds, 'Leslie says you're pleasant.'

'Thanks,' I reply. My cheeks heat up both with the awkward placement of that comment and also how vague it is. What does *pleasant* mean? Scenery is pleasant. The scented hand towels you get in seafood restaurants are pleasant.

I glance over at Circe's cheek and the tips of her eyelashes as she blinks. She turns back towards me and just as she's about to speak her focus shifts over my shoulder. I follow her stare. A willowy young woman is coming up the driveway. She wears a black maxi dress and clog sandals that buckle around the top of her slim feet. Her wooden soles go *clop-clop* on the cement. She comes over to where Circe and I are sitting to pick up a piece of red thread from the pile beside us.

'Would you like a drink?' I ask her.

'Oh, yes please,' the woman replies. 'That would be nice.' I bring her a carton of red longan tea.

'Thank you,' she says as she sips through the straw. 'I was feeling very heaty. Are you Amisa's daughters?'

'Not me, her,' Circe replies. 'She's Szu, and I'm Circe.'

'It's very nice to meet you, Szu,' the woman says. 'Wait, which one is Szu?'

'I am.'

'Ah, I see,' she says. 'How grown up you are!'

Circe and I exchange a look.

The woman is very statuesque. She smells like classy boutiques, and up close I see the foundation patted all over into her face, spread over her pores and slightly smudged in the humidity. She could be anything between her late twenties and her early forties.

'Did you work with my mother too?' I ask. Out of the corner of my eye I notice that my aunt is sitting ramrod straight and watching us.

'Not me,' the woman replies. 'Iskandar Wiryanto is my dad. He worked with your mother.'

She's smiling but her eyes are serious.

'Can I help you?' my aunt asks. She's come up behind us. She sits down one chair away from the woman.

'I was just chatting with your granddaughter.'

'She's my niece,' Aunt Yunxi says, unsmiling. 'Have we met?' she continues. 'I'm Yunxi.'

205

'I'm Novita,' the woman says, embarrassed. 'My father directed the *Ponti* movies.'

'Ah, of course. Iskandar Wiryanto,' says Aunt Yunxi. 'I heard so much about him. How is he?'

'He passed, ten years ago.'

'I'm sorry.'

'It happens,' Novita replies, taking in the funeral awning. 'I didn't know Amisa had family in Singapore. We spent a lot of time together.' Novita directs this statement at me, not Aunt Yunxi. 'Would you like to hear a story about your mom, Szu?'

'Got no time,' says Aunt Yunxi.

'Uh. Sure,' I reply, even though I don't like the way the woman addresses me as if I'm six, not sixteen. 'What story?'

Beside me, Circe leans forward in her chair.

'Oh, a funny one,' Novita says. She glances towards my aunt. 'I'll keep it brief. I was five when they filmed *Ponti!* The first time I met your mother on set, she approached me wearing this light-brown samfoo, her hair in braids. Even dressed so plainly, she looked like a princess. Just so perfect. We played marbles on set. Anyway, the second time I visited the set, my father points at this cluster of huge banana trees and says, hey, Novita, why don't you go over there? Maybe I've hidden a present. So I do that. And just when I get really close the leaves rustle, and your mother leaps out at me, growling. This time she's all in white and her mouth is bloody. I screamed and ran as fast as I could, but I didn't see the metal pole.'

'Jeez,' Circe says. Novita looks around at her audience

of three, including my frowning aunt who has her arms crossed.

'Then what?' asks Circe.

'I knocked my front tooth out. I still remember the crunch. I saw stars. Blood everywhere. We were never able to find it. We looked all over.'

'So Mrs Ng scared the tooth out of you,' Circe says, and laughs.

'Oh yes!' Novita says, and clasps her hands.

I imagine my mother parting the leaf blades, feral, angry. It makes me shiver. Aunt Yunxi has a hooded expression on her face. Her mouth is pursed.

I grimace at Novita. I don't know what to say. I assume she's mistaken Circe for me again, as if we're completely interchangeable. Novita brings her hand up to tuck her hair behind her ear and I notice her fingernails, dirty, with chipped bright-red polish.

'Well, thanks for coming to pay your respects,' Aunt Yunxi says. 'But I'm afraid we are packing up.'

I glance at the clock; it's only 10 p.m. Last night we wrapped up long past eleven.

'What a shame,' Novita says. 'Szu, I have so much I want to tell you about your mother.'

'Another time. Thanks for coming,' Aunt Yunxi says. 'I'll show you to the gate.'

My aunt gets up from her chair and stands there staring at Novita like she's a picture she wants to take off the wall. Novita picks up her bag and slings it back over her shoulder. She reaches over Circe to throw her drink carton in the black bin. When she looks back I am surprised to see that her eyes are reddened and a little wet. She stares at me for a moment.

'It's nice to meet you,' she says. 'I'll see myself out.'

We watch her totter down the driveway. She shuffles away much more self-consciously than she came, holding herself stiff as a board. I keep expecting her to veer around and shout something crazy. But she reaches the gate, unlatches it, and avoids our eyes as she turns to shut it behind her.

'That was awkward,' Circe mutters.

'Shouldn't *you* be on your way too?' Aunt Yunxi asks.

*

That night I dream of my mother with her hair in an uncharacteristic high ponytail, like one of the volleyball girls at school. Her expression is mild and almost peaceful. She walks up the corridor that runs along the kitchen to my bedroom, to hers, and ends at Aunt Yunxi's door at the bottom of the hall. She skims and traces the left wall with her fingertips. The smell of burnt tuberose fills the hallway, acrid and distinct. Under Aunt Yunxi's door a red light is glowing. The light gets brighter and brighter and frames my mother's smooth, sunken cheeks in orangey red. She reaches out to turn the handle, changes her mind and turns towards the extraterrestrial glow of the kitchen. That striking woman from earlier tonight is standing in front of the counter, as tall as the fridge. I can't remember her name. She stares at my mother, her big eyes doleful as a puppy's. My mother reaches towards her and takes her hand. The woman stoops as she follows. When they are out in the corridor the woman seems to grow; she has to curve her back and hunch up her shoulders. My mother leads her past our doors and towards Aunt Yunxi's room. When they reach the door frame with its lip of light they turn about and come back down the hallway again. My mother's bare feet are silent but the woman's clog shoes clop across the tiled floor. I half open my eyes and stir in bed. My bedroom is bathed in the watery blue of so-late-it's-morning. Two feet away, the *clop-clop-clop* sounds out just on the other side of my bedroom door. I blink awake and try to move; fail, listen, panic. By the time my hand meets my face the clopping is replaced by the drone and thump of garbage trucks.

18

AMISA

1978

The first Monday after Didi died, Amisa auditioned for the role of Ponti. It took place on the same day as Didi's funeral, but she couldn't bear to go. She stood before Iskandar and his producers in a hollow-eyed daze, did as he said. The motions felt effortless; she had nothing to lose. They offered her the role on the spot. The next morning she quit her job at the Paradise Theatre. Filming started six weeks later, in January.

Every morning as she brushed her teeth she looked in the mirror and thought: Full-Time Actress and Most Beautiful Woman in Asia. Her ego bloomed like the tacky purple flowers printed on the shower curtain. Her hope yawned out over the horizon. She loved the calm eye of the recording cameras, the blinking lights, the costume changes, the gallons of fake blood, fake knives, fake leaves, fake walls, the hustle and hassle of people all gathered to shoot her. The only problem was that she was finding the actual acting harder than she thought.

Some nights Wei Loong came to watch her filming after work. Having him there should have comforted her, but instead she felt even more stilted. Iskandar Wiryanto no longer treated her with the same gushing reverence as at their first meeting. One week into the shoot, he had already revealed himself to be a tyrant, a small-time despot, an ego-maniac. But she had signed a contract for three films and would have to see it through.

At the start of week two, they were filming in a field at 2.30 a.m. Even her husband's presence failed to quell Iskandar's anger.

'You are driving me mad! This is not working. Useless. Unusable. We are all doomed.'

Iskandar knocked the clapperboard out of the assistant's hand and marched towards Amisa. She stood in front of the film crew with the lights trained on her, in a thin white dress, barefoot. Her legs were covered in mud and she had twigs in her long black hair. Make-up made her face chalky, her eyes rimmed in bruises, and she shivered even though it wasn't cold.

'Here. Stand here, like that, on the mark,' he said, pointing. 'And you've got to make a show of it when you come out of the tree. Make it more expressive. Right now you are really like a corpse. This is the big reveal. Have some energy. Be graceful, like a dancer, a scary dancer.'

'I don't know what you mean. I can dance, but I don't know what's a scary dancer.'

'*Expressive dancer!*'

'What is that? Why must you always say so cheem?'

'Are you stupid?'

'No, I'm not, and you can't talk to me like that.' She crossed her arms and jutted out her jaw.

'Come with me,' he said. He grabbed her arm. Her husband just looked on, as did the two camera assistants and the surly electrician Ah Choon who had a mild smirk on his face. Iskandar Wiryanto led her past the piled-up equipment and empty catering table, over to his tan-brown Ford Cortina in the car park.

'Get in,' he said.

'Why?'

'Because I say so.'

Reluctantly, she sat in the passenger seat. He got in beside her and slammed the door. It was dark in the car and its vinyl upholstery reeked of smoke and pickles.

'Where are we going?'

'Nowhere, that's the point. Listen, Amisa, I know we have our differences. But I have so much faith in you. I know you can do something special.' His voice was slow and soft and his moustache moved as he talked so she could only see the bottom of his mouth, like a ventriloquist's puppet. 'You have to channel the right energy and really focus. Stop just standing there and looking pretty only. Be like how you were on your audition. Remember when you cried and howled, and you were so furious that we thought you were going to scratch our eyes out? Hamid and Chek Bee and Roddy and I were blown away. Completely floored. Try and equal that.'

'My brother just died, back then,' she said. She stared at her small pale hands on her lap and the remembering subdued her.

'Look at me.'

'Don't tell me what to do.'

'Why not? I'm your director. It's my job. And we signed a contract.'

She turned towards him slowly, her face catching a slice of yellow light. 'What do you want?'

'Your power. *Ponti!* needs some of that. Without your power there is no film: my vision is ruined. Don't just rely on your looks. That's the easy way out. Be my Pontianak, my murderous ghost, inside and out. Go deeper. Channel all the shit you want to shout about. You feel a lot, Amisa, I can tell. It's all seething under that perfect face of yours, waiting to be coaxed out. Life is loss, right? You're only twenty, but don't you have regrets, don't you worry where the time has gone? You might tell me, no, Iskandar, I'm so young and pretty, *saya tidak mengerti!* But I'd know you are lying. Because everybody has regrets. And everybody wonders where time has gone.'

She sighed and looked out of the window, at the car park with its reed-grown, sordid lots.

'Your brother would be happy for you to do well,' he continued, softly. 'I know he would. Trust me. You can be great. You have something special.'

Iskandar Wiryanto was fifty-five and still reminded her of a hawk-eagle. She felt a pang in her chest partly engendered by that likeness. Inside the stuffy car, it dawned on her for the first and only time in her life: this strong, disorienting twinge that straddled fear and pleasure. She respected him, she supposed. He scared her, and nobody else commanded that. She wanted to prove him right. What was special about her, behind her incredible face? Did she really have a lodestone of wonderfulness nested inside: something chimeric that sparkled and warped, a brilliance waiting to be called? She didn't know, but he seemed sure.

She started going over to the Wiryantos' house after shoots some evenings or late afternoons, depending when they wrapped and what time they started. This was common knowledge amongst the crew and her co-stars, and Amisa adopted the same prideful unabashedness that she had in her village. So what if people thought she and Iskandar thrice weekly typified a film-industry cliché: the ingénue leading actress sleeping with the ageing director – the most appealing penis being the one attached to the most power. So what if most of the crew and co-stars hated her, and Novita, the director's five-year-old daughter, followed her around set like an annoying little ghost she couldn't shake off.

The Wiryantos lived in a sprawling, professionally decorated bungalow in East Coast with two separate wings. Mrs Wiryanto occupied the left wing, which smelt of lilacs and citrus. Amisa only peeked in once; saw a labyrinth of walk-through cupboards filled with steam-pressed designer gowns and endless shoes in fancy boxes.

Novita had a round room in the middle, full of toys still perfectly new and wrapped up in plastic. Mrs Wiryanto encouraged her daughter to be a collector, rather than someone who messed and crinkled things up. The right wing was Iskandar's domain, where he conceptualized and wrote his scripts. He occupied a huge book-lined study with a parquet floor, big television, a record player and a board for his script ideas. It was into this room that Amisa followed him during her visits, and he always locked the door behind her. His daughter waited outside, scratching at the woodgrain from time to time like a small dog that hadn't been fed.

Inside, everyone thought they were fucking like animals. It would have seemed so; she emerged from the house with messy hair, dazed eyes. Even Wei Loong, she was sure, must have pictured filth in there with the same limp, helpless anger that made her detest him. Ah Choon the gaffer, Anson the second camera operator and Poh Heng the special-effects man were the worst gossips of all. One day, she heard them conferring behind a bougainvillea bush at lunch break. They were saying the lewdest things in Hokkien about what she and Iskandar got up to in his house; what Iskandar was sticking in her front and back doors; how many times; what their little Indo-Chinese baby would look like with such a lunatic for a dad and a dumb, moody bitch for a mother; whether poor Novita had to plug her ears with cotton wool to drown out the horrible sounds. Amisa didn't bother to shove her way through the bushes and confront them.

The truth was, she wished their speculations were true. By then, it was what she wanted. She surprised herself. She had fallen in love with the most hideous man she had ever met. Unbeknownst to almost everyone else, the handsome leading actor Abdul Aziz was the one who snuck in and out of Mrs Wiryanto's wing, and one time they even ran into him in the corridor wearing nothing but a towel, his glistening broad chest exposed. Iskandar waved cheerfully to him and told him, 'Have fun, just be careful.'

What Amisa and Iskandar did in the locked room did not fit the mode of a conventional affair. Because he didn't lay a finger on her.

It went like this. They entered the room. She put down her bag. He drew up a chair and sat. He pointed and made her lie in the middle of the floor, with her arms and legs spread out. Most times she was fully clothed; other times he made her take all her clothes off and get into a pair of faded white trunks that looked like adult diapers. She would cross her arms over her breasts and he would say, Don't be stupid, put them down. And he would talk to her. That was it, just talk, but how potent his talk. Spirals of speech about how boring she was making herself and how much better she actually was. How she was a dead grey soul in a beautiful shell, or a sublime soul in a flawless but awful husk of being, depending on his mood. How her beauty meant nothing in a murderous world where men just wanted to fuck and kill her and nobody cared what she thought. And where women saw her as a challenge, or a husband thief. He brought up her brother, her mother, her sister, her village and how they disapproved of her. He made her tell him how many men she had slept with, an estimate, and he sneered. He was so impossibly cruel that after a while she just took it, came to expect the degradation, felt it was somehow deserved. He made her repeat lines of the script to him over and over until the words stopped making sense, and then he laughed at her English pronunciation and told her it didn't matter what she sounded like, they were dubbing the films over anyway with a voice actress from Los Angeles called Savannah Roberts, and Amisa couldn't sound better or more intelligible even if she tried for a million years. He broke her spirit and built her up again within the hour by soothing her with his honeyed voice, telling her impassioned stories about the tangled wilderness of Sumatran jungles; the slaughter of hundreds of thousands of communists; the terrible ways that Suharto's dictatorship prevailed; how he had had no choice but to leave forever, his life now scattered across Asia and Europe, his artistic vision to make these horror films that would put Indonesia and Singapore on the world map. He had so many myths to tell, an unquenchable thirst to cram his moods and memories into ninety pages of script and make it explode across the screen. The character of Ponti he based on his own dead mother, who bore a slight resemblance to Amisa. He would make her unbelievably famous. Her face would grace billboards in Hong Kong, Paris, Hollywood; she would fly across the world in private jets; she would be his muse and they would attend the Golden Horse Awards and the Oscars together. She would be immortal.

One day, she got up and reached her arms towards him, half naked and so lissom and entreating with her hair all mussed, pert breasts and sparkling eyes. She was giving it her best shot. He put his hands up in a gesture of polite disgust and supplication. He was so good at saying and doing things that were both commanding and placatory all at once.

'Put it away! You're very beautiful, but you're just not my type,' Iskandar said. 'You are getting so much better,

Amisa. But this is a strictly professional relationship, and I'd like to keep it that way. Besides, I'm too old for you, and I think your flavourless husband is good for your health. You're a chilli padi and you need something bland. Don't touch me, lah. Like I said before, I'm a happily married man.'

Amisa sputtered like a faulty engine and didn't know what to do with her arms. Her breasts suddenly embarrassed her, as did the febrile arousal she could feel vaporizing off her skin. She put her clothes on, stung by the first sexual refusal she had ever received in her life. She had thought she was invincible. She had thought no man could resist her.

He drove her home that evening with his daughter buckled in the back seat. Amisa maintained a sullen silence, curtly ignoring Novita's questions about what was that tree, what was that building? Iskandar sighed at the wheel and switched the radio on to Gold 90.5.

'It's a balmy Friday, 5th October, 1978. Temperature is 32° Celsius, with variable clouds. There's a traffic jam on the PIE owing to a road obstruction. I hope you're all having a wonderful evening otherwise. Here's a track to relax to, from Fleetwood Mac,' the presenter drawled.

Amisa wasn't paying attention; instead she watched the city rush past her, grids of office lights and long rows of sea apple trees, onward towards Toa Payoh and her sulking husband. The song started innocuously enough: gentle chord progressions, subdued female voice in the popular folk twang.

But exactly thirty seconds in, when Stevie Nicks drew out the word 'landslide', Amisa recoiled as if she'd been hit in the face. She started to sob. She couldn't help it. Every subsequent line and shift of the song took on an unbearable potency. The voice issuing from the dashboard speakers sounded so private and subdued, as if its owner was trying and failing to keep her grief to herself. Infected by the symptoms of this lilting American melody, how incurably sad Amisa felt. *Didi*, she thought. *Didi, Didi, Didi*. With each verse, Amisa's cries jagged and amplified inside the car. Iskandar glanced at her and turned the volume up, up, up, as Novita looked on, confused and fraught. At the traffic junction the drivers of the cars on either side of them glanced over at the baffling tableau: man blasting a folk song, beautiful woman crying, baffled child in the back seat.

From then on, when the moment called during their evenings together, Iskandar knitted his eyebrows as he put the needle on the record and the black vinyl started to spin like a blade. 'Landslide' vibrated from the walls of his study, that husky voice everywhere, the hurtful chords. He played it on set, too, when he wanted to break her, over and over until everyone was sick to death of it and said it made them bleed from the ears. But nobody could deny that the song did something. The actress's cold eyes would darken, and Ponti began to embody this exquisite awful sadness. The change was immediate and apparent. He wrung her of every ounce of emotion until one day, finally, filming was done.

'That's a wrap,' Iskandar said. 'I have always wanted to say that.' The cast and crew clapped politely, sighs of relief all around. Amisa sat half in and half out of her stupid banyan tree, completely spent.

*

Iskandar had huge plans for the premiere. And the distribution. And for promoting the film. As it turned out, so did a Filipino director called Bobby Suarez, who had been shooting a movie at the same time. It was titled *They Call Her Cleopatra Wong* and starred a winsome girl named Marrie Lee who had feather-cut hair and a searchlight smile. If you put their headshots side by side, you would rather be friends with Marrie Lee than Amisa Tan.

Marrie Lee played Cleopatra Wong, a female Interpol agent who high-kicked and stunt-fought her way to the bottom of a conspiracy involving impostor monks. It was a Philippine–Singapore international co-production and super-spies were sexy and trendy. Nobody cared about pontianaks – so dated; superstitions were being sieved out; fewer people wanted to engage with ghosts. There was only room for one local film to be screened this year; not enough support and interest; financial decision; nothing personal or about the quality of your film, man. Those were the reasons the distributors cited, and the small, independent cinemas that flatly refused to screen the film. Besides, there had recently been a film called *Pontianak* directed by Roger Sutton. Eventually they found one theatre that would take it: a two-screener in Bishan. At the premiere, Amisa wore a black bias-cut dress and grinned skull-like for the cameras. The auditorium was half empty. She sat in between Iskandar Wiryanto and Wei Loong, who fell asleep during the last half-hour of the film.

They shot *Ponti 2* shortly after, cast and crew dejected, but the Wiryantos paid them relatively well, enough to put food on the table. And that sufficed to make people put up with someone as difficult and deluded as Iskandar Wiryanto. The first film went nowhere, ditto the second. By the time they shot *Ponti 3: Curse of the Bomoh* in 1981, it was like watching a tree fall in the most distant forest in slow, laborious motion. Even the script was so terrible that it was as though Iskandar had given up on the writing process and knew it wouldn't go anywhere. Filming it was like watching paint dry and slow-clapping at the end result. Nobody dared to say it, but the trilogy was a vanity project, an elaborate and costly present from Mrs to Mr Wiryanto, facilitating his wishes and the delusions of grandeur that seemed to slip further from realization with each successive attempt.

At home, Wei Loong and Amisa shared a bed but hardly touched. He was sore about Iskandar despite her protest-ations of professionalism; he didn't believe that Iskandar had never entered her smooth, yielding body, not even kissed her. Why, then, did she go over to his house so often? The crew all laughed at him; he was a conscious cuckold. They shared meals in silence, filled the hours before sleep with television. It was hard to remember that any kinship or affection had ever existed between them.

The week after they wrapped *Ponti 3* Amisa returned to

the Paradise Theatre, now called the Everitt Cineplex. She asked for Rocky and was directed to his office upstairs. He didn't look surprised to see her.

'Always knew you'd be back,' he said.

19

SZU

2003

It's the final evening of the funeral and I've had enough. I glance at the clock and try not to let it be too obvious that I'm watching the time. The white blouse I've been wearing every day has started to smell. Circe arrived an hour ago, uncharacteristically on time. Dressed in a black T-shirt and jeans, she's subdued, solemn.

The clock reads ten minutes to ten when my father comes down the driveway. I draw a sharp breath and my whole body feels limp and light. My father has been gone for nine years and as he gets closer he looks younger, not older, than I remembered. His hair is mostly black and slicked to the sides with pomade. He is tanned and wears a dark short-sleeved shirt and pressed trousers. Somehow when I imagined him in the present I always pictured him as scrawny and destitute, a castaway with crustacean whiskers and a balding pate.

'Hello, Szu,' he says. His voice is new, carroty. I remembered it all wrong.

I stand there and gawp at him for a second. I feel a prickle in my chest both expansive and painfully specific.

I turn to Circe mechanically and stage-whisper, 'That's my dad.'

She is silent, just looks at me and back at him with checkout blankness.

'Szu Min,' my father says, like he's testing out the sound of my name. He looks at me straight on and my jaw tenses.

I turn away and almost knock into Aunt Yunxi.

'How good of you to show up,' she says to him. Although her tone is even, calm, conscious of our visitors, people turn to watch us. Humans have this spectating instinct for drama.

'I don't know what your purpose is,' Aunt Yunxi says in a flat voice, in Hokkien. 'But it's not the right time.'

Is it possible that my father disappeared into a time machine and has only now found his way back? He hasn't aged a day; he looks well fed and well slept. I press my toes into my canvas shoes and wriggle them out of reflex, just to check I'm not dreaming.

'I saw the obituary in the papers,' my young-looking father replies in Hokkien. 'I want to pay my respects. I used to live here, this was my house.'

'Not any more,' my aunt says.

My father lets out a long exhalation. He is holding a pair of sunglasses in one hand and he reaches up to place them on his head as he stares at my aunt.

'The obituary wasn't put there for you,' Aunt Yunxi continues, arms akimbo. 'Look, Ah Loong, why don't you pay your respects? Then go. Now is not the time to make a scene.'

'Who are you to talk to me like this?' my father asks. 'To act so high and mighty? What gives you the right?'

His tone thickens the air. Everyone stares.

'Does Szu know?' my father asks, looking at me like we're on the same team.

My aunt just ignores him. Two of our guests have come to her side, burly men with oily comb-overs and thick forearms.

'Please go,' Aunt Yunxi says. Her tone is flat and polite.

'Please go,' I repeat. 'You shouldn't be here.' My voice catches on the last word.

'Don't you think you should tell her?' my father asks my aunt. She just glares at him.

He turns to me.

'She's not your real aunt,' he spits out, eyes afire. 'Did your mother ever tell you? Did you guess? They just used to live together. She's not even related—'

'Cut it out!' a man calls out from the side. 'How can you be so disrespectful?'

'This woman is a scammer,' my father continues, gesturing towards Aunt Yunxi. 'Always has been. She was a bad influence on your mother. She only moved in so she could live in the house and do her black magic here. She can't be trusted.'

'Go away,' I say, in English. 'Stop bad-mouthing my aunt.'

He looks at me, surprised, with his bulgy goldfish eyes and his Adam's apple moving up and down in his throat. I'm only a little shorter than he is. He's half of who I am but I feel no more akin to him than I did to my mother.

'You shouldn't be here,' another man says to my father in Mandarin. He comes forward and moves towards him, but before anything happens my father backs off and begins to walk away. It's like a slow, embarrassing nightmare repeating itself. I'm eight all over again and keep expecting him to turn around. He walks speedily, with purpose, as if he's on his way to an important meeting. I misremembered him kind. Cowardly, but kind. Now I bore holes into the back of his head. My heart is thumping and I can hear the blood whistling around my ears as I watch him leave. The gate clangs; he's left it slightly ajar. I consider running after him, but I don't know if I would hug him or hit him.

Circe and I retreat into the house. She's animated by the drama. I can tell by her jerky movements and the brightness in her eyes.

'Jeez,' she says. 'Are you okay? So that guy was your dad? That was mega awkward.'

'Yep.'

'He looks so young.'

'Yeah. Tell me about it.'

'He's pretty inconsiderate turning up today. Of all days,' Circe says.

'Of all days,' I repeat, my voice catching. In my head I'm picturing how I should have shouted at him, had the courage to be brave. I should have yelled: *Just leave, since you're so good at it*, and everyone would have applauded me.

Circe circles her left foot in one direction and then the other. 'What do you think of that stuff he said about your aunt not really being your aunt?' she asks. 'That's crazy.'

'He's probably right,' I say.

'Well—' Circe starts to speak.

'Szu, can you come outside?' my aunt calls from the patio. 'I need you.'

*

Later on, the men from the funeral home show up. They pull up in the van and get out, a tumble of tired faces. Soon after, the monks arrive.

The presiding monk has liver spots across his face and on the back of his shorn head. As he performs his final rites around the coffin, chanting and singing sutras, I watch his orange robes sway. The younger monk joins in. Their voices are low, soothing. They commence the ritual of closing the coffin. Nobody is meant to look – bad luck – but while everyone's eyes are shut I open my left, the way a giant whale would at the bottom of the sea. Submarine silence. Nobody sees me ruin the ritual. Six men lift the casket up, steady it on their shoulders. And then they proceed down the driveway and through the already-opened gates.

*

The rest of the afternoon passes in a flurried blur. In the viewing room at the crematorium we watch the incinerator hatch open. The coffin slowly slides in. It looks so small from the viewing gallery, as if it could fit a pet or a doll. When most of the coffin has slotted in the doors close and my hand twitches, wanting to reach for my mother. The monks keep chanting. I wonder how many rites they do a week, how often boredom overrides devotion. I find myself holding Circe's small, cold hand and I don't know how to make my thoughts go quiet. I think about my mother's downcast face and her uncommon smile. My eyes start to water and I can see distortions in the air, like I'm right up close to the fire.

*

The next morning Aunt Yunxi and I return to collect the remains. The crematorium assistant ushers us into a small room bathed in cruelly cheerful sunshine. I squint at the tray in front of us, set on the cement counter. My aunt passes me a pair of long brown chopsticks and tilts her chin towards the pile of grey. My mother's bones have broken down so much in the fire that they look like they came from a bird. We pick up what we can make out and place it in a smaller tray, to be transferred to the urn. The more I search for pieces of her the more my vision smudges.

'It's okay,' Aunt Yunxi says. 'We can take our time.' She puts down her chopsticks for a moment and pats my shoulder slowly.

When we have finished collecting the bones, the assistant places them in the urn. We follow a different assistant down the hallways of the columbarium, which has gleaming marble floors and ceiling-high niche shelves. It would be easy to get lost in here if we didn't take down the location, so we don't forget where to find her. My mother goes into the fifth row up, three down the aisle, her full mouth unsmiling, eyes clear and serious.

*

Monday morning is strip-lit and overcast; the stuff of doomsday movies. Circe leads me through our school corridors like I'm famous and she is my po-faced security guard. My eyelids droop with the excruciation of Real Life. Everyone is watching us. After a week away, the Whampoa Convent of the Eternally Blessed has a penitentiary air to it. The sugar-plum pastel paint job is intolerable. Grilled windows and the hush near the staffroom, rounding down towards our classroom where girls in the hallway hang back and whisper in our wake. Priya and Elizabeth offer me smiles and *I'm-sorry*s. Trissy and Clara look at me like I've just been dredged up from the sea.

'Where's their sympathy?' I ask Circe. Not so secretly, I am relishing my force field of bereavement, the immunity from overt teasing, and the goodwilled attention and condolences from the kinder girls.

'Some bimbos are too dumb and shallow to feel anything,' Circe whispers. 'They're not worth bothering about.' But she's the one who keeps glancing around as she puts her small hand lightly on my back and walks me to class.

In Geography Mrs Lee gives out our continuous assessment scripts. I've scored 44 per cent and I don't bother to read any of the remarks in detail, just stare at the angry red ballpoint looping over my answers. 'Keep trying, Szu,' reads the note on the final page. It sounds like a motivational card. Emptily hopeful. I look out of the door into the long, rectangular PE field. The dark-green trees sticking out behind it have lightened over the past few months and the fog has settled. Now some of the tips of the branches are light green, as if dried out. It's the end of August. No more wild dogs. Just tender, ugly mud and earthworms roving under foot. The haze coming and going, inciting illnesses, clogging our lungs in our sleep. After class I tear off the final page of my script and scrunch it small in my palm. I throw it into the wastepaper bin on the way out.

After school Circe and I take the train to Bugis, but the movie we want to see is sold out so we buy giant cups of Diet Coke and sit by the giant pillars in the cinema lobby because this is habit even if the place seems warped and sullied in a tired, sorry way. Trailers for remakes of remakes play on loop on the screens over the popcorn stands. The explosions blast out of sync. When I look away the glare and flashes make my eyes hurt.

'Didn't ask you how you did for Geography,' I say to Circe.

'Oh, I did okay,' Circe replies, rattling the ice cubes around her Diet Coke.

'How much? I got 44.'

'Hm.'

'What did you get?'

'71.' She looks up at me from under her eyelashes.

'Wow! That's amazing. Why didn't you say earlier?'

'It's okay,' Circe replies. 'It's no big deal,' she adds, even though it is: I thought we were failures together. She tilts her head away to gaze at a group of girls sailing up the escalators from another secondary school with orchid-purple uniforms. They are in hysterics, one loud, clear voice bubbling into breathless giggles. When people laugh hard it sounds like they are having genuine fun, especially if you don't know what the joke is about.

'Their uniforms suck,' I try, but Circe doesn't respond.

In the shadow of the pillar I feel like I'm pulling her down into the carpet with my mildewed, mushroomy weight. We sit there for five, ten, twenty more minutes. The explosions play on a loop. The orchid-purple girls file into a theatre, still laughing uproariously. I try and think of something interesting to say.

'Bugis is so lame,' I mutter.

'Is it?' Circe asks.

Before my mother passed away this would have been enough for Circe to start on a gleeful tirade. And I would nod and agree, and we would cackle. Now she turns towards me, purse-lipped, with a glaze over her face. Her eyes sweep down to my wrists and knobbly knees, sticking out under my dark-green skirt.

'Do you want to get a snack?' she asks. 'I'm craving sweet corn. Or tau huay.'

'I'm good,' I say. My stomach rumbles. 'I feel kind of bloated,' I add, which is true. My tummy makes a low burbling sound, and this time I'm grateful for the nearby explosions before the gravelly-voiced trailer narrator drawls his lines.

'Let's get up, my legs are numb,' Circe says. She dons her school bag without looking at me. I'm the one who gathers and bins our emptied Diet Cokes. I trail Circe to the snack stall. She orders soya bean milk and a red bean pancake.

'Can you hold this for me?' she asks, passing me the

warm paper packet containing the coaster-sized pancake. She adjusts the straps of her school bag and sips the soya bean milk. 'Have some,' she says.

I shake my head at the straw.

'Red bean?'

I shake my head again. When I pass her back the packet she exhales sharply and rolls her eyes, all this so quickly I can't and anyway wouldn't dare comment on it.

*

When I get home my aunt has just finished clearing out my mother's room. The walls are shiny and it smells of bleach.

'Isn't it unlucky to clean so much?' I ask.

'How was school?'

'I failed Geography.'

'Oh,' my aunt replies. 'A test? You failed a test? You can retake.'

'No. It doesn't work like that. It's too late.'

'Why?'

'You won't get it.'

'Hmm,' she says. 'Never mind. Don't worry, Szu. It's bad for you. Worry until head ache. Still bad for you.'

My aunt has her sleeves rolled up over her skinny arms, and a bottle of glass cleaner in one hand. She sets it down on the table and turns towards me.

'Szu, can you sit for a minute?'

I slump my backpack down and take a seat opposite her. She watches me as I reach down to take off my socks.

'We have not had a chance to talk about this,' she begins. 'I was not surprised to see your father, the other day. He was trying to pay his respects, but he did not go about it in the best way.'

There's a pause. 'Doesn't matter,' I finally say.

'Are you sure, Szu Min?'

'Yes, Aunt Yunxi, I'm sure,' I say.

'Do you want to talk about it? Ask me any questions?'

'It doesn't matter. I don't want to see him again.'

Aunt Yunxi frowns and purses her lips. She sighs and shakes her head.

'I don't care,' I say. My voice sounds feeble, wheedling. I hate it.

'Poor girl. I worry about you.'

'You don't have to,' I snap. I gather my things quickly and get up. When I lock my bedroom door I listen as she moves about in the other room. She's opening and closing drawers more loudly than she needs to.

*

It's been three weeks since my mother died. Already Circe avoids the topic, or doesn't really continue the conversation when she asks me why I'm quiet and I tell her the same thing, I'm sad. It's getting boring to listen to, I can tell.

After school we run into some swimmers by the tuition centre glued to their boyfriends. I spot them first, a cluster of perfect tans and gazelle legs, resolving into eight strong-shouldered superhumans with bright, inscrutable smiles. Rather than endure the indignity of being ignored by them, Circe and I break into an ostrich trot round the back of the building, and then we sit on the terracotta-coloured steps.

'Do you ever think about finding your father? Tracking him down?' Circe asks. It's the first thing she has said to me since we made our hasty retreat. We don't discuss why or how we hurried away.

'He didn't leave any details.' Sweat sticks around my shoulders and I'm out of breath, dizzy.

'Surely we can find him,' she says. 'We can hire a private investigator. Don't you watch TV?'

'I don't have a TV, remember.'

'Oh yeah. Okay, well, I have the Internet.'

'Nah. Forget it.'

'What about that woman? Novita? She might know something. We can find her number and call her.'

'There's nothing to know. She was just some crazy person. Making life hard for my aunt.'

'Aren't you curious?'

'Don't care.' I crane my neck in case the swimmers have followed us around the corner.

'You always say that,' Circe replies. 'When you obviously do. It's tiring.' What she means to say is: *I'm* tiring. What I want to say but don't is: *you're not Nancy Drew; my family is not some mystery-of-the-month project, so fuck you.*

The air between us is heated and pungent, like car exhaust. We look out at the main road with its endless stream of buses and taxis. When I glance at Circe she's stormy-faced, jaw set, looking at the dried-out leaves of the nearby tree swaying in the slight, selfish breeze.

'I still think,' she says, 'that if I were you, I'd at least be curious.'

'It's not so easy,' I say, and I can feel my blood rising.

I speak quickly; the words come out faster than I can stop them. 'You just think it's easy cos it's not your problem. Things are so much harder from inside the problem than outside. There's no quick, magic fix sometimes.'

'No shit, Sherlock.'

'You don't get it.'

When she looks at me her eyes are furious.

'The first time he left,' I start, before she can say anything, 'I told myself for ages that he was having a bad day. And I'd done something wrong. Or my mother had said something wrong. And he wasn't a bad man. He was just too angry or embarrassed to come back straight away. But to see him again like that, all of a sudden, and then he just went away. Didn't even try to stay.'

Circe's eyes are wide and dry, her mouth hangs open.

'What's the point? Why even come back?' I'm shuddering.

Circe reaches into her bag for a tissue packet and hands me two pieces. 'Here. I'm sorry, Szu,' she says. 'I don't know what to say.'

I shake my head and wipe my eyes with the back of my hand, flushed and furious. Circe looks to the right and then back at me again. I follow her stare towards the lissom flickers of ponytails. The swimmers stroll to the bus stop, armed with boyfriends and small pots of frozen yogurt.

20

AMISA

1982

Amisa fidgeted in her plastic chair by the theatre doors. It had been a year since they filmed *Ponti 3*. By now her life should have changed, but it was the stuck, drowsy same. She was twenty-four and could pass for younger. She had three films to her name, but her name didn't matter. *Ponti*s *1* to *3* were reels of film that could fit into the back of Iskandar's car; they were things that had gotten made and now what? What next?

The *Ponti 3* premiere was scheduled for tonight. Iskandar had hired out a screen in the Everitt Cineplex from 7 p.m. At 6.30 Wei Loong arrived.

'Your dress,' he said, handing her the rattan bag.

He wore a beige shirt with a starched collar. When she came out in her blue party dress he took her arm, staring ahead, his face smile-like. Over the next hour people started to arrive: friends of the crew, Wei Loong's colleagues, Yunxi, and finally Iskandar, in a cream suit. He looked tanned and very old, his skin leathery, his eagle eyes wise and sharp. Mrs Wiryanto followed close by, her hair in a stiff, hairsprayed updo, wearing a twinset the colour of champagne. Novita was the last to enter the lobby, nine years old now, all skinny limbs and buck teeth. She was almost the same height as Amisa.

'Hello, Amisa.'

'Hello, little princess.'

'How come I haven't seen you for a long time? Why you never come to my house any more?'

'I don't know,' Amisa replied, pursing her lips. Even though she did know: filming was over, and so, it seemed, were the invitations to the Wiryantos'. She glanced at Iskandar and felt a swell and sink in her chest. He was talking to one of his associates. It seemed as if his back was angled conspicuously towards her. He turned and caught her staring. She smarted.

'How's my star?' he asked, all cavalier lightness. 'And how's the proud husband?'

'We are good, thank you,' Wei Loong replied. She felt his hand drift to her waist.

The theatre smelt of stale popcorn and musty cushions. Amisa must have swept these floors hundreds of times. She sat stiffly between Wei Loong and Novita. Iskandar Wiryanto was a wife and child away. The lights dimmed.

'Bigger! Scarier! We've got to scale everything up,' Iskandar had said, insisting she wear a clunky mask of foam latex, applied by the nervous make-up artist, a girl no older than nineteen, who stippled the edges of the latex onto Amisa's skin. She looked garish, barely recognizable, but in a way that seemed sloppy and unintentional. Just two eyes glaring from behind a rubbery mask with a hooked nose like a fairy-tale witch's, nowhere near anybody's idea of a Pontianak.

On the large screen, she popped out from a cupboard. Hands extended over her head, cartoonish. Novita chuckled beside her, and in that moment, Amisa hated the girl. That big reveal had taken hours to shoot. The titular Curse of the Bomoh was to make her even uglier. How her back ached from stooping inside that mahogany cupboard, waiting to spring the doors open, to howl. She had boils and welts painted and glued down on her arms and legs.

She peered over at Iskandar. He propped his elbows on the armrests of the plush chair and had his fingers bridged in front of his face, like a chess player considering his next move. Did he think the film was any good? Amisa could barely bring herself to keep her gaze on the screen. Finally the credits rolled. Wei Loong clapped and clapped when her name came up.

AMISA TAN .... PONTI

Her hands lay still and she kept a lidded gaze on the screen as other names followed. She wondered how many actresses all over the world had stared at their name in the credits and seen the hard, often horrible work encrypted in that line of dots: the long shoots, the bad takes, the standing in the sun and rain. Very many, she assumed. She felt cowed by the unoriginality of her thought.

'You make a good monster, Amisa,' Mrs Wiryanto said to her afterwards, in the lobby.

'Thank you. I'm so glad you enjoyed it,' Amisa replied. Her cheeks ached as she smiled.

*

At the start of 1983, the Wiryantos moved to Hong Kong. Iskandar said the film industry was more virile over there and he could find better collaborators. He would call her, he claimed, once things were set up.

For the first year that she didn't hear from him, she forgave him out of the painful habit of unrequited love. Such a love endures so much cruelty, is even fortified by it. The weakening of her spirit kept that bad grip strong. She knew the way he was, how he consumed ideas and discarded them at the drop of a hat, how when he was focused on a project everything and everyone else just fell away, even his own daughter. What chance did Amisa have?

She looked out for news of Iskandar's films in the papers, but it never appeared. She tried dialling her birthday digits, and then the foreign number he left her, but one line was disconnected, and the other was either engaged, or five long beeps promised an answer, before the connection cut out.

She turned twenty-six, then twenty-seven. Even though she still tried for auditions, no studio in Singapore or Malaysia would offer a leading, or even substantial, role to a woman pushing thirty with no star wattage, much less no experience besides three totally unknown horror films that had barely screened and, as such, hardly existed. Nobody had heard of her, nor of Iskandar Wiryanto, nor of the Ponti films; nobody cared enough to help her out. She tried lying about her age, but the industry was tightening its rules, and work permits required her IC or her passport, both of which bore her stubborn, damning birthdate.

She wanted so badly to be a somebody and an every-thing, not a nobody and a nothing, but the trench between the two states was deep and wide and a stubborn mystery to traverse. She went for a meeting with a man she found through the classified ads, who claimed he could get her an audition for a Hong Kong telemovie. He operated out of the back office of the yellowing, notorious Sandstone Plaza, already a bad sign. He was a Chinese man in his late thirties with a queasy, seasick face: darting eyes, greenish pallor.

'I'll help you if you help me,' he said. At least he cuts to the chase, Amisa thought, as she looked up at him from under her eyelashes. She waited three seconds before nodding coyly.

He took her to the Fragrance Hotel and booked a room on the hourly rate. The air conditioner leaked onto her bare shoulders and the pilling blue pillow that reeked of old sweat and body lotion. The vent made an eerie keening sound and it masked her own flat, desultory moans as the man flipped and pounded her like she was a burger patty. This was sexless sex, a body performing its urgent, ugly motions; two strangers jarring and grifting for conquest. Amisa thought of her younger days lying down in the fields with the swarthy men and avid boys in Kampong Mimpi Sedih. She'd considered herself victorious then; possessing the upper hand. Not so now. She felt a twinge of fondness for Wei Loong and how meaningfully he still handled her. *Too* meaningfully, in fact, fixing her with a mushy, trustful look that didn't flatter his features. But being fucked like

240

this, the bedsprings tawdry and telling, didn't feel good
either.

*

Over the next few years she tried attending open calls for
Channel 8, but rejected the two roles she was offered. She
refused to put talcum powder in her chignon, to kowtow
to concubines. She would not play the part of the frowning
matriarch, the suffering mah jie, the amah, or the hand-
wringing spinster sister. She wanted to be at the glowing
centre of each story, to love and hate and fight and win
completely and without condescension, no concession to
screen time, no expense spared. Why did getting older have
to put a stop to her wanting? Surely it grew as she grew.
Why did no one respect that?

One afternoon, she was at the box office staring at her
hands and wondering if they looked soap-worn when Wei
Loong came bounding through the double doors. He
grinned widely.

'It worked. After nine bloody years, it worked!'

'What are you talking about?'

He waved a slip of paper in front of her: the Toto,
embossed with the light-red Singapore Pools logo, receipt
fonts printed with the number he had bought every week
since the beginning of their marriage: 23081958, bonus
numbers 190476. They had won.

'We can move out of our flat. We can buy a house, get
a garden of our own. A fucking driveway. I've never had a
garden. Have you?' Wei Loong was more attractive and
enthused than she had seen him in years.

He twirled her away from the counter. Yes, the possibilities were opening up: fuck the film hall, fuck the ticket stubs, fuck the peanut shells she had to sweep up every evening, fuck the dirty toilets, fuck the ficus tree, fuck their noisy neighbours, fuck their beige bedroom.

They bought a house in a cul-de-sac at the end of a leaf-strewn driveway. It was more than they had ever dreamed of. There was a garden full of sagging trees and bug-filled plants. Everything awake, alive.

On the day they moved into the house they went out to the patio. Light came down in diagonal stripes on the dirty tiles. Rain- and mud-stained, brown streaks on yellowed cream, with a Nyonya patterning. Wei Loong lifted her up by the waist and his hands hurt her a little, fingers poking her ribs. He swung her around and held her in the air like a prize. And then he put her down and she laughed because that was what people did in films.

21
SZU

2003

After school I pass out in bed and only wake up four hours later, when it is dark outside. I blink open my body in its crumpled uniform. I feel that angry grogginess of hours lost.

As if she senses that I'm awake, I hear Aunt Yunxi's room door open. She pads down the corridor in my mother's slippers and blocks out the light in my door frame. I pretend to be asleep when she comes in and puts her hand on my forehead.

'Cold snap,' she pronounces in Hokkien, with her raspy stage voice. 'It keeps coming back.'

I continue to feign sleep as she goes to the kitchen, opens the fridge, the creaky cupboard, pours and shuts and comes back clinking a spoon against a bowl. Double-boiled soup to balance me out. Chinese pears, wolfberries, white fungus, snow peas, celery, piss-coloured and smelling of death.

'Your heart is afraid and you have offended a spirit,' Aunt Yunxi says. 'I can't tell which one.' She puts her hand on my chest, moves it up towards my throat and down again, roughly, like she's feeling for something foreign. Her palm is warm and calloused. In the frog-eyed dimness I study her knuckles and the way the veins protrude, so many decades of life running through her, all that pain and treasure. Now that I'm thinner we've started to look alike. Even if she's not really family, the same way women living together sync their periods I feel like I'm absorbing her features, and maybe in forty years I'll be another version of her.

'You should stop spending time with your friend,' she says softly. 'She is a spoilt girl with a weak soul. She's bad for you.'

'Don't talk about Circe like that,' I reply, even though I've started to agree with her.

'Szu Min. Szu. I'm worried about you.'

'I'm okay, really.'

'That's not true.'

My eyes glaze. I feel her staring at me with her forehead all scrunched up, mouth a worried line. If I focus on how old my aunt looks, my soul softens. Right now I don't want to be nice.

'If you don't eat, you'll lose your strength,' she nags. 'And let bad things in. Like greedy spirits. Or a terrible cold. I know you're still bothered. About your mother, about your father. A lot to think about for a young person like you.'

'I am thinking of nothing,' I reply. 'Thanks for the soup.'

When she leaves the room I wait until she is out of earshot before I spoon bits of pear and fungus into the bin and cover them with graph paper. Tomorrow I'll get rid of the rest.

*

The afternoon of our last prelim exam, I walk out of the hall with an executioner's gait. The big, actual O levels are next month. I feel like the final girl halfway through a horror movie, eyes wide, peering around a corner, falsely safe because her ordeal needs further complication.

Circe asks me to come along to K-Box with her new-found choir cronies to celebrate. I accompany her just to curry the last scraps of good favour, even though I know it won't make much of a difference, and she knows that kara-oke combines two things I hate: singing and socializing.

In the red-and-black K-Box reception three choir girls are waiting. They finished their prelims earlier and God knows how long they've been here, with their purposefully undone laces, bobbed hair and neutral expressions. Tsarina, Rong En and Angela. We've shared a school for four years but I have never hung out with them before, much less had a proper conversation. Circe and Tsarina are second sopranos in the choir and they have been spending time together lately in early practices for a choral festival. Circe's speaking voice I am accustomed to, but Tsarina Chong sounds like she has a throatful of phlegm and helium. Oh, she's horrible, and she waves at me like I should feel so bloody blessed. Angela and Rong En don't even acknowl-edge my presence. I fall back into step as Circe and Tsarina lead us down the narrow black corridor, past darkened, flickering soundproofed rooms, until we reach our booth.

Our session consists of two hours of singing, inclusive of one jug of soft drink and a bowl of 'assorted snacks' which turn out to be the saddest peanuts on earth. I don't want to sing and the other girls just shrug at my lack of participation.

'You're so extra,' Tsarina says. 'You're like someone who goes to a theme park and doesn't ride the roller coasters. Wait and hold bags only.'

'Ha ha, that's funny,' I chuckle.

Circe glares at me and starts to scroll through the song catalogue. I get it, I'm her accessory, a human comfort blanket filling the role of the silent boyfriend, if only we had boyfriends. After an everlasting five minutes of ordering and selection the singing begins.

Tsarina and Rong En go first. They have the same level of competent but not-amazing voices and that's probably why they are friends. Circe is up next. She picks a Stefanie Sun song, her inflections forced from pretending her Mandarin is worse than it actually is. She thinks that being bad at Mother Tongue makes her cooler. Tsarina and Rong En and I are laughing at Circe. Subtly at first, and then more raucously. Tsarina and I exchange sideways glances, in on the same joke, and I can hear Circe's voice waver as she tries to focus on the song and not lose her temper. And it's all so funny. But then I notice the other girls shooting me a look because they've stopped laughing and my shoulders are still shuddering, almost involuntarily. I wipe the tears from my eyes and clear my throat. I stifle my hiccups and direct my attention to the red walls and the bowl of peanuts on the table. A soft burning pain flexes my stomach.

'You sure you don't want to have a go, Szu?' Angela asks, one claw around the microphone. I shake my head.

'Say one ah!' she exclaims, and clears her throat. 'Okay!' Her cheerfulness is an impermeable rainbow bubble. She's chosen a Mariah Carey song. During the lengthy instrumental I turn away and expect the worst. And then she starts to sing. Ten seconds in it is clear she is really good, miles better than the other three, and she will always be blessed unless she smokes a pack a day like my mother did. She makes it seem easy, executing impressive vocal slides while the other choir girls lean tight-lipped into the faux-leather seat and flinch with every inflection. The song lasts forever. Every time I think it will end Angela carries on, smart-ass gesticulating like she's doing an unplugged performance on live TV.

I think of the choir terms Circe mentioned to me: *glissando, tremolo, portamento,* rolling off my mental tongue like flavours of fancy ice cream, and the thought of dessert makes me sick. Circe grins encouragingly at the screen, cheeks straining, her eyes hard and shiny. Every few seconds Tsarina grabs a fistful of peanuts and chews like a cowboy. I watch the ticker on screen counting down as Angela's ostentatiously great voice floods the room. It wasn't a competition but she wins.

Afterwards, Circe and I stand at the entrance for a good ten seconds watching the other girls leave. If I weren't here like her weird tall appendage, maybe she would be following them to MOS Burger to chat about confounding church boys and choral things.

'I guess I better head back to do some revision,' Circe

says as we descend the escalator. 'Also I'm running out of allowance. So I can't afford to stay in town.'

She's never used the money excuse before. We reach the bus stop in silence. She seems irritated with me, even though I feel like I've been good today.

'I'm having bad dreams,' I say, because dreams used to interest her due to her sleeping problems. She's facing away from me, waiting for the 77. My bus is the 518. 'My mother keeps popping up,' I continue, and this is true. I also think if I mention my mother Circe will have to at least pay attention.

'It's normal to dream things.' Circe replies.

'Some nights she looks peaceful,' I continue. 'Other nights she looks so sad and I can't stand it and I wake up sad, too. It feels as if she's trying to tell me something. But I can't figure out what it is.'

'Hm,' Circe replies, craning her neck a little, keeping her eyes on the road. 'I wouldn't overthink it.' She squints at the number on the approaching bus but it says 7, not 77. 'Lately I've been thinking.'

'About what?'

'Isn't it crazy that we are stuck here on earth, and we won't make it out of here alive?'

'What do you mean?' I feel quietly peeved at her dismissal of my dream.

'I was watching this thing on TV the other day about NASA. And it occurred to me that the only way to get off this planet is to die or become an astronaut.'

My eyebrows rise. 'Hm. Yeah. Guess so. What made you think that?'

'I dunno, just feeling random. Anyway, have you heard of any Singaporean astronauts? No, right?'

'No . . . and since when were you interested in all this space and planet stuff?'

'Why not? I'm being serious.'

'It's cool, I guess.' I look at the floor. 'I don't mind being on this planet,' I continue uncertainly.

'Why, though?'

'I don't know . . . it's too hot here, but it's okay.'

Circe stands back as if assessing me, and blinks like she's getting dust out of her eyes.

'You hate being here,' she says.

'No, I don't.'

'Yeah, you do. Earth-hater.'

Even though it's a dumb conversation it is still progress, almost like how we used to be. For the past few weeks topics have skirted around exams and how busy she is. Circe seems so insistent about this. For a moment I space out at the wide green trees across the road as cars rush past. And then something occurs to me.

'Hey, wait a minute, didn't you read that on the Internet a while ago? That earth astronaut thing? I remember. We were on your PC, at your house.'

'Don't remember.' Circe's chapped mouth twitches.

'Yeah, I think you showed me someone's Livejournal or something. It was on a blog. The thing about how we won't make it out of this planet alive and we only have this time on earth, etc. Some American chick wrote it. I remember!'

Circe's face drops. She looks older, stern. She frowns

and takes a deep breath. When she speaks her words are soft and slow, loaded with last straws. 'What's your problem?'

'Er, I don't know what you mean.'

'*God*, you're so frustrating.'

It's Thursday early evening and brutally busy in town. The bus stop by Tangs Plaza feels more exposed than most – right by the wide, rushing road, people everywhere. The *77* pulls up and people spill out and shove past us. A middle-aged man with a blue tie accidentally strikes me on the arm with his satchel.

'Ow,' I say, rubbing my shoulder. 'Shit. Chill, it doesn't matter.'

Circe crosses her arms. People keep jostling. I step to the side. She's still frowning.

'You know what?' she asks. I shrug, weakly. Her eyes dart from my face to the arriving bus. The crowd begins to form a long queue. 'I've tried my best,' she says. 'I've tried to be understanding. But it's so hard to be around you, Szu. It's not just hard, it's *painful*. It's like this big, dark pain follows you everywhere. You're no fun to hang out with. You feel sorry for yourself all the time. And you hate everything. At least I try. You think you're better than everyone.'

'So do you,' I reply instinctively. Her eyes narrow. 'That's not true,' I correct myself. I clench my fists, which have gone cold.

'I care about my future,' she replies. 'I can't do this any more.'

'Do what?' I bark. My face is flushed with adrenaline. I want to hit her.

'Babysit you,' Circe spits out. She turns away as the bus door hisses open. She shoves past a salt-and-pepper-haired auntie. The auntie tuts and whips her head around to glare at me as if I've done the pushing.

My eyes are stinging as I watch Circe board and beep her EZ Link card. Her blue, beat-up Jansport backpack weaves and bobs down the body of the bus. It is too crowded to sit so she holds on to a handrail and faces away from me. Her stance makes her look even shorter. As the bus pulls away I spot my own crumpled face reflected in the window.

It happened so fast that we hardly made a scene. I feel like this is the last time we will ever speak. Tonight it's not just the haze that gives the air on Orchard Road this choked, impersonal finality. People push me around and hit my calves with their shopping. Maybe Circe is right and I hate being on this planet because I am useless at living here. Except for my aunt, no one would notice if I left or dropped dead. I have no parents nor siblings nor friends. The future is a failed exam. I feel wispy as a dandelion and haven't eaten for thirty-six hours, so I'm not surprised when I trip and fall forward with a thud. It sounds dull but feels sharp, and in the moment before I black out my belly aches so much, as do my brittle bones and the pit of my heart.

22

AMISA

1987

Late January 1987 the baby was born. She was a little girl and Wei Loong liked the name Szu Min; it had been his grandmother's. Amisa agreed to it, exhausted from carrying around and painfully expelling this wriggling red bundle. Ng Szu Min resembled Wei Loong more than her; it was hard to find her trace in that mushed-up face with the small brown eyes like rocaille beads.

In June Amisa found out in the newspapers that the Everitt Cineplex, former Paradise Theatre, had been demolished to make way for a mega-mall. The shophouse where she had stayed in Geylang had been sold en bloc and converted into offices. Nothing was recognizable. Not even her own child. She waited for that savage tenderness, the instinctual stirring of maternal affection, but even staring at Szu made Amisa feel bloated and foggy. For the first time she understood her own mother with an undeniable, visceral intensity. Her swollen feet were foreign to her. Her skin itched and dry patches began to form on her hands and ankles. She spent ages in the bath lamenting her wrecked body while its fault cried in the nursery room.

Wei Loong would rattle the door, furious.

'Since you like acting so much, why don't you act like a mother?' he said.

'Why don't you act like you have balls and a spine, then?' she would reply. Her words echoed in the bathroom. Ugly things like: 'Where were you earlier? You're not home half the time. Go out and drink beer only. You don't even know how to wipe your baby's ass. Go on! Who's the model father? Fucking hypocrite.'

Her voice turned hoarse, cawing. After she spat out the angry things she would run her fingers through her wet hair and scowl at him. He would glare back, before the baby's cries summoned him to the other room.

Some mornings she took her daughter to the nearby community park. Smiled at the other women with their prams and flat brown slippers. Amisa was a woman pushing a problem. The problem gurgled as they took two laps around the park.

*

1995. It had been a bad year before it even began, and every passing day confirmed its rottenness. Late afternoon, stalemate weather: soupy air bearing down on her photo-sensitive skin, her aching, peeling shoulders. The smell of wasted food from the big bins outside travelled from room to open-windowed room. The child was asleep next door, ceiling fan on full. Amisa sat up in her bed and watched Wei Loong carefully applying pomade to a stray cowlick. He would be forty soon. His hair had started thinning in a patch on the left-hand side of his head. He stood in front of her dressing table, handling a black comb with painterly seriousness.

'Where are you going?' she asked, trying to be jocular. 'Why the effort?'

'To meet old army friends.'

'Army friends like who?'

'You won't know them. Not like you ever come out any more,' he said, softly. He shot a furtive glance at her. She tilted her head at him like an eastern grass owl, and did not blink until he, as usual, looked away first. She stretched out her legs under the thin green sheets, one strap of her negligee slipping off her shoulder.

'Bye now,' Wei Loong said. He came over and pressed his mouth briefly to her right cheek before he left the room. The sight of her half naked in mussed-up blankets did not have the same irresistible appeal as when they first met eighteen years ago. This was only natural, she thought. Not like she missed his groping, incessant hunger for her, anyway.

The sound of his engine travelled all the way down the driveway. Amisa pushed herself up and sat on the edge of the bed, leaned her face into her hands. If she had ever loved him it was because he had loved her. That was how it had been in the beginning. But now that he did not love her there were nobody's feelings to be hurt. In a way, it felt freeing. She was a person of no tactical importance to anyone, except, perhaps, the smaller person in the room next door. There was probably some youngish mistress somewhere, waiting for Wei Loong's pomade embrace, his genuine suckerfish kisses. So-and-so could keep him. Amisa had no energy to be angry or jealous about a third party interfering in her antique marriage to the antiques restorer. In a second she would get up properly and see if Szu was still asleep, or if she wanted a snack.

*

2003. Amisa's whole body hurt, up to her eyeballs, and she was so, so tired. She needed a drink, and she was out of cigarettes. The sun glared in the garden and would scorch her skin if she went out at this hour. Yunxi was stuck in the session room with a neurotic and profoundly irritating woman who needed spectral life advice about even the smallest matters: what to have for dinner, and whether the tax man was out to overcharge her. Still, she always paid for her extra-long consultations.

Amisa sat up in bed and watched the light shifting on the dusty windowpane. Perhaps because Wei Loong had left for good and she no longer bothered with men, she indulged in wondering about Iskandar Wiryanto. He had left Singapore almost two decades ago. He would be an old man now.

She said these lines to him in her head: *Do you know who I am, Iskandar Wiryanto? Nobody does. I'll never be famous. I am forty-three, and utterly unknown. Also obscure: Iskandar Wiryanto. Your name means nothing to anyone else.*

She got up and felt the blood rush to her head, and her legs almost gave way. Water, she probably needed water. She went to the hallway and stopped outside Szu's door. Her daughter had her friend over again, that annoying girl whose name Amisa could never remember.

Teenage habits mushroomed and rotted in the fierce hothouse privacy of that bedroom. Stuck to its wooden door was a DO NOT ENTER! DANGER ZONE sign and below that a half-scratched-off Spice Girls sticker that had gradually lightened under the glare of Szu's embarrassment. ('I never loved the Spice Girls,' she now claimed. 'They were okay only.')

When Szu was eight, just before Wei Loong left, she begged her parents to buy her that huge sticker from a stationery shop in Bras Basah. It had touched and amused them so much (at that point, it was one of the few things that touched and amused them), how desperately Szu wanted that huge, ugly sticker. She pleaded for it as a matter of life or certain death. Back then, Amisa marvelled at how little it sometimes took to make a child happy – even one as solemn as their Little Bunny. It had taken just S$1.99 and a piece of colourful, adhesive paper to make Szu feel over the moon. But that was then. Now all that was left of the sticker was nail-clawmarks and the shadow of one arm casually slung over another, a shock of hair, bleached teeth on faded faces.

Amisa knocked. She heard shuffles, murmurs. She rapped the door twice and opened. Szu was sitting on her chair, and her friend sat cross-legged on her bed. Fuzzy music played. They were flipping through magazines, which Amisa disapproved of. Szu reddened.

'Hi,' she said.

'Ah girl, can you go to the shop for me?'

'Now?'

'Yeah.'

'Oh,' Szu replied, meaning: *no*.

'Your friend can stay. While you're away, I'll talk to her. We can have a nice chat.'

'It's okay, Auntie, I'll go with her,' the friend mumbled.

'Please, it's Mrs Ng,' Amisa replied, and fashioned a smile. The girl shyly returned it. 'What was your name again?'

'Circe.'

'Ah, yes, Sissy, of course. Like Sissy Spacek.' The girl didn't reply. Amisa got out S$120 from her pocket and handed the crumpled notes to Szu.

'Two packs of Marlboro Reds and a bottle of Jim Beam. Chop chop.'

'Are you sure?' Szu asked.

'Of course I'm sure,' Amisa replied. 'The uncle knows you're my daughter, he's my friend, will close one eye. Just pay when no one is looking. And you can use the change to get a snack for you two. Something low-calorie though, you girls got to be healthy.'

Szu took the money and got up. Amisa squeezed past her and sat in her chair. At the doorway Szu turned towards Amisa and Circe. Circe moved, as if to follow.

'No need for both of you to go, this is not a military operation. You stay,' Amisa said, fixing the friend with a pursed smile.

'Er. Okay,' the girl replied. She didn't want to be rude.

They said nothing as Szu walked down the hallway and left the house. Amisa thought of asking the girl what she did, but of course, she was just at school. She did schoolgirl things and had schoolgirl worries. She had all the time in the world to figure out in what direction to swim, and how, and when.

Amisa studied her daughter's only friend. She was small and skinny with a long nose like an Afghan hound. It conferred an air of distinction on her young face; Amisa liked people with striking noses. The girl looked down at her lap, and then up again.

In that instant the dull-purple walls of the room seemed to funnel down to a point of warm brightness. It was the look in Circe's eyes: scared, both powerful and pleading. She had the desperate yet resigned stare of someone on the run, in the jungle, starving to death. Someone who had been through bad and sad things and who needed help she didn't realistically expect to receive. Almost forty years had passed since Amisa had come across the oily man and woman, and she never thought she would see them again. And yet here they were, looking at her with gladness and recognition.

Amisa took Circe's hands in her own, and Circe started to pull away but changed her mind and left them there.

'You're going to make it out alive, don't worry,' Amisa said, gripping her. 'I know how people are. They don't give, and they never listen. But you're different. I'm different, too. I know you've been through hell. I believe you.'

A shadow passed, and when the sunlight cut back through the feeling faded and they were strangers again. Amisa briskly withdrew her hands. The girl's mouth was a bamboozled circle.

'Um. Enjoy the rest of your afternoon, Sissy,' Amisa said. 'I'm going to take a nap. When Szu comes back, tell her to leave the things outside my door.'

23

CIRCE

2020

It is Saturday afternoon. I'm in FairPrice, hung-over and pushing my empty trolley with a dreamy laboriousness. There is something calming about supermarkets in times of mild, self-induced physical crisis. Ambling down the produce aisle I eye up the verdant bunches of chye sim and butterhead lettuce without taking anything; the keen fresh vegetable and pesticide smell calms me.

Last night I went out to this new bar in Amoy Street called Kopi O))) which looked and felt just like a dingy old kopitiam, down to the unstable plastic chairs and stray cats, except it served S$25 chendol espresso martinis and the staff wore a uniform of printed black wife beaters and too-tight jeans. Julius tried to set me up with his friend Deon, a margarine-hued man in his late thirties with a moustache of sweat on his upper lip.

Julius didn't tell me he was setting me up but I knew from the moment I arrived. It was coded in the way his advertising friends shifted their weight in their spiffy shoes and sipped their drinks, and how quickly everyone left a conspicuous radius around Deon and me. Three martinis in, the sugar was making me sick and I didn't want to partake any further in this disappointing social fumble. I was all talked out from five days' worth of tense and boring conversations at work. Besides, Deon wasn't interested in me either. I noticed the tiny downturn in his eyes when he first said hello, and the way he kept looking over my shoulder while we were talking.

I've never been much of a drinker, so right now I am suffering the effects of the alcohol grievously. My head pulses and my mouth tastes like shit. I am squeezing an exorbitant Hass avocado that feels like a boob when my brother calls. I haven't heard from him in weeks, possibly months. Seeing *LESLIE* flashing up on my phone is so unlikely that I stop my trolley to answer.

'Hello? Did you call me by accident? This is Circe.'

'Yeah, I know. Hi, Sisi.'

'What's up?'

I balance my phone in between my jaw and shoulder and resume pushing the trolley. I can hear the strain in Leslie's voice even as he tells me about how his youngest son Ezekiel has started swimming classes and the little prodigy Thaddeus just had a piano recital. I have always hated his kids' names. I think they sound pretentious, but who am I to talk? My parents named me Circe.

'Rach's been so busy with work lately. And it's been crazy for me as well.'

'Uh-huh, uh-huh,' I say, trailing past the pulses. I round off into meat and dairy.

'Have you called Mom?'

'Yeah, last week,' I lie.

'She hasn't heard from you. You're meant to go to

Thomson Medical with her on Monday. Check-up for her gallstones, remember?'

'You have a car.'

'*Yeah*, but I'm tied up with this project and the kids right now. I'm swamped.'

I hate his tone. 'I thought Ma's appointment was the week after next. Look, I've been busy too. I got a lot going on.'

I hear my brother adjust the phone and gather his breath.

Even in his late thirties, Leslie still looks young. If he went around claiming he was twenty-five, nobody would bat an eyelid. He has alabaster skin and delicate features and wears sunblock with full SPF. He is unable to grow much facial hair and has the distinctively long Low nose that looks dignified on him and harsh on me.

We arrange that I'll accompany my mother for her surgery next week.

'How's Julius?' he asks.

'Fine, he's fine,' I reply. I breathe out sharply and feel a bloom of heat still sitting on my clavicle. Leslie seems to think that Julius and I are dating, living in sin. While he rambles on I start filling up my trolley, chucking in Gardenia bread and sutchi fillets and tofu and beetroot and minced pork and a packet of pepper.

I'm deciding between discounted jumbo packs of toilet paper when Leslie says, 'Oh. You won't believe who I ran into the other day. Blast from the past.'

'Who?' I pick the cheaper brand, my throat constricting.

'Szu Min! Your friend in Sec Four. Your tall twin.'

'Wow. Small world. Where?' My hand grips the silver handle of my trolley.

'Railway Mall. She was with her kid. Hello?'

'Yeah, I'm still here,' I say, shifting my phone from left to right. I resume pushing the trolley. 'She's got a kid?'

'Yeah. A little girl, around Ezie's age. Very sweet.'

I picture Szu as a distended, pastier version of her teenaged self, drifting about her old neighbourhood in a maternity dress, her belly a batik-covered half-moon. Having a daughter who grows up as gangly and morose as she was; Szu being responsible for an entire human being. It seems a little absurd, almost obscene.

'How was she? Szu, not the kid.'

'She seemed well. You know, I always liked Szu. She always seemed older than her age. She was smart.'

'Where got. She had her head in the clouds.'

'You're so bad,' Leslie says in that prefectorial tone of his, and I hear him inhaling to start to say something but then he drops it. It is remarkable how potently a family member can cram years of disappointment into three seconds of silence on the phone.

'Anyway,' Leslie continues. 'She asked after you. She gave me her card.'

'Oh, cool.'

'Maybe you should get back in touch. Such a shame, what happened between you.'

I don't know what to say for a moment. I even feel insulted by his directness. He's never brought it up before. There wasn't much to bring up in the first place. Still.

'Yeah, maybe . . . Listen, I've got to go. I'm getting

263

another call,' I say, and mumble goodbye and hang up. I abandon my trolley and hurry out of the supermarket. Errands can wait. I need some air and my head hurts.

I board a bus home and brood out of the window, trees and clouds and flyovers. My thighs stick to the seat. From time to time a pair of teenage girls in the bay of the standing area let out peals of laughter. One is taller than the other; she wears braces and has short hair. The smaller one has a pinched kiddy face. We enter a long tunnel. The smaller girl shows something to the tall one on her phone; they peer into the cryptic glow of the screen and look back at each other with derisive grins. Cocooned in some small, secret knowledge, they are their own squirrelly and absorbing universe of two.

*

When I think about the Age of Szu, it often surprises me how brief it actually was. A little less than a year elapsed and then she and her aunt and mother were gone. How weirdly indelible the smells and shadows of that cul-de-sac, the Marlboro fog and wafts of incense, the mouldy fish tank bubbling like a cauldron, the altar with its rotating gods, the locked room.

When I met Szu and she told me she had no friends I found it hard to believe; she was intelligent and interesting, which was a rarity in that convent full of preening Stepford-Wives-in-training. Szu and I were citizens of nowhere. We never felt a belonging. Not with the happy nor the popular nor even the outliers, the rebels. We were too gawky to be mysterious, too cautious to be wild, and too self-conscious to stand out. We thought our alienation was unique, and felt secretly enlivened by our discontentment; it meant we weren't sheep.

After Amisa died things shifted. Szu stopped eating regularly or even trying to study. She grew scarily thin and too intense. At first we tried to act like how it had been during the first few months, such relieved companionship. Yet by the end of that year, being friends with Szu was like carrying around a heavy, sloshing bucket of water. Her grief weighed me down and I couldn't escape its drip: not in the cinema, not studying in cafes, not even on my own. She followed me around school and in the afternoons afterwards, like a phantom with her blanched face and hollow eyes. She started wearing her hair in a bubble ponytail just like mine and mooched about my house all day drinking gallons of Diet Coke and draping her sadness over my things. She developed a sour, musty odour that caught me in surprising whiffs. She shed her hair everywhere, leaving tangled black strands all over my bedspread. She was infatuated with Leslie. When she thought I wasn't looking, she stared at him with a bawdy, open hunger. It disturbed me.

When we started dating, my ex-husband and I had a conversation about former relationships. I told him that in a way, even before my boring boyfriend in junior college, Szu felt like my first test of patience: a tenuous, milk-toothed kind of love that evolved into the toil and torpor of a difficult marriage. You could say it was prophetic. I'm not exaggerating when I say that we were only sixteen but I felt like we had been through decades.

When Szu and I shared a bed, in the darkness I could

sense the thoughts and moods pulsing from her stone-still form, a telegraphed presence so strong it felt like an extra being. When my feet skimmed hers she was cold as ice. I turned away simulating sleep, and put my face on my hands. Nothing worked; I couldn't block her out. She was like sarin gas, leaked poison.

Szu and I had one argument (if it could even be called an argument – as always she was annoyingly reticent, con-ciliatory, muted) and after that she kept away from me. For a couple of weeks I slipped into a rhythm of normality: revision, choir practice, new friends from choir, a couple of bland but pleasant girls whose names I barely recall now. Occasionally I spied Szu's shuffling gait out of the corner of my eye, those sallow limbs like chopsticks, and I just looked the other way. She grew thinner and more sunken, her voice strangled-soft if she was ever called upon to speak. Her deterioration was both frightening and affirm-ing to me; on the one hand I worried but on the other I felt that I had made the right decision. Even the bullies left her alone. Our big exams were close and it was one step too far to pick on a girl who was clearly unwell, who had only recently lost her mother.

Things might have carried on this way through our O levels and until we graduated and went our separate ways, had she not collapsed in the concourse one hazy morning that smelt of burning. It happened just before assembly. I was standing elsewhere and I remember a cluster of people forming a space for her, the murmurs of distress. Our first O-level exam was the week after. Two days later she fainted again, during a Chemistry revision session. I wasn't there

266

but I heard about it within the hour. Something about an ambulance and emergency services. They took her to hospital; she was too ill to sit the exams. Everyone in our level was intrigued and a little envious of her exemption and all of a sudden they remembered that Szu and I were supposed to be best friends.

'How is Szu, heard any news?' Clara and Meixi and Elizabeth Kwee asked.

'Um, she's recovering,' I said, supposing this was true.

Then, midway through the exam period, I received a call at home. It was Aunt Yunxi. She spoke in English, her voice crackling.

'Can you come and visit? Szu is not well.'

*

Going down Szu's driveway, I remembered the wake with its strangers and interruptions, and the irretrievable ease of our early days. The garden stank of rotting vegetation. Crickets and cicadas trilled. Swarms of gnats followed me, flirting with my hair.

Aunt Yunxi was waiting at the door. She looked the same, stale and dusty as tinned food and very thin. She wore a patterned mauve blouse-and-trouser set. She did not return my smile; just let me in through the sitting room with its lit altar.

'Be careful, floor is wet,' she said. A blue bucket stood in the corner of the kitchen. I caught a glimpse of the fish tank, which lay empty. The glass of the tank was still dirtied green with mossy stones at the bottom.

'You want something to drink?'

'No thanks, Auntie.'

I could feel her displeasure. I knew that she knew I had neglected her niece. Szu's bedroom door was open and I walked down the corridor at a gingerly pace, trying to seem casual but chock-full of guilt and dread. Szu lay in bed, facing the wall. Her long black hair was tucked under the bobbled pillow. Her toes stuck out of the edge of the bed frame. The rest of her was covered in a thin checked blanket that I hadn't seen before. The scene reminded me of Amisa in hospital, the impersonal antiseptic tang of the air, that palliative print.

Her breathing sounded shallow. She had the scuffed, bony elbow of an old woman.

'It's me!' I called out. Szu didn't move. The air in that purple bedroom was stagnant. I sat on her swivel chair and put down my school bag. After a few seconds she stirred and turned towards me. She had a serene expression but her skin betrayed her, worn and jaundiced. She attempted a smile and I smiled back, but I didn't mean it. Where was my kindness? Szu Min was sick and she wasn't going to take her exams at the same time as everyone else. Her aunt was creepy and possibly a charlatan. And both her parents were gone. Life sucked for her, but all I could think of was how burdened I felt, as if my time was being wasted. I had my e-Maths and History exams the next week and my head was full of facts and numbers. I wanted to do well enough to move on.

Szu let out a long, deep breath.

'I think I'm dying,' she said.

'No, you're not,' I replied. 'You're bluffing, right?' I

didn't believe her but my eyes filled with tears. Suddenly I felt incredibly and frankly sorry about the last few months; I wanted to reach out and hug her, but she seemed so frail.

'Auntie says I've offended some spirits, and I've breathed in bad air. I have light bones and a light body and if I am not careful I will die young.'

'Is that what the doctors said?'

'Don't remember. It doesn't matter, anyway.'

She looked away and lay back so she was facing the ceiling. She closed her eyes. I wondered if she wished I wasn't here or if she was waiting for me to say something, even to apologize.

After a few minutes I started to talk. I went on and on and the only sign Szu was registering me was the grand, guileless way her eyes stirred behind their lids as if she was rapid dreaming. Perhaps thinking she was asleep encouraged me. By that point, I was past caring how she would judge me and I had no consideration for the effect my words might have. Whatever my reasons, that day I decided to tell her something I'd never mentioned before and which I've never told anyone since.

*

I was eight years old, a quarter of a century ago. One afternoon in September, it rained so hard the mud by the roadsides rose and swelled. As I looked out from the windows of my school bus the big longkang along the main road coursed with drain water the colour of milk tea. By the time I got home the sky had ruptured into a torrential monsoon shower.

269

We lived in our old flat back then, in our old life; this was just before my father's business took off. It was on the third floor of the block. I tried the front door and it was locked. I pressed my ear against the window and heard the flat thrum with unmanned smugness. I shivered and rattled the brass handle as if it would budge. My mother must have forgotten that choir practice was cancelled and I would be coming home three hours earlier. I was too young, apparently, to be trusted with my own set of keys.

My parents had recently fired Melati. She was our maid, a quiet twenty-one-year-old from Indonesia who had probably lied about her age to her agency and was eighteen at most. I adored Melati because she was funny and kind to me, but she had one fatal flaw. She could not stop eating sweets all day. This snacking habit was considered unacceptable even though she worked hard and the boiled sweets and chocolate were bought with her wages, and she sometimes shared.

Without Melati the door was a dead end. I shivered outside the double-locked door, shit brown with a green grille. I tried to rattle it even though I knew my efforts were useless. My fists felt soft and weak. I must have stood there in my soaked pinafore for over half an hour, school bag by my feet. I stared at my Bata shoes, and then at the dirty concrete, and finally the rippling grass two storeys below. I thought of the unthinkable pain I would feel if I jumped. I anticipated it as abstractly as adult romance. How my legs would crumple. How my body would fold.

I kept to the sheltered walkway, one foot in front of another, a game, pretending I was on a zigzag balance beam instead. My school bag sopped through my back, my textbooks heavy and useless. I felt hungry and cold. I went all along the corridor and then up the stairwell. I couldn't have climbed more than a few floors. But later on, when I tried to get the events straight, it was like something in my brain just couldn't compute. The corridors and identical dun-and-apricot-coloured blocks merged and warped into an infinity of stairwells and hallways, like an M. C. Escher drawing. It's funny how we get so used to the environment we live in that going down a different pathway becomes as unnatural as writing with your non-dominant hand.

Being on the other side of our block of flats, which Leslie and I hadn't bothered to explore for a while, was enough to unsettle me. The floor I found myself on looked just the same as our own, down to the brown bristle welcome mat a couple of doors ahead, and the single potted plant in the corridor. My skin felt clammy and in need of a wash. The rainstorm kept up its angry piston beat. I scratched a mosquito bite on the back of my neck, unsure of what to do next.

A door opened halfway down to the right, exactly where our flat would be, except this wasn't our floor. First the inner lock, and then the grille came unlatched. An auntie popped her head out. She had white hair and a foggy face. She reminded me of a turtle because of her slow, reptilian stare and the sagging skin of her neck. We had lived in this building for years but I had never seen her. She beckoned for me to come over.

'Ah girl. You're Circe, aren't you?'

'How do you know my name?'

271

'Your mother told me to let you in if you were locked out,' she said. 'Don't just stand there, you'll catch cold.'

I stayed where I was, even as she came out and beckoned. She stood opposite me, arms akimbo. She was old, and quite fat. I could see the lumps of her tummy where her blue blouse clung to her, and the dappled flesh under her arms.

'Your ma told me to look for you. Glad you came here.'

'You know my mom?'

'Yes, of course. She said to have you over for tea.'

She spoke like a teacher who had been educated overseas, yet it was hard to place where her accent came from. I guessed Hong Kong or Taiwan.

I peered behind her and into her flat. It was dark in there, not even a TV on. I could see the floral edge of a sofa, and the floor was speckled. Now I must say here that I'm not stupid: I remembered what we had been taught since kindergarten about dangerous strangers, even if Singapore is one of the safest places in the world. The instructional videotape told us to refuse everything offered and to step away slowly, claiming parents were close. I felt flattered that if this woman was a kidnapper, I was deemed worth it and cute enough for criminal calculation. Usually the missing children on TV were British or American, blonde baby beauty queens or mop-fringed cherubs.

'Come in, lah,' the woman said. 'Stop dilly-dallying. Your ma Magda told me to take care of you. I know her from Bible study. She never say? I'm Madam Chang, by the way. Nice to meet you.'

Madam Chang herded me in. Her living room was

dingy as hell. She gestured towards a rattan chair. The room's only illumination came from a small aquarium in the corner. Algae grew across the top and bottom of the glass. Two big, bloated goldfish with ragged tails drifted about. They were pearly white with a tinge of red, as if their scales had faded. One of the fish had cataracts.

'Would you like some juice? Or some Milo?'

'Maybe some Milo,' I replied. 'Thanks, Auntie.'

She went into the kitchen. Through the din of the rainstorm I heard the pad and hum of the fridge door. She returned with a cold carton of Milo. I took it from her, and suspecting that it could be spiked or poisoned, dropped it on the floor. Madam Chang picked it up and gave it back to me. Again, I let it fall. Making the same mistake twice seemed to upset adults and teachers. If she grew angry then she couldn't be trusted.

'You are naughty,' Madam Chang said as she placed the carton on my lap, but she smiled as she said this and her yellow teeth shone. She sat on the rattan chair beside mine, with her hands placed flat on her knees.

I smiled at her primly and shrugged. I shook the carton of Milo before I poked the straw in, wondering how long my parents would take to come back, and how long the rainstorm would last. As I sipped the Milo I stared at the goldfish with the cataracts, bobbing unsteadily. It looked like it would go belly-up any moment.

'You're looking at my jinyu, huh? Guess how old they are?'

'Dunno.'

'Come on, guess.'

'Two?' I took another sip, making a small gurgling sound with the straw. The Milo tasted slightly bitter.

'Wrong!' Madam Chang said, and grinned at me. 'Try again. Come on!'

I shrugged.

'They are both 150 years old. Husband and wife, you know. They lived through the war and the British people. If I had more space these fishes would be the size of ducks. Or even pigs.'

I said nothing and looked at the tiled floor.

'Do you like school?'

'It's okay,' I replied.

'Don't say like that,' Madam Chang said. 'Okay only? You're lucky you get to go. I never got the chance. My father made me stay inside all day. My sisters, some of them so clever, but they weren't allowed books, they had to cook and clean and sew. I had to learn everything on my own. Don't say the government bad to you to make you go to school.'

I rolled my eyes internally. I knew what pattern she was: Preachy Propaganda Auntie. I loathed being lectured.

'Can you read? Can you do maths?' I asked, because I hated both those things. 'I'm good at maths,' I lied. 'I got full marks for my last test.'

'Wah, so clever,' she said. 'Are you hungry?'

'I'm okay,' I replied, but Madam Chang got out of her seat. It cost her a great effort.

I stared at the pile of women's magazines neatly stacked on the coffee table. Madam Chang returned with a plate containing some love letter biscuits. I took one just to have something to do. When I bit into the biscuit it crumbled completely and scattered all over my uniform.

'How come you know my mom?' I enquired, as I helped myself to another. 'I'm in the yard all the time. I've never seen you.'

'I keep to myself,' Madam Chang replied.

I was about to ask her why when she fixed me with a serious expression. Her eyes were very shiny, and very black. All of a sudden she seemed sad, and her sadness sucked the light out of the room. It had a weight to it, a heft.

'You are a very special girl, Circe,' she said. Her voice was brittle. 'Not everyone is like you.'

The aquarium light shifted from purple into teal and the walls took on a waving quality. In a matter of moments, Madam Chang seemed to grow younger as the room turned the green of cartoon slime, nuclear waste. Now she didn't look any older than fifty. She had this serious, yearning expression. She reached towards me, made to touch my cheek, and I flinched, not because I thought she would hit me but because when her hand got close I felt a force I can only describe as extreme vertigo, or what I would find out years later is called a hypnic jerk, that jolt you get when you're falling asleep.

In the laser-green light, Madam Chang told me she was thousands of years old. I can't remember her exact words, just the gist of it. Even her voice changed. She had a storyteller's rasp now, almost theatrical. She was born in the Qin Mountains, forever ago. When she was very small, five priests and an astrologer came to her house. They had

275

searched the land for someone like her for a long time. They inspected her body and declared that she met all the requirements. She had twenty perfect teeth and a neck as curved as a conch shell and lampblack eyes and bovine eyelashes. She was five years old. The men took her to a giant room full of the fly-ridden heads of slaughtered animals. They snuffed out their torches and left her there, locked in the darkness alone. At the crack of dawn, when they found her sitting calm and cross-legged amidst the carcasses, they declared her a goddess.

From then on she could only leave her chambers for ceremonial occasions. She only saw her sisters. She was considered so sacred that her feet could never touch the common ground or her powers would leave her. She was carried everywhere on an elaborate beaded palanquin and people wept when they caught a glimpse of her. They made her offerings of giant fruit, rice, flowers, sometimes crayons, even though everyone was dirt poor. Happy and reverent tears looked just the same as sad ones. She was lonely and sick of making people cry. Her legs grew soft and weak as stalks. Life carried on this way until she shed her first blood and she was told that, just like that, she and her family would return to the anonymity of their own village. It was very hard for her to be normal after years of being treated like a divine being on earth. Even to walk with certainty, big bold steps, when she was accustomed to a shuffle.

The men who married goddesses like her were cursed to early deaths, but she didn't want to believe it. She grew up, fell in love. Her husband, Mr Chang, worked in a mine. They made joy for each other for four perfect years, and then he fell ill. He had dust in his lungs and the sinseh could do nothing to help. One night, when the moon was so full it flooded the window, Madam Chang woke up with a gasp. She remembered that trial night with the bloodied buffalo heads staring into her soul, their victims' eyes and long, dusty lashes. How moving, how cold. She wondered why it marked her as special to have endured that. Now she was powerless. Her husband's laboured breathing rattled beside her. The sinseh said he had not long left. Her heart hurt and she was seized with the impulse to get away from this sickbed and the pain that filled every corner of the house. She decided to go walking up the mountain.

She wandered along the winding dirt path, lingering with the slow steps of one reluctant to return home, but who soon must. Something small gleamed ahead, winking like a signal. In the middle of the mud she found a pearl. It had a glowing pink lustre. It was perfectly beautiful. She had never seen anything like it. Without thinking she put it in her mouth, tilted her head back and swallowed. It tasted foul. Almost at once, she began to feel her bones lighten and her whole body had the sensation of dissolving like foam. Her once sacred, now calloused feet lifted from the ground. Her shoes slipped off and then she floated up and away. She rose above the trees more quickly than she could shout. She watched the village and the mountains shrink to the size of her thumbs.

'And then what?' I asked Madam Chang.

Her hand brushed my knee. The light from the fish tank turned blue and lit up the lines across her forehead.

'I kept floating until the whole earth looked like a scroll full of ink smudges. I went past clouds and birds. All the way until I reached the moon,' she said. The living room was now cast in astral blue.

'Up there I had no need for shoes. It's not so special, the moon, just rock and cooled lava; it smelt of gunpowder. Like fights, like volcanoes. I heard a sound in the distance, as if someone was chopping wood. How strange, I thought. That definitely sounds like a woodcutter. I kept moving along, trying to get closer. I walked for many hours but didn't seem to be making any progress. Just when I was going to give up, I heard a thump and a rustle. I looked around and saw a white rabbit peeking out of a crater. First the little ears, and then the round eyes . . .'

'No way!' I exclaimed. 'That's the story of Chang Er, the moon goddess. The Mid-Autumn Festival is next week, right? The mooncake festival.'

'Next week?' Madam Chang said, and peered at me with a small, shy smile. Her pupils were huge. 'Mooncakes?'

'Come on, Chang Er? Everybody knows this one. It's in my Chinese textbook . . .' I continued, though less insistently. 'Even got a TV series about her last year . . .' My voice trailed off and I stopped talking because now she was staring at me as if I'd offended her. Her eyes turned hard and beady for a moment. And then she relaxed.

I could almost picture her as that young goddess with a delicate nose and a rosebud mouth, drifting towards her lunar exile. Why were there a woodcutter and a rabbit on the moon? The myth made no sense. Why and how did she come back to earth? I wondered these things but I didn't want to know. Instead I put down my carton of Milo.

'I got to go home,' I said.

'Cannot,' Madam Chang replied. 'Your parents are out. You shouldn't be alone.' Thunder rumbled, and lightning lit up the locked grille.

I tried to calculate whether I could make a break for the door. My limbs felt leaden, slow. Madam Chang got up and reached across me, towards the table. She grabbed the topmost magazine: *Nuyou*. She flipped to the middle. The pages made a sound like smacking.

The spread opened to show a brown-haired Eurasian model posing on a chair: nothing unusual, but all these pieces of paper fell to the floor.

'Look at these,' Madam Chang said. 'I made them myself.' I didn't want to touch anything. She pressed a few pieces firmly into my hands. They were thin as tissue. I held one up to the light, my hand shaking. It was cut in the shape of a bird. Another was shaped like a prowling paper cat.

'Cat,' I said. I tried to get up but I was stuck.

'Do you like them? I made for you,' she said. She smoothed out a piece with her two hands, turned to me. She put her face right in front of mine.

'Circe. Listen,' she said. 'Time is a wild animal. Time is a tiger. Time is an ox. Time is a rat. *Xiao lao shu*,' she said in Chinese, waving the stencil almost comically. 'You're a little rat.'

The light changed to yellow. A goldfish plopped in the tank. The person who called herself Madam Chang looked old again. She moved around behind me. I froze. She put her hands on my shoulders. I dropped the stupid stencils.

'You're young now, but one day your body will change,' Madam Chang said. Her hands moved gently around my neck. My eyelids felt heavy. Her voice sounded garbled, as if filtered through the fish tank. 'Your skin will loosen. You will drop hair. One day you will wake up with your bones all wrong and find it hard to move like you used to, and you can't run from that.'

When my mother returned around 5.30 with Leslie in tow, she found me slumped in the corridor outside our flat. I had fallen asleep with my school bag as my pillow, legs curled up, arms splayed at angles. The rainstorm had died down to just a small, steady trickle. It was almost dark. My uniform was all crumpled and I had a smear of blood on my right leg but no cut; she checked. Later on my mother would tell me, 'The smudge looked like you smacked a huge mosquito just as it was biting you.'

My mother put me to bed.

'Where is she?' was the first thing I asked when I came round.

'Who?' my mother asked. I was running a high temperature. She pressed a cold towel to my forehead.

'Madam Chang. The auntie who lives upstairs. From your Bible study group. Is she here?' I looked around furtively, eyes bulging. My temples pulsed.

'No, I don't know what you're talking about. I don't know such a person. You're not feeling well. Go back to sleep.'

By the time my father came home from work, I felt even

worse. They took me to the doctor who concluded that I had dengue fever. Fever can cause hallucinations; my forehead was hot as a stove.

My parents asked around the block but nobody had heard of a Madam Chang. I was too scared and weak to go with them to look.

'It was the same door as where our flat would be, just a different floor,' I said. 'Moon lady with the fish tank.'

They looked at me as if I was mad.

'Bible study group.'

'Stop saying that!' my mother cried out. 'For the millionth time, there is no Madam Chang in my Bible study group!' She considered for a moment. 'We do have a Mrs Chan, though.'

'Not her,' I replied. 'She's nice.'

'Did this Madam Chang do anything to you?' my father almost bellowed. 'Anything unusual?'

My mother tutted. 'Teck, don't say like that. She won't understand.'

My father's face was like thunder. He grabbed my arm and my palm opened into nothing. Without understanding fully, I knew the rough of what he meant. The speculation reddened my cheeks.

My parents tried every flat in the block. My father couldn't find a place like the one I described, with a fish tank in the corner, a floral sofa, rattan chairs, and grey floors. He scolded that it was my fever talking, that I had dreamt it all up. I was already known for telling tall tales, exaggerating. Then my mother spotted a living room on television that matched my description precisely – it was the set of a maudlin Channel 5 'dramedy' called *Bukit Panjang* that showed every Thursday at 8 p.m. Even if it looked slightly different, all the components were there.

I could go look upstairs for myself if I wanted, they said, but I did not. For the remaining year we lived there, I never took the stairs up to the other floors again. Leslie was spooked by the smear of blood on me, and focused on the idea of a ghost that had given me the fever. In the end my mother concluded that I had scared myself. There were simple, often boring explanations for everything, she said.

*

By the time I stopped talking, Szu had a wide and peaceful smile across her face. She looked like a kid who had just heard a cosy bedtime story. I felt irritated. What I had just told her did not comfort me. Now that I had gotten the words out, I felt like they were wasted. I stared at the dusty floor.

'Is that why you have trouble sleeping?' Szu asked.

I looked up at her. Her eyes were bright and irritating.

'Well, yeah,' I said. 'Sometimes I have bad dreams and wake up in the middle of the night. And can't get back to sleep.'

'I see,' Szu replied. 'Bad dreams of Madam Chang?'

'No. Just random nightmares. Anyway, it's better now.'

'No Madam Chang?'

'No.'

'And you just never saw her again? This woman who lived on the moon?' Szu interlaced her fingers over her stomach, very proper, like a little princess. Her wrists were tiny. Her expression was thoughtful and alert, eyes rising out of a crisp and pointy face. Almost like a ballerina. She looked a world away from the big-boned, galumphing girl I had met at the start of the year.

'Nope,' I replied, blithely. 'Didn't want to look for her, either.'

I didn't bother to mention the article in the newspaper I stumbled upon a week after the incident. I kept the clipping for years, tucked away in a Hello Kitty folder: 23 September 1995, *Top Stories.*

Two patients had escaped from Woodbridge Mental Hospital and remained at large, hiding out somewhere, or maybe they had crossed the Causeway, who knows. VULNERABLE ADULTS, the article said. Below were two grainy photos. One of the escapees was a frazzled Indian man in his forties with a villainous moustache and a granite stare; the other was an unhappy-looking Chinese woman in her late sixties, not called Madam Chang, but she bore a resemblance. The two women could have been cousins. Sisters, at a stretch. I couldn't shake the connection out of my head.

I thought I would show that newspaper clipping to the police one day, triumphant, and they would catch her. But that never happened. And my parents never asked me any further questions. It was horrible, no one believing me. Not even my brother, who was ten and supposed to be my best friend. When I turned thirteen I burned the clipping with a lighter.

'It's funny, a woman on the moon,' Szu said. 'Like what you brought up about the astronauts. Madam Chang left earth and came back. What if you could leave earth and come back? Was Madam Chang real, or a ghost? What if you could ask a ghost what they know, why they were like that? Is that possible?'

She was prattling. I shrugged and picked at a hangnail.

'What if what my aunt does is genuine?' Szu continued. 'All my life I never believed it. I saw too much backstage business, their expenses books, the way they discussed clients, and all that . . . but what if it's for real?'

'Who the hell cares?'

'You care. You said so yourself. At the bus stop, in town. Maybe this planet is just one place to be in, of so many others. And you can hop around. And time travel isn't just made up.'

Szu was babbling bullshit. And she was so fixated on the stupid moon, which was missing the point, even though I couldn't quite describe what the point was. I felt slighted.

'You've got me thinking . . . who knows . . .' she said.

I stopped listening and watched her with a mixture of tenderness and disgust. She reminded me of a diseased animal with her furry skin and reddened eyes. Just like a rabbit afflicted with myxomatosis, which was a word we both learnt when we were friends all of half a year ago because it was a song on a Radiohead album. It seemed to me that all the knowledge I held on to at sixteen was either too awful or too embarrassing to forget, or just useless facts, lazy and incidental. Everything else I simply lost track of. Our placid afternoons of listening to music together seemed far-fetched now, fictional.

'My mother used to think I was special, in a good way,'

Szu continued. 'When I was little I took a long time to learn how to talk. But once I got the hang of it, I started growing really fast. Taller, and chatty. And then she didn't like me any more. I could see it happening but I couldn't do anything to change it. It was beyond my control. I wasn't special enough.'

I crossed my arms and leaned back in the chair. I'd heard this diatribe from her many times before.

'Even you are more special than I am,' Szu said softly.

I pitied her too much to be offended. I flashed a brief smile, and shook my head. Szu released her stare and tilted back to the wall. I guess I should have told her that we were both unique, some small, kind reassurance to make her feel better. It was clear that she was still consumed by the mean mystery of her mother, a lifelong rejection she had outlived but not necessarily outlasted. Something flipped, knotted and hardened deep inside my guts. I wanted to tell Szu that her mother, for all her faults, had seemed to acknowledge my horrible encounter with Madam Chang even without me telling her, and that she had been so extraordinarily kind about it. Even just that once, but I'd never forget it, and never forget her. How she told me we were both different as she clasped my hands in her slight, cold palms. And I felt it then, a bond that even her own daughter didn't share with her, and Amisa sensed it in me too, even if she ignored me ever after. What linked us was something real and true and rare. Szu wouldn't understand.

'I've got to go,' I said instead. 'I've got tuition soon.'

It was a lie but hopefully Szu didn't notice. I patted my

hands on my lap and stood up. She kept quiet and drew a sharp intake of breath as I hoisted my backpack and tucked my feet back into my shoes.

'Don't go,' she said in a quiet voice. 'Please.'

I paused.

'I can't action that,' I replied. 'Not today. You'll be okay. You just need some rest. See ya later, Szu.'

No response. Just the still curve of her cheek. Lank strands of hair across the blanket. She sniffed twice.

As I made my way down the corridor I glanced at Amisa's emptied bedroom: door gaping, curtains drawn, dark furniture. It was depressing to see it so exposed, just a square room not much bigger than her daughter's, scent of mothballs with a hint of floral freshener. That old, mysterious haunt. It didn't provide any answers. Szu felt cheated of explanations, and I felt sorry for her. But life just happened and it wasn't fair, wasn't my fault. Memory tussled us backwards with idiot hands, just the past insisting on its pastness because it didn't know what else to do.

At the kitchen doorway I said goodbye to Aunt Yunxi. She was hacking a watermelon to pieces and she turned towards me with a wary look. She made a sound of acknowledgement: ugly, almost guttural. It was only when I hurried all the way out of the cul-de-sac, veered right and reached the bus stop, that it hit me with a pang that Szu might have been crying. I didn't know yet, nor did I truly expect it, but that was the last time I saw her.

24
SZU

2020

I'm watching the 8 p.m. news with my husband Ben and my daughter Elizabeth when my phone vibrates. I tilt the screen to read it:

> Hi Szu,
> This is Circe here, from secondary school? Long time no see. I got your number from Leslie. He says he ran into you the other day. Nice to know you're back in town. I was wondering if u were free to catch up sometime?

I glance up at the television. Wide shot of nebula, cut to scientists talking. Chang'e 6, the unmanned lunar orbiter from China, just landed on a lava plain on the moon. The footage shows the shuttle in the black thickness of space, and then the camera cuts to a diagram indicating the location of its landing.

'*The landing site is a vast lava plain called Mare Imbrium, the Sea of Rains. Data gathered from the orbiter will be used to refine key technologies for further missions . . .*'

I glaze over at the newscaster's magenta lipstick and sleep-deprived face and ponder the message. Elizabeth tussles my arm and I smile at her. I was holding her hand when I ran into Leslie at Railway Mall the other day. Elizabeth and I were on our way to buy cornflour and onions. Leslie, my first crush; I was surprised by how much he'd changed, when really, isn't that how time works? He looked like a grown, tired man, but I couldn't help but paste the ghost of his eighteen-year-old self over his features. We made small talk and bade our farewells and I remembered the sad, truncated way I'd said goodbye to his younger sister.

It's been seventeen years since I saw her last. Circe left my childhood bedroom in a criminal hurry, tossing excuses in her wake. I knew she meant well but she was afraid of and for both of us. And she had just shared something ugly and important. But I didn't know what to say, nor how to help her. I was at the start of my worst, way back then. It's hard to find the strength to be giving or forgiving in times like that. It was a worst that would take me years to wade out of. I can name it plainly with a developing detachment, now that I'm well: my eating disorder, the way I tried to use the numbness I felt from denying myself to blanch and stymie the gushing, greedy chaos of everything else. It sounds dramatic, but that was a dramatically bad year. When I was ill everyone at school pretended not to notice. They thought kid gloves were the kindest way to handle me. I felt like I lost my mother at sixteen, and my father all over again. All I had, at the end of it, was Aunt Yunxi. Even she knew we couldn't completely rely on her amulets, her twists of dried roots and white fungus.

'I told you your friend is bad news,' she said at the time. 'Abandoner. Don't worry, I'll summon a long wriggling worm inside her, because that's what she is, a little worm herself.'

I laughed, weakly.

I withdrew from school. We moved out of the house two weeks later, and went to Penang to meet my aunt, my real aunt, for the first time. Jiejie is the kindest woman in the world and took Yunxi and me in without question.

Not that Yunxi needed her help – she's the most resilient person I know. Shortly after I moved in with Jiejie, Aunt Yunxi went on one of her expeditions again – this time to Tibet. She comes and goes as she pleases. And when she came back from one of her trips, a few years back, she announced to all of us that she had renounced her mediumship, and was now a born-again Christian. It makes me happy that she's happy. Now she lives with two church friends in Georgetown. She still behaves like the same person she was in her other life, with her hoarse, funny voice, her jolty mannerisms. I remember her trying to explain to me many years ago about the difference between shamans and mediums. How shamans have the power to let their spirits leave their bodies, lift off and walk far from home. They travel across great distances, encountering wonders we'd never otherwise see or know. Mediums are the reverse: they invoke, inviting gods and spirits into their bodies and feeling them as violently as a flagellation. I think Yunxi was trying to tell me that if our body is a vessel we have to treat it with respect while we have it to ourself. But I'm not sure: she's always been a roundabout type.

Ben flips the channel and the trailer for *Ponti 2020* comes on. I make a face but before he changes it again I shake my head and we turn to watch it together. Eunice Prinze looks nothing like my mother. The new Ponti runs barefoot from one end to the other of the glittering hull of Marina Bay Sands. New Ponti wears a maxi skirt. New Ponti haunts crisp-collared expats on Boat Quay. New Ponti tells the (predictably white) leading man, 'I've lived through things you wouldn't believe. Trust me.'

'How can I trust a monster?' he asks.

'Will you take a gamble?'

'For you, yes.'

I roll my eyes as they kiss to synthy muzak.

'Maybe it's not bad. We can hate-watch it at home,' Ben says.

'Yeah, definite hate-watch material,' I tell him. 'At least they're trying to push the film. So much effort. Remember those weird stencils the PR company sent us?'

'And the hamper at the end! I think they feel guilty that they are butchering your mother's legacy.'

'Hm. Maybe.'

The trailer ends and an American crime serial comes back on. Elizabeth starts hitting the blue cushion with her fists.

'Stop that, you little monkey!' I tell her.

I turn back to my phone.

> Hey Circe!
> Good to hear from you. Leslie
> says you're doing well. It would be
> great to catch up. I'm free any day
> next week except Wednesday, so
> just say when.

I hit send and watch the blue bar grow.

*

I've started part-time film-making classes, Wednesday evenings from 7 to 10 p.m. It's a foundation course. This week for homework we have to do some basic editing.

Perhaps because the remake is coming out soon, or because I'm a masochist, I've picked footage from the original *Ponti!* I have it in front of me, digitized, scrubbed to clarity. I'm fixated on one particular sequence that comes from twenty minutes into the film.

We open with a shot of a grotesque banyan tree, its limb-like aerial prop roots and obscuring vines. Stillness. One beat of shadow. Leaves stir. And then the monstrous human thing that is my mother begins to emerge. First her thin white hands. And then her bloodied, beautiful face. Followed by the rest of her, an elegant attack of white dress and scarred legs. I'm obsessed with this moment. I keep looping it back and rewatching, as if she'll grant me answers after a thousand repetitions. Amisa, Ponti, Xiao-fang hides from and reveals herself to me over and over, in the hypnotic shifting of frames. Her moonbeam skin comes into focus, before disappearing into the darkness again. The hope in her face breaks my heart. Rewind. The hate in her face breaks my heart.

I'm thirty-three now. As the gap narrows, twelve years between my age and my mother's when she died, I approach the notion of my forties with a tentative faith. So we are put on this planet and we won't make it out alive. But while I'm right here, I can try to be kind. As my mother the horror-movie actress blooms out from the vines, I press pause and detest her and miss her, all at the same time. But most of all I talk to her. I remember my silly incantations before I entered the school gates. How I willed words to work, lines of protection. As if she can hear me from the other side, I lean in to the screen and tell Ponti the same thing I wish on my daughter every night. So it's a hot, horrible earth we are stuck on and it's only getting worse. But still. I want to care for you always. May you be safe, may you feel ease. May you have a long, messy life full of love.

I unpause the footage but this time it doesn't respond. I click again. The screen stutters and stalls into an imperfect blur.

ACKNOWLEDGEMENTS

I am deeply grateful to:

Jean McNeil and George Ttoouli for guiding and encouraging me from the very start.

Deborah Rogers, who I never got to meet but who gave me the lifeline, means and self-belief to finish this book.

Emma Paterson for being the most empathetic and incisive agent, reader and person.

Sophie Jonathan and Ira Silverberg for taking extraordinary and exacting care of my work. Yours in Ponti, thank you.

The teams at Picador and Simon & Schuster, everyone at Rogers, Coleridge and White as well as Lucinda Praine.

Dr Karen Schaller, Henry Sutton, Giles Foden and Trezza Azzopardi at the University of East Anglia.

The David TK Wong Fellowship, the Booker Foundation, and the Elizabeth Kostova Foundation for supporting me.

Elizabeth Berry, Zoe McCarthy, Owen Fung, Jennifer Eakins, Cecilie Olsen, Caitlin Ingham, Peter Bloxham, Tom Offland and Joan Chan for wonderful, humorous friendship.

Suzanne Ushie for being my first reader and best writing companion always.

Avni Doshi for being the best fellow fellow there could be while this story was incubating (and helping me name Amisa).

Soumya Poudaval for reading the first draft and reality-checking the school scenes.

My family – the Teos and Ongs – for everything.